D0258137

NORTH EAST LINCOLNSHIRE
LIBRARIES

WITHDRAWN

NORTH EAST
LINCOLNSHIRE
LIBRARIES

CLE		GRL	
CB		RLN 14/oc	
CCL		ISO 7/09	
CCR			
RA		VAL	
HUM			
HMM			
ROUTE	CE 12/11		

216178

CREEPERS

CREEPERS

David Morrell

THORNDIKE
WINDSOR
PARAGON

This Large Print edition is published by Thorndike Press®, Waterville, Maine USA and by BBC Audiobooks Ltd, Bath, England.

Published in 2006 in the U.S. by arrangement with Morrell Enterprises, Inc.

Published in 2006 in the U.K. by arrangement with Headline Book Publishing.

U.S. Hardcover   0-7862-8497-8 (Americana)
U.K. Hardcover ISBN 10 1 4056 1388 2   (Windsor Large Print)
U.K. Hardcover ISBN 13 978 1 405 61388 0
U.K. Softcover ISBN 10 1 4056 1389 0   (Paragon Large Print)
U.K. Softcover ISBN 13 978 1 405 61389 7

Copyright © 2005 Morrell Enterprises, Inc.

All rights reserved.

The text of this Large Print edition is unabridged.
Other aspects of the book may vary from the original edition.

Set in 16 pt. Plantin by Christina S. Huff.

Printed in the United States on permanent paper.

British Library Cataloguing-in-Publication Data available

Library of Congress Cataloging-in-Publication Data

Morrell, David.
    Creepers / by David Morrell.
        p.   cm. — (Thorndike Press large print Americana)
    ISBN 0-7862-8497-8 (lg. print : hc : alk. paper)
        1. Asbury Park (N.J.) — Fiction.   2. Large type books.
    I. Title.   II. Thorndike Press large print Americana series.
    PR9199.3.M65C74 2006
    813'.54—dc22   2006001517

To Jack Finney and Richard Matheson,
whose imaginations never fail to inspire.

". . . places you're not supposed to go."
— subject of the Web site *infiltration.org*

". . . Hell is empty,
And all the devils are here."
— Shakespeare, *The Tempest*

9:00 p.m.

1

Creepers.

That's what they called themselves, and that would make a good story, Balenger thought, which explained why he met them in this godforsaken New Jersey motel in a ghost town of 17,000 people. Months later, he still would not be able to tolerate being in rooms with closed doors. The nostril-widening smell of must would continue to trigger the memory of screams. The beam from a flashlight wouldn't fail to make him sweat.

Later, as he convalesced, sedatives loosened the steel barriers he'd imposed on his memory, allowing frenzied sounds and images to dart out. That chilly Saturday night in late October. A little after nine. That was the moment when he could have turned around and saved himself from the mounting nightmare of the next eight hours. But in retrospect, even though he'd survived, he surely wasn't saved. He blamed himself for failing to notice how hyper everything felt. As he approached the motel, the crash of the

11

waves on the beach two blocks away seemed abnormally loud. A breeze scraped sand along a decaying sidewalk. Dead leaves rattled across cracked pavement.

But the sound that Balenger most remembered, the one that, he told himself, should have made him retreat, was a mournful rhythmic *clang clang clang* that drifted along the area's abandoned streets. It was harsh, as if from a fractured bell, but he would soon learn its true origin and how it represented the hopelessness he was about to enter.

Clang.

It could have been a warning to ships to stay away and avert disaster.

Clang.

Or it could have tolled for a funeral.

Clang.

Or it could have been the sound of doom.

2

The motel had twelve rooms. Only unit 4 was occupied, a pale yellow light seeping past its thin curtain. The exterior was run-down, as much in need of paint and repair as all the other buildings in the area. Balenger couldn't help wondering why the group had chosen it. Despite the hard times the community had suffered, there were still some decent places in which to stay.

The cold breeze made him tug the zipper on his Windbreaker all the way to his neck. A broad-shouldered man of thirty-five, he had short, sandy hair and an experience-etched face that women found appealing, although there was only one woman he cared about. He paused outside the room, wanting to control his thoughts, to prepare his emotions for the role he needed to assume.

Through the flimsy door, he heard a man's voice. It sounded young. "The guy's late."

A woman's voice, also young. "Maybe he isn't coming."

13

A second man, much older. "When he contacted me, he was enthused by the project."

A third man. Young, like the first two. "I don't think it's a good idea. We never took a stranger with us before. He'll get in the way. We shouldn't have agreed."

Balenger didn't want the conversation to proceed in that direction, so he decided he was as focused as he was going to get and knocked on the door.

The room became quiet. After a moment, a lock was freed. The door came open the length of a security chain. A bearded face peered out.

"Professor Conklin?"

The face nodded.

"I'm Frank Balenger."

The door closed. A chain rattled. The door came open again, revealing an overweight man of sixty silhouetted by light.

Balenger knew the man's age because he'd researched him thoroughly. Robert Conklin. Professor of history at the State University at Buffalo. Vietnam war protestor during his graduate-school years. Jailed three times at various political events, including the 1967 march on the Pentagon. Arrested once for possession of marijuana, the charge dismissed for insufficient evidence. Married: 1970. Widowed: 1992. One year later, he became a creeper.

"It's after nine. We began to wonder if you were coming." The professor's gray hair matched his beard. His glasses were small, his cheeks heavy. After a careful look outside, he shut and locked the door.

"I missed the earlier train from New York. Sorry to hold you up."

"Quite all right. Vinnie was late arriving also. We're getting organized."

The professor, who looked out of place in jeans, a sweater, and a Windbreaker, indicated a thin man of twenty-four, who also wore jeans, a sweater, and a Windbreaker. As did the two other young people in the room. As did Balenger, who'd followed the instructions he was given, including the directive to make certain the clothes were dark.

Vincent Vanelli. B.A. in history: State University at Buffalo, 2002. High school teacher in Syracuse, New York. Unmarried. Mother deceased. Father unable to work, suffering from smoker's-related emphysema.

Conklin turned toward the remaining two people, a man and a woman. They too were twenty-four, Balenger knew from his investigations. The woman had ponytailed red

15

hair, a sensuous mouth that some men would have worked not to stare at, and a figure that the sweater and Windbreaker couldn't hide. The good-looking man next to her had brown hair and a solid build. Even if Balenger hadn't researched his background, he'd have known that the man enjoyed exercise.

"I'm Cora," the woman said, her voice pleasantly deep, "and this is Rick."

Again, only first names, although Balenger knew that their last name was Magill. They had B.A.s in history from the State University at Buffalo, 2002, and were now in the graduate history program at the University of Massachusetts. Met in 2001. Married in 2002.

"Pleased to meet you." Balenger shook hands with everybody.

An awkward moment ended when he pointed toward objects laid out on the worn bedspread. "So these are the tools of the trade?"

Vinnie chuckled. "I guess, if the wrong person came in here, he'd get suspicious."

It was an amazing array of equipment: hard hats with battery-powered lights attached to them, flashlights, candles, matches, spare batteries, work gloves, knives, knapsacks, rope, duct tape, water

16

bottles, hammers, a crowbar, digital cameras, walkie-talkies, trail mix, energy bars, and several small electronic devices Balenger couldn't identify. A Leatherman all-in-one tool (pliers, wire cutters, various types of screwdrivers) sat next to a first-aid trauma kit in a red nylon bag. The kit, labeled Pro Med, was the equivalent to what SWAT teams and military special-operations units carried, Balenger knew.

"Anticipating trouble? Some of these could be considered burglary tools."

"The furthest thing from our minds," Professor Conklin said. "Anyway, there's nothing to steal."

"As far as we know," Cora said. "Not that it would make a difference. We look but don't touch. Of course, that's not always possible, but that's the general idea."

"To quote the Sierra Club," Rick said, " 'take nothing but photographs; leave nothing but footprints.' "

Balenger removed a notebook and pen from a Windbreaker pocket. "How long have you been creepers?"

"I hope you're not going to use that word in your article," Vinnie objected.

"But it's part of the slang, isn't it? 'Mice' are law-enforcement officers, right? 'Ball busters' are large pipes you're forced to

17

straddle to get over. 'Poppers' are the crow-bars you use to pry up manhole covers. And 'creepers' are —"

" 'Infiltrators' is an equally dramatic term, with a less harsh connotation, although it does imply we're breaking the law," Professor Conklin admitted. "Which, strictly speaking, we are."

"Why not call us urban explorers or urban adventurers?" Cora said.

Balenger kept writing.

"City speleologists," the professor suggested. "Metaphoric cave investigators descending into the past."

"We'd better set some rules," Rick said abruptly. "You work for —"

"*The New York Times Sunday Magazine*. They brought me on board to write features about interesting cultural trends. Movements on the fringe."

"On the fringe is exactly where we'd like to stay," Cora said. "You can't identify us in your article."

"All I have are your first names," Balenger lied.

"Even so. This is especially important for the professor. He's got tenure, but that doesn't mean his dean won't try to take it away if the university finds out what he's doing."

Balenger shrugged. "Actually I'm way ahead of you on that point. I have no intention of using your names or specific details of your backgrounds. It'll add to the supposed danger if I make it sound like you're members of a secret group."

Vinnie leaned forward. "There's no 'supposed' danger about this. Some creepers have been seriously injured. Some have even died."

"If you identify us," Rick emphasized, "we can go to jail and pay heavy fines. Do we have your word that you won't compromise us?"

"I guarantee none of you will be damaged because of what I write."

They glanced at each other, uncertain.

"The professor explained to me why he thought the article deserved to be written," Balenger assured them. "He and I think the same. We've got a throwaway culture. People, plastic, pop bottles, principles. Everything's disposable. The nation's suffering from memory disorder. Two hundred years ago? Impossible to imagine. A hundred years ago? Too hard to think about. Fifty years ago? Ancient history. A movie made *ten* years ago is considered old. A TV series made *five* years ago is a classic. Most books have a three-month shelf life. Sports organizations no sooner build stadiums than they blow them up so they can replace them with newer, uglier ones. The grade school I went to was torn down and replaced by a strip mall. Our culture's so obsessed with what's new, we destroy the past and pretend it never happened. I want to write an essay that convinces people the past is important. I want to make my readers feel it and smell it and appreciate it."

The room became quiet. Balenger heard the *clang clang clang* outside and the waves crashing on the beach.

"I'm beginning to like this guy," Vinnie said.

3

Balenger's muscles relaxed. Knowing there'd be other tests, he watched the creepers fill their knapsacks. "What time are you going in?"

"Shortly after ten." Conklin hooked a walkie-talkie to his belt. "The building's only two blocks away, and I've already done the reconnaissance work, so we don't have to waste time figuring how to infiltrate. Why are you smiling?"

"I just wonder if you realize how much your vocabulary is like the military's."

"A special-ops mission." Vinnie clipped a folded knife to the inside of a jeans pocket. "That's what this is."

Balenger sat on a cigarette-burned chair next to the door and took more notes. "I found a lot of material on the professor's Web site and the other major ones on the Net, like infiltration.org. How many urban-explorer groups do you think there are?"

"Yahoo and Google list thousands of sites," Rick answered. "Australia, Russia, France, England. Here in the U.S., they're

21

all over the country. San Francisco, Seattle, Minneapolis. To urban explorers, that city's famous for its maze of utility tunnels known as the Labyrinth. Then there's Pittsburgh, New York, Boston, Detroit —"

"Buffalo," Balenger said.

"Our old stomping grounds," Vinnie agreed.

"The groups often flourish in areas with decaying inner cities," Conklin said. "Buffalo and Detroit are typical. People flee to the suburbs, leaving grand old buildings without occupants. Hotels. Offices. Department stores. In many cases, the owners simply walk away. In lieu of taxes, the city assumes ownership. But often the bureaucrats can't decide whether to demolish or renovate. If we're lucky, the abandoned buildings get boarded up and preserved. In downtown Buffalo, we sometimes infiltrated places that were built around 1900 and abandoned in 1985 or even earlier. As the world moves on, they stay the same. Damaged, yes. The decay is inevitable. But their essence doesn't change. With each structure we infiltrate, it's as if a time machine takes us back through the decades."

Balenger lowered his pen. His look of interest encouraged the professor to continue.

"When I was a child, I used to sneak into

22

old buildings," Conklin explained. "It was better than staying home and listening to my parents argue. Once, in a boarded-up apartment complex, I found a stack of phonograph records that were released in the 1930s. Not long-playing vinyl, what used to be called LPs, with a half-dozen songs on each side. I'm talking about discs made of thick, brittle plastic, easily breakable, with only one song on each side. When my parents weren't home, I enjoyed putting the records on my father's turntable and playing them again and again, scratchy old music that made me imagine the primitive recording studio and the old-fashioned clothes the performers wore. For me, the past was better than the present. If you consider the news these days — elevated threat levels and terrorist attacks — it makes a lot of sense to hide in the past."

"When we were undergraduates in a class the professor taught, he asked us to go with him to an old department store," Vinnie said.

Conklin looked amused. "It involved some risk. If any of them had been injured, or if the university found out I was encouraging my students to commit a crime, I could have been dismissed." His pleasure made his face look younger. "I guess I'm still marching against the rules, wanting to raise hell while I'm still able."

"The experience was eerie," Vinnie said. "The department store's counters were still there. And a few pieces of merchandise. Moth-eaten sweaters. Shirts that mice had chewed on. Old cash registers. The building was like a battery that stored the energy of everything that happened inside it. Then it leaked that energy, and I could almost feel long-dead shoppers drifting around me."

"Maybe you belong in the University of Iowa's creative-writing department," Rick kidded him.

"Okay, okay, but each of you knows what I mean."

Cora nodded. "I felt it, too. That's why we asked the professor to keep us in mind for other expeditions, even after we graduated."

"Each year, I choose a building that I feel has unusual merit," the professor told Balenger.

"Once we infiltrated an almost-forgotten sanitarium in Arizona," Rick said.

"Another time, we got into a Texas prison that was abandoned for fifty years," Vinnie added.

Cora grinned. "The next time, we snuck onto an abandoned oil rig in the Gulf of Mexico. Always excitement. So what building did you choose this year, Professor? Why did you bring us to Asbury Park?"

"A sad story."

4

Asbury Park was founded in 1871 by James Bradley, a New York manufacturer, who named the community after Francis Asbury, the bishop who established Methodism in America. Bradley chose the ocean resort's location because it was convenient to get to from New York to the north and Philadelphia to the west. Methodists established summer homes there, attracted by the shaded streets and the grand churches. The city's three lakes and numerous parks were ideal places for strolls and family picnics.

By the early 1900s, the mile-long boardwalk was the pride of the Jersey shore. When thousands of vacationers weren't lying on the beach or splashing in the water, they ate salt-water taffy and visited the copper-and-glass carousel house or else the Palace Amusements building, where they rode the Scooter, the Twister, the Tunnel-of-Love boat, a merry-go-round, and a Ferris wheel. Ignoring the Methodist foundations of the community, many also went to the ornate casino that now occupied the southern end of the boardwalk.

Through the first World War, the Roaring Twenties, the Depression, and most of the second World War, Asbury Park flourished. But in 1944, symbolizing what was to come, a hurricane destroyed much of the area. Rebuilt, the resort strove for its former greatness, straining to keep it during the 1950s and almost retaining it during the 1960s when rock concerts filled the boardwalk's Convention Hall. Walls that had felt the swaying chords of Harry James and Glenn Miller now reverberated with the pounding rhythms of The Who, Jefferson Airplane, and the Rolling Stones.

But in 1970, Asbury Park could no longer resist its decline. While rock and roll was a force of the times, so were Vietnam, anti-war protests, and race riots. The latter stormed through Asbury Park, smashing windows, overturning cars, looting, and setting fires that spread until the flames gutted the community. Thereafter, local families fled the devastation while vacationers migrated to newer spots along the shore. In their place came the counterculture: hippies, musicians, bikers. Then-unknown Bruce Springsteen often played in local clubs, singing about the desperation of the boardwalk and the urge to head down the road.

In the 1980s and 1990s, political instability and real-estate bankruptcy doomed efforts to rebuild the community. As more residents fled, entire blocks became uninhabited. The Palace Amusements building, dating back to 1888, practically synonymous with Asbury Park, succumbed to the wrecking ball in 2004. The decaying boardwalk was deserted, as was the famous Circuit in which bikers and hot-rodders once cruised north on Ocean Avenue, sometimes at sixty miles an hour. In the old days, they veered west for a block, then roared south on Kingsley Avenue, slid east for a block, and resumed their race north on Ocean. No more. Gone. A visitor could stand all day in the middle of Ocean Avenue and never fear being struck.

The rubble and ruin resembled the aftermath of a war zone. Although 17,000 people claimed to be residents of Asbury Park, it was rare to see any of them in the blight of the beach area where, a hundred years earlier, a multitude of vacationers frolicked. In place of carousel music and children's giggles, a loose piece of sheet metal banged in the wind, a clang of doom from an uncompleted ten-story condominium building.

Evidence of the city's dismal renewal effort, the project ran out of money. Like the historic buildings around it — the few that remained — the development was abandoned.

Clang.

Clang.

Clang.

5

Balenger watched the professor unfold a map, then tap a finger on a section two blocks north.

"The Paragon Hotel?" Cora asked, reading.

"Built in 1901," Conklin said. "As its name indicates, the Paragon claimed to be the model of excellence. The finest amenities. The most painstaking service. A marble-floored lobby. Exquisite porcelain dinnerware. Gold-plated eating utensils. A telephone in each room at a time when the only phones would normally have been in the lobby. A heated indoor swimming pool when that was a rarity. A steam room, which wasn't common either. An early version of a whirlpool spa. A ballroom. An art gallery. An indoor roller-skating area. A primitive air-conditioning system based on forced air being blown over ice. Also, a full heating system, which was unusual, even for the finest beach hotels — after all, their clients were summer visitors wanting to *get away* from the heat. Four recently invented, gearless electric elevators with push-button controls. Room service was available twenty-four hours a day. The elevators plus a system of electric dumbwaiters guaranteed prompt delivery."

"Throw in some cocktail waitresses, and you've got Las Vegas," Vinnie said with a grin.

Balenger tried to blend with the group by looking amused.

"The Paragon was designed by its owner, Morgan Carlisle, who inherited the family fortune after his wealthy parents died in a fire at sea." The professor's explanation made Vinnie's grin dissolve. "Carlisle was only twenty-two, eccentric, withdrawn, given to fits of anger and deep depression, but he also showed brilliance in whatever he tried. He was a genius constantly verging on a nervous breakdown. It's ironic that a steamship line was the source of his fortune and yet he had a morbid fear of traveling. He was a hemophiliac, you see."

The group peered up from the map.

"The bleeding disease?" Cora asked.

"Sometimes called the 'royal disease' because at least ten male descendants of Queen Victoria were afflicted with it."

"The slightest bump or fall causes almost uncontrollable bleeding, right?" Balenger asked.

"That's correct. Basically, it's a genetic disorder in which blood fails to clot properly. Without showing symptoms, females pass it on to males. Often the hemorrhaging isn't external. Blood seeps into joints and muscles, with crippling pain that forces the victim to stay in bed for weeks."

"Is there a cure?" Balenger made a note.

"No, but there are a few treatments. In Carlisle's youth, an experimental procedure involved blood transfusions that temporarily supplied him with clotting agents from normal blood. His parents were terrified that an accident might cause him to bleed to death, so they kept him under strict control, almost a prisoner, supervised by the servants. He was never allowed outside the family home in Manhattan. His mother and father loved to travel, however, and frequently left him alone. It's been estimated that they stayed away six months every year. They returned with photographs, paintings, and stereoscope images showing him the wonders they'd seen. He was so programmed to stay indoors that he developed agoraphobia and couldn't bear the thought of going outside. But after his parents died, he mustered all his frustration, courage, and anger, and vowed that for the first time in his life, he'd change locations. He'd never set foot on the Fifth Avenue sidewalk outside his home, but now he was determined to design a hotel and live in it, at a fabulous, beyond-imagining ocean resort that all Manhattan was talking about: Asbury Park. The model he used came from one of those stereoscope images his parents brought him. A Mayan ruin in the jungles of Mexico."

Balenger noticed how intense the group's eyes became.

"Carlisle decided that if he couldn't see an actual Mayan pyramid, he would build one for himself," the professor continued. "The structure was seven stories tall: the height, width, and depth of the original pyramid. But he didn't slavishly imitate. Instead, he decided that each level would be set back, the upper floors getting smaller, until only a penthouse stood at the top, a modified pyramid shape that anticipated art-deco buildings in the 1920s."

Rick frowned. "But if he had agoraphobia . . ."

"Yes?" Conklin studied Rick, waiting for him to draw the logical conclusion.

Cora was quicker. "Professor, are you telling us that Carlisle moved into the hotel, lived in the penthouse, and never left?"

"No, *you* just told *me*." Conklin put his hands together, pleased. "One of the elevators was for his private use. Day or night, but mostly at night, when the guests were asleep, he had a small version of the world at his disposal. Given the cost of the hotel, the enterprise never had a chance of making a profit. Even the rich would have balked at the prices Carlisle would have needed to charge. Those with moderate means would have stayed away entirely. So Carlisle made his prices competitive. After all, the point was to surround himself with life, not make a profit."

Balenger asked the logical question. "How long did he live?"

"To the age of ninety-two. The general misconception about hemophiliacs is that they're weak and sickly, and indeed some are. But one treatment involves keeping physically active. Non-contact exercises such as swimming and stationary bicycling are encouraged. A muscular torso supports painful joints. Mega-doses of vitamins with iron supplements are recommended to prevent anemia and strengthen the immune system. Steroids are sometimes used to add muscle mass. Carlisle pursued all these with a vengeance. By all accounts, he had an arresting physical presence."

"Ninety-two years old," Cora marveled. A sudden thought struck her. "But if he was twenty-two in 1901, then he lived until —"

"Add seventy more years. 1971." It was Rick's turn to complete Cora's thought. Balenger noticed that, even this early in their marriage, they shared that trait. "Carlisle was there when the riots and the fires happened the year before. He probably watched them from his penthouse windows. He must have been terrified."

" 'Terrified' is an understatement," the professor said. "Carlisle ordered shutters to be installed on the inside of every door and window in the hotel. Metal shutters. He barricaded himself inside."

Balenger lowered his notepad, sounding intrigued. "For more than three decades, it's been boarded up?"

"Better than that. Carlisle's reaction to the riots did us a favor. The interior shutters worked better than any outside boards would have. Vandals and storms have destroyed the glass on the windows. But in theory, nothing got in. This is a rare opportunity to explore what may be the most perfectly preserved site we'll ever find. Before the hotel's destroyed."

"Destroyed?" Cora looked puzzled.

"After Carlisle's death, the hotel became

the property of the family trust with instructions to preserve it. But after the stock market crashed in 2001, the trust suffered financial problems. Asbury Park seized the building for unpaid taxes. A developer bought the land. Next week, a commercial salvager will come in to strip the hotel of whatever's valuable. Two weeks after that, the Paragon has an appointment with a wrecking ball. But tonight, it'll have its first guests in decades. Us."

6

Balenger sensed the excitement in the group as they turned on their walkie-talkies. The crackle of static filled the room.

Conklin pushed a button. "Testing." His distorted voice came from each of the other units.

In sequence, Rick, Cora, and Vinnie did the same, making sure that their units could send as well as receive.

"The batteries sound strong," Cora said. "And we've got plenty of spares."

"Weather?" Rick asked.

"Showers toward dawn," Conklin said.

"No big deal. It's time," Vinnie said.

Balenger shoved work gloves, trail food, water bottles, a hard hat, an equipment belt, a walkie-talkie, a flashlight, and batteries into the final knapsack.

He noticed the group studying him. "What's wrong?"

"You're really coming with us?" Cora frowned.

Balenger felt pressure behind his ears. "Of course. Wasn't that the idea?"

"We assumed you'd back out."

"Because crawling around an old building in the middle of the night doesn't appeal to me? Actually, you've got me curious. Besides, the story won't amount to much if I'm not there to report what you find."

"Your editor might not be pleased if you get arrested," Conklin said.

"Is there much chance of that?"

"Asbury Park hasn't seen a security guard in this area in twenty years. But there's always a possibility."

"Sounds like a slight one." Balenger shrugged. "Hemingway went to D-Day with a fractured skull. What keeps *me* from doing a little creeping?"

"Infiltrating," Vinnie said,

"Exactly." Balenger picked up the last item on the bed. The folded Emerson knife was black. Its handle was grooved.

"The grooves insure a tight grip if the handle gets wet," Rick told him. "The clip on the handle attaches the knife to the inside of a pants pocket. That way you can find it easily without fumbling in your pocket."

"Yeah, just like a military expedition."

"You'd be surprised how handy a knife can be if your jacket gets caught on something when you're crawling through a narrow opening or when you need to open the seal on a fresh set of batteries and you've got only one hand to do it. See the stud on the back of the blade? Shove your thumb against it."

The blade swung open as Balenger applied leverage with his thumb.

"Useful if you need to open the knife one-handed," Rick said. "It's not a switchblade, so in case you're caught, it's perfectly legal."

Balenger made himself look reassured. "Good to know."

"If we were exploring a wilderness area," the professor said, "we'd tell a park ranger where we planned to go. We'd leave word with our friends and families so they'd know where to look if we failed to contact them at a specified time. The same rule applies to urban exploration, with the difference that what we'll be doing is against the law, so we need to be circumspect about our intentions. I've given a sealed envelope to a colleague who is also my closest friend. He suspects what I've been doing, but he's never put me on the spot by asking. If I fail to phone him at nine tomorrow morning, he'll open the note, learn where we've gone, and alert the authorities to search for us. We've never had an emergency requiring that to happen, but it's comforting to know the precaution's there."

"And, of course, we have our cell phones." Vinnie showed his. "In an emergency, we can always call for help."

"But we keep them turned off," Conklin said. "It's hard to appreciate the tempo of the past when the modern world intrudes. Questions?"

"Several." Balenger was anxious to get started. "But they can wait till we're inside."

Conklin looked at his former students. "Anything we've neglected to do? No? In that case, Vinnie and I will go first. The three of you follow five minutes later. We don't want to look as if we're in a parade. Walk to the street, turn left, and proceed two blocks. There's a weed-choked lot. That's where you'll find us. Sorry to get personal," he told Balenger, "but please make sure you empty your bladder before you leave. It isn't always convenient to attend to bodily functions after we infiltrate, and it violates our principle of not altering the site. That's why we carry these." The professor put a plastic bottle into Balenger's knapsack. "Dogs, winos, and crack addicts urinate in old buildings. But not us. We don't leave traces."

10:00 p.m.

7

In the darkness to Balenger's right, the crash of the waves on the beach seemed louder than when he'd arrived. His heart beat faster. The October breeze strengthened, blowing sand that stung his face. *Clang. Clang.* Like a fractured bell, the strip of flapping sheet metal whacked harder against a wall in the abandoned building two blocks farther north. The sound wore on Balenger's nerves as he, Cora, and Rick surveyed their desolate surroundings. Cracked sidewalks. Weeds in ravaged lots. A few sagging buildings silhouetted against the night.

But in the foreground were the seven stories of the Paragon Hotel. In the starry darkness, it did resemble a Mayan pyramid. As Balenger approached, the hotel seemed to grow, the symmetry of its receding levels capped by the penthouse. In moonlight, it so resembled art-deco buildings from the 1920s that Carlisle seemed to have been able to peer into the future.

Balenger turned toward his companions.

"You said the three of you were in Professor Conklin's history class in Buffalo. Do you still keep in touch between your yearly expeditions?"

"Not as much as we used to," Rick answered.

"Holidays. Birthdays. That sort of thing. Vinnie's in Syracuse. We're in Boston. Stuff gets in the way," Cora added.

"But in those days, we sure were close. Hell, Vinnie and Cora used to date," Rick said. "Before she and I got serious."

"Wasn't that uncomfortable, the three of you hanging out together?"

"Not really," Cora answered. "Vinnie and I were never an item. We just had fun together."

"Why do you suppose the professor chose the three of you?"

"I don't understand."

"Over the years, he must have had plenty of other students to choose from. Why you?"

"I guess I always assumed he just liked us," Cora said.

Balenger nodded, thinking. And maybe the professor liked Cora in particular, liked to look at her, invited her then-boyfriends to make her feel comfortable and disguise the interest of an aging man whose wife was dead.

Balenger tensed, seeing a figure rise eerily from the weeds. It rose straight up and stopped at stomach level, as if materializing from the earth.

He took a moment to realize that the figure was Vinnie and that he seemed to levitate from a shadowy opening in the ground.

"Over here."

Balenger saw a circular hole, a manhole cover next to it. Vinnie disappeared below-ground. Balenger and Cora went next, descending a metal ladder bolted to a concrete wall.

The *clang* of the sheet metal in the condominium building became fainter. The air got cooler, with a smell of moisture and must. Balenger's boots sounded on concrete as he reached the bottom.

The darkness thickened. Metal scraped as Rick came down the ladder and tugged the manhole cover into place. It was a mark of his strength that he was able to do so. Finally, the darkness was complete, and the outside *clang* could no longer be heard.

Balenger became conscious of the sound of his breathing. He couldn't seem to get enough air, as if the darkness were something pressed against his face. Although the tunnel was cold, he sweated. He relaxed only slightly when the light on a hard hat gleamed. It was above the professor's bearded face, the hat's brim casting a shadow down Conklin's heavy cheeks. A moment later, the light on Vinnie's hat went on.

Then Balenger heard Rick arrive at the bottom, heard the scratch of zippers and cloth as Rick and Cora took their hard hats from their knapsacks. Balenger did the same, feeling uncomfortable from the weight he put on his head.

Everybody spread out, trying not to crowd each other. At the same time, Balenger sensed they wanted to remain close. Their five headlamps bobbed and veered as they studied a tunnel. Puddles reflected their lights.

"The city's so eager for urban renewal," Conklin said, "all I had to do was hint I was a developer and ask for the charts of storm drains and utility tunnels. The clerk even made photocopies for me."

"And this leads to the hotel?" Vinnie asked.

"With a few detours. Carlisle put in this tunnel arrangement. He had a long-term vision and knew that his hotel's electrical system was bound to need updating. To avoid periodic excavation to get at incoming wires, he had these tunnels constructed for ready access. To keep animals from chewing the wires, everything's bundled in these pipes. The tunnels also act as a drainage system. In wet weather, the area near the beach can get marshy. To avoid that, Carlisle had drainage tile buried around the hotel. Rain and snowmelt seep into these tunnels and exit under the boardwalk. That explains the puddles down here. The drainage system is one reason the hotel lasted more than a century while others had their foundations rot."

They took thick belts from their knapsacks. The belts had loops, clips, and pouches, reminding Balenger of the utility belts that electricians and carpenters wore. He was also reminded of police and military belts. Walkie-talkies, flashlights, cameras, and other equipment were quickly attached to them. Balenger did the same, adjusting the weight around his hips. Then everyone put on work gloves.

"We're wearing Petzl cavers' headlamps," the professor told Balenger. "They're capable of switching between halogen and LED bulbs, depending on how much light you need. At the extreme, the batteries can last two hundred and eighty hours before they need changing. That's one thing we don't need to worry about. But there are others. Safety check," he told the group.

Vinnie, Cora, and Rick pulled small electronic devices from their knapsacks. Balenger remembered seeing them on the bed earlier, unable to identify them. His companions pressed buttons and watched dials.

"Normal," Cora said.

"We're checking for carbon monoxide, carbon dioxide, and methane," Rick told Balenger. "All of them are odorless. I've got a slight reading on methane. It barely registers."

"Regardless," the professor said, "if you feel dizzy, sick to your stomach, headachy, uncoordinated, let us know immediately. Don't wait till you think you might be in trouble. By the time symptoms are serious, we might be too far into the tunnel to be able to evacuate. We'll check the meters often."

8

Balenger listened to the echo of their foot-steps and breathing. In the lead, the pro-fessor glanced periodically at a diagram.

The tunnel was only five feet high and forced them to stoop. Rusted pipes ran along the walls and the ceiling. As the group splashed through puddles, Balenger was thankful for the advice to wear waterproof construction boots.

"Smells like the ocean," Vinnie said.

"We're just above the high-tide mark," Conklin explained. "During the 1944 hurri-cane, these tunnels were flooded."

"Here's something for your article," Vinnie told Balenger. "Walt Whitman was one of the first urban explorers."

"Whitman?"

"The poet. In 1861, he was a reporter in Brooklyn. He wrote about exploring the abandoned Atlantic Avenue subway tunnel. That tunnel was dug in 1844, the first of its kind, but already, seventeen years later, it was obsolete. In 1980, another urban ex-plorer rediscovered the same tunnel, which had been blocked off and forgotten for more than a century."

"Look out!" Cora yelled.

"Are you okay?" Rick held out a hand.

"A rat." Cora tilted her helmet's light up toward a section of pipe in front of them.

A pink-eyed rat glared and scurried away, its long tail sliding along the pipe.

"I've seen so many, you'd think I'd have gotten used to them by now," Cora said.

"Looks like it has a friend."

Ahead, a second rat joined the first and raced along the pipe.

Now a half-dozen rats scurried. Now a dozen.

Balenger tasted something bitter.

"If they spend their lives down here, they're blind," Conklin said. "They're not reacting to the lights but to the sounds we make and the scent we give off."

Balenger heard their claws scratching along the pipe. The rats vanished into a hole through which an adjoining pipe emerged from the wall on the right.

A rectangular opening appeared on the left. Their wavering lights revealed a wide rusted pipe that blocked the lower way.

"We go through here," Conklin said.

Vinnie, Cora, and Rick checked their air meters.

"Normal," Vinnie and Cora said.

Rick breathed hard. "The methane's still borderline."

The professor kept his light aimed toward the rusted pipe. He asked Balenger, "Did you take my advice and get a tetanus booster?"

"You bet. But maybe I should have gotten something for rabies or distemper."

"Why is that?"

"The rats are back."

Five feet farther along, several glared from a pipe. The headlamps illuminated the red at the back of their sightless eyes.

"Are they checking out the new neighbors," Rick wondered, "or figuring how to bite a chunk out of us for dinner?"

"Very funny," Cora said.

"That big one looks like he could eat a couple of fingers."

"Rick, if you want sex in this century . . ."

"Okay, okay. Sorry. I'll get rid of them." Rick pulled a water pistol from his jacket and stepped toward the rats, who remained in place, refusing to budge from the pipe. "Here's the deal, guys. It's either my wife or you." He frowned. "For God's sake . . ."

"What's the matter?"

"One of them has two tails. Another's got three ears. Some kind of genetic defect from inbreeding. Get the hell out of here." Rick squeezed the pistol's trigger, spraying liquid over them.

Balenger heard several shrieks that tightened his spine as the misshapen rats stampeded into another hole beside a pipe. "What's in the water pistol?"

"Vinegar. If we get caught, it seems a lot more innocent than mace or pepper spray."

Now Balenger smelled it. His nostrils felt pinched.

"I don't suppose anybody took a photograph," Conklin said.

"Shit." Vinnie gestured in exasperation. "I was just standing here, not doing anything. Sorry. It won't happen again."

Vinnie's camera, a compact digital Canon, was in a case attached to his belt. He pulled it out and turned it on, pressing the flash button to capture the image of a one-eyed rat poking its head from a hole next to a pipe.

Spiderwebs filled the space above the wide pipe. Rick's gloved hands brushed them away.

"I don't see any brown recluses." Balenger knew that Rick referred to a hermit species of spider whose bite could be fatal. The young man squirmed over the obstacle, his legs briefly straddling it, hence the description of these kinds of pipes as "ball busters." His shoes crunched down on the other side, where he rose, knees bent, and aimed his helmet's light along the new tunnel. "Everything's fine . . . except for the skeleton."

"What?" Balenger asked.

"Of an animal. Can't tell what kind. But it's bigger than a rat."

Vinnie climbed over the pipe and crouched next to him. "That belonged to a cat."

"How do you know?"

"The low forehead and the slightly forward shape of the jaw. Plus, the teeth aren't big enough to be a dog's."

One by one, the rest of the group squirmed over the pipe, their clothes scraping on rust. Conklin came last. Balenger noticed that the elderly man breathed with effort, his weight making it difficult for him to get over.

"How come you know so much about animal skeletons?" Cora asked Vinnie.

"Just cat skeletons. When I was a kid, I happened to dig up one in my backyard."

"You must have been a charming kid, digging up your parents' yard."

"Looking for gold."

"Find any?"

"An old piece of glass."

Balenger kept staring at the skeleton. "How do you suppose the cat got in here?"

"How did the rats get in here? Animals find a way," the professor said.

"I wonder what killed it."

"Couldn't have been starvation, not with all the rats around here," Vinnie said.

"Maybe the *rats* killed it," Rick said.

"Funnier and funnier," Cora told him.

"Well, *this* isn't funny. Here's another skeleton." Vinnie pointed. "And another. And another."

Their headlamps flickered over the numerous bones.

"What the hell happened here?" Balenger asked.

The tunnel became silent, except for the sound of their breathing.

"The hurricane," Cora said.

"What do you mean?"

"The professor said the hurricane flooded the tunnels. These four cats tried to get away by following this tunnel upward. See how it rises? But the water caught them anyhow. When it finally receded, their bodies were blocked by that pipe. Instead of floating away, they sank to the bottom here."

"You think these bones date all the way back to 1944?" Balenger asked.

"Why not? There's no earth to help them decompose."

"Cora, if you were still in my class, I'd give you an A." The professor put a hand on her shoulder.

Balenger noticed that the hand stayed longer than necessary.

9

The new tunnel took them past more pipes and spiderwebs. Shadows bobbed in the lights. A couple of times, Balenger banged against the ceiling and was grateful for the hard hat. He splashed through another puddle. Despite the water, dust irritated his nostrils. His cheeks felt grimy. Everything smelled stale. The cramped area seemed to compress the air, making it feel thick.

Vinnie, Cora, and Rick kept checking their meters.

"Isn't there an easier way to get in?" An echo distorted Balenger's voice.

"The windows are sealed from the inside with metal shutters, remember?" Conklin said.

"But the doors . . ."

"The same thing. Metal. We could try to pry something open, I suppose. We have a crowbar and Rick's strong arms. But there'd be noise, and if a security guard came around, the damage might be obvious."

The tunnel ended, a new one opening on the right.

Rick checked his air meter. "The methane's still borderline. Anybody feel sick?"

Vinnie answered for them. "No."

As they turned the corner, Balenger stiffened, confronted by gleaming eyes. Heat shot through his nervous system. The eyes were a foot above the tunnel's floor. A huge albino cat.

Vinnie's camera flashed. Hissing insanely, arching its back, the cat whipped its right paw at the lights, then charged away, disappearing into the darkness. Balenger frowned, noticing that the animal's hind legs had something wrong with them. Their rhythm was grotesque.

Vinnie's camera flashed again. "Hey, kitty, you're going in the wrong direction. Dinner's the other way. I've got some rats I want you to meet."

"Damned big animal." Cora got over the shock. "Maybe he stuffed himself on rats. Seemed to me he could see our lights. He must have a way in and out. Otherwise, his optic nerves would have stopped working."

"His hind legs," Balenger said.

"Yeah." Vinnie showed the group the back screen on his camera: the photograph he'd taken. "*Three* back legs, two growing out of one hip. Dear God."

"Do you see this sort of thing often?" Balenger asked.

"Mutations? Occasionally, in tunnels that haven't been used in a long time," the professor explained. "More often, we see open sores, mange, and obvious parasite infestation."

" 'Parasite'?"

"Fleas. When you got your tetanus booster, did you tell your physician you'd be traveling to a third-world country and wanted to take antibiotics with you, just in case?"

"Yes, but I didn't understand why."

"A precaution against plague."

"Plague?"

"It sounds like a medieval disease, but it still exists. In the U.S., southwest areas such as New Mexico see it in prairie dogs, rabbits, and sometimes cats. Very occasionally, a human being contracts it."

"From infected fleas?"

"As long as you follow the recommended precautions, you needn't worry. None of us has ever gotten sick from plague."

"What *did* you get sick from?"

"Once I was in a tunnel that had standing water as this one does. Mosquitoes. I got West Nile fever. I recognized the symptoms and went to a doctor early enough.

Not to worry. Now that it's autumn, the mosquitoes are dead. And we've arrived. This is it."

10

Balenger braced himself, focusing his light on a rusted metal door.

Rick pressed down on a lever that formed the door's handle. Nothing happened.

He tried again, straining, but got the same result. "Locked. Maybe rusted in place."

"Professor?" Vinnie asked.

"This is always the moment I dislike," the elderly man said. "Until now, we've merely been trespassing. When we look for ways to infiltrate a building, I love it when we find a board that's fallen from a hole in a wall: a place to squeeze through. Nothing's been altered. Nothing's been destroyed. But now we're about to do something more serious. Breaking and entering. Assuming we can in fact enter. I'd very much like to see what's inside, but I can't encourage any of you to break the law. It has to be your choice."

"Count me in," Vinnie said.

"You're sure?"

"My life isn't that exciting. I'll never forgive myself if I miss this chance."

"Cora? Rick?"

"In."

Conklin looked at Balenger, keeping his light away from Balenger's eyes. "Perhaps you shouldn't continue. You have no obligation to us."

"Yeah." Balenger made himself shrug. "But the hell of it is, when I was a kid, I always found a way to get into places where I wasn't supposed to go. You've got me wondering what's on the other side of that door."

Rick took a crowbar from his knapsack and drove it into a rusted area between the door and the jamb. The impact rumbled along the tunnel. Bracing himself, he pulled on the crowbar. The door scraped open an inch. He tugged the crowbar harder and forced the door open enough for even the professor to squeeze through.

Balenger entered cautiously, his light scanning a massive utility room. After the smothering space of the tunnel, the open area was welcome. It felt good to be able to lift his head, to straighten his back and neck. Switches, levers, dials, and gauges occupied the shadowy wall to the right. Pipes filled the murky ceiling and the remaining walls. Huge metal cylinders stood in the center. Balenger assumed they were water heaters. The chill area smelled of metal and old concrete.

"Carlisle kept updating the infrastructure," the professor explained. "This is from the 1960s."

Aiming his headlamp, Rick scanned the levers and other devices. "Impressive. He certainly was organized. Everything's so clearly labeled, an idiot would know what to do. The hot water system is isolated for the different floors. So is the air-conditioning. Here are switches for the swimming pool: heater, pump, purge."

Balenger searched behind the boilers.

"A door's over here." Vinnie crossed the room. "Probably leads into the main part of the hotel."

"Hey, guys!" Cora yelled.

They turned, their lights swiveling.

"Maybe this is one of those Venus-Mars things, but *that's* really going to bother me." Cora aimed her light toward the open door and the tunnel they'd left. "If that five-legged cat gets in here, or those rats with two tails . . ."

Vinnie chuckled. He and Rick shoved the door closed. Specks of rust dropped from creaky hinges.

"Now let's see what's beyond the other door," the professor said.

They crossed the utility room. After Rick tugged the next door open, they stood spellbound, their lights revealing something that rippled.

"Amazing," Balenger said after a moment, cold humidity drifting over him.

Vinnie flashed another photograph.

"For heaven's sake, they didn't empty it." Cora stepped closer.

The reflection of their lights shimmered across their faces.

"But after all these years, wouldn't the water have evaporated?" Rick asked.

Something plopped on Balenger's hard hat. Worried about bats, he jerked his light toward the ceiling, but all he saw were beads of moisture. Another drop splashed on him.

"As long as the doors seal the area, there's no place for the evaporation to go," the professor said. "The water's trapped in here. Feel how humid the air is."

"Dank is more like it," Balenger said.

Cora shivered. "Cold."

What they stared at was the hotel's swimming pool. To their astonishment, it still contained water, green from algae growing in it.

And it rippled.

Vinnie's camera flashed.

"Something's in the water," Cora said.

"Probably an animal that heard us coming and jumped in to hide," Conklin said.

"But what kind?"

The algae kept rippling.

"A muskrat perhaps."

"What's the difference between a rat and a muskrat?"

"A muskrat is bigger."

"Just what I needed to hear."

Rick found a slimy pole on the floor. It had a net at the end: a pool skimmer. "I could poke around in the water and see what I catch."

"You mean what drags you in," Cora said.

Vinnie laughed.

"No, I'm serious," Cora said. "This door was closed. So is the one on the other side of the pool." Her light streaked across the scum and indicated the other door. "So how did that thing — whatever it is — get in here?"

Lights flashed in all directions, searching for another entrance.

"Rats can work their way into almost any place," the professor said. "They're determined and tough enough to chew through concrete blocks."

"And what in God's name is *this* stuff?"

Balenger pointed toward what resembled a white carpet on a wall.

"Mold," Cora said.

The scummy water rippled again.

"Rick, let me know when you find the creature from the green lagoon."

"You're leaving?"

"I've run into enough rats for one night. I'm a historian, not a biologist. If I stay here longer, I'll grow moss."

While Cora rounded the pool, Vinnie took another picture. With an unnerving clatter — "Ooops. Sorry." — Rick dropped the pole. Everyone followed. Trying to stay balanced on the slippery tiles, they joined Cora at a set of swinging doors.

Rick pressed against a rusted metal plate on one of them. With the now familiar squeak and scrape, the door yielded.

11

They entered a cobwebbed corridor in which a door on each side had a tarnished plaque with the word GENTLEMEN engraved on one and LADIES on the other. Farther along was a dusty counter behind which rubber sandals were scattered.

"When people abandon a house, they usually take everything with them. It's their stuff, and they want to keep it," Rick told Balenger. "But when it comes to closing a hospital, a factory, a department store, an office building, or a hotel, everybody's in charge, and nobody is. It's assumed that somebody else will take care of the final details, but it often doesn't happen."

They passed elevator doors whose metal was rusted. Stairs led up.

Conklin pointed. "Take a close look at the stairs."

"Marble," Vinnie said, then turned toward Balenger. "Most places we infiltrate, the floors have nails poking through. That's why we warned you to wear thick-soled boots."

At the top, they came to another pair of swinging doors.

"Looks like mahogany," Cora said. "A sturdy wood. Even so, these doors are rotting." She indicated a crumbling area at the bottom of each.

When she pushed at the doors, they didn't budge.

"There's no lock," Rick said, puzzled. "Something on the other side must be jamming them." He used his knife to pry one of the doors in his direction.

The doors suddenly flew open. With a crash, Rick hurtled back, slamming into Balenger, knocking him down. Several things cracked and snapped, cascading. Cora screamed. Large objects banged around them, burying Balenger.

In darkness, he felt something blunt and hard jabbing into his chest and stomach. A mushy, fetid substance weighed against his face. Heart racing, he struggled to free himself. He heard Rick cursing. He heard wood breaking, as if it were being thrown against a wall. Abruptly, he saw the light from head-lamps and pushed something heavy with rotting fabric off him.

"Rick! Are you all right?" Cora screamed.

Coughing, struggling to his feet, Balenger

saw Cora yank at a tangle of large objects, hauling them off Rick.

Vinnie's hands were on Balenger, helping him up. "Are you hurt?"

"No." Balenger felt nauseous from the odor of what had pressed on his face. He tried to wipe away the smell. "But what —"

"Rick?" Cora pulled him up.

"I'm okay. I just —"

"What fell on us?" Balenger demanded.

"Furniture," Conklin said.

"Furniture?"

"Broken tables and chairs. Sections of sofas."

An animal made a terrible screeching sound. Balenger saw a rat scurry from a hole in a decaying sofa. A second rat streaked after it. A third. Balenger's stomach thrust bile to his mouth.

"Somehow, all kinds of banged-up, shattered furniture got piled against that door," Conklin said. "When Rick opened it, the movement was enough to dislodge everything."

Balenger rubbed his aching chest where what he now realized was a table leg had jammed into him. Adrenaline shot through him. "But how did the furniture get broken? How did it get thrown there?"

"Maybe a crew started to do some renovating and was told to quit," Conklin suggested. "These old buildings have all kinds of puzzles. In that abandoned department store in Buffalo, we found a half-dozen fully dressed mannequins sitting in a circle of chairs as if having a conversation. One of them even had a coffee cup in its hand."

"That was somebody's idea of a practical joke." Balenger scanned the darkness. "Fine. So is *this* a practical joke? Is somebody telling us to stay away?"

"Whatever it is," Vinnie said, "it happened a long time ago." He showed Balenger a broken table leg. "See this break?"

Balenger aimed his headlamp at it.

"The wood's old and dirty. If this were a fresh break, the inside of the leg would be clean."

Conklin smiled. "You get an A, also."

Rick picked up his knife. "Well, at least we got the doors open."

Balenger noted Cora's relief that Rick wasn't injured. But he also noted the way Vinnie looked at Cora, pained that her affection wasn't directed toward him.

The young man subdued his emotions and raised his camera. Its flash made an animal scamper.

The open doors beckoned. Past the murky outlines of more broken furniture,

Balenger and the others paused in astonishment.

"Now this is what makes the effort worthwhile," Rick said.

12

They stood in the shadows of a vast lobby. The ceiling was so high that their lights barely reached it. The floor was grimy marble. At several pillars, there were tangles of battered furniture: cracked chairs, tables, and sofas, once-plush upholstery moldering.

"A clean-up crew that was told to stop is still the logical explanation," Conklin said.

Some pillars were surrounded by rotting velvet divans. Elaborate crystal chandeliers drooped. Balenger kept a distance, concerned that they would fall.

Vinnie took a photograph of a chandelier, but its crystals didn't reflect the camera's flash. Everything in the lobby was dull and smelled of dust, while another acrid hard-to-identify smell hovered. Cobwebs hung like ragged curtains. A mouse scurried from a settee. Suddenly, a panicked bird catapulted from one of the chandeliers. Balenger flinched.

"How did *that* get in here?" Vinnie said.

A cricket screeched.

Rick coughed. "Welcome to *Wild Kingdom.*"

"Or Miss Havisham's memorial chamber in *Great Expectations.* Stay away from animal nests," Conklin warned.

"Believe me, I intend to," Balenger said.

"What I'm concerned about is the urine smell."

Now Balenger recognized the odor. Again he wiped his face, trying to lose the feeling that something mushy and fetid still pressed against his mouth.

"If you get too strong a whiff of the urine, there's a risk of hantavirus." Balenger knew the professor referred to a recently identified flu-like virus sometimes found in rodents' nests. Harmless to its animal hosts, the disease was potentially fatal to humans. "Not that you need to be paranoid about it. From time to time, cases turn up in the American West, but it's rare around here."

"That certainly relieves my mind."

Conklin chuckled. "Perhaps I should change the subject and talk about the lobby. As I mentioned, Morgan Carlisle took pains to update the infrastructure of the hotel." The professor's voice sounded hollow in the huge area. "But he never changed the design of the interior. Apart from the damage, this is the way the lobby appeared when it was first constructed in 1901. Periodically, the furniture wore out and needed to be replaced, of course. But the look of it never varied."

"Schizoid," Rick said. "The exterior anticipates art deco of the 1920s. But the furnishings are turn of the century. Victorian."

"Queen Victoria died in 1901 as the Paragon was being built," the professor explained. "Although Carlisle was American, he felt that the world had changed and not for the better. This was the style of the New York mansion in which he was raised. The exterior symbolized where his parents went and he was not allowed. The interior represented the place in which he felt safest."

"Yeah, schizoid. No wonder the hotel had trouble making a profit. It must have seemed old-fashioned even when it was built."

"Actually, it achieved the status of a theme hotel." Conklin gestured toward their surroundings. "Because the interior remained firmly entrenched in 1901, over the years 'old-fashioned' became viewed as 'historical' and then a kind of 'trip back into time.' The staff wore uniforms in the style of the turn of the century. The porcelain dishes and gold-plated eating utensils remained the same, as did the menu. The music in the ballroom was from that era, and the musicians wore period costumes. Everything was from another time."

Balenger studied the shadows. "Must have been a hell of a shock when a guest went upstairs, turned on the TV, and saw Jack Ruby shoot Lee Harvey Oswald. Or firefights in Vietnam. Or the riots at the Democratic convention in Chicago. But maybe Carlisle didn't allow televisions in the rooms."

"Reluctantly, he did. Guests didn't want to go *that* far back in time. But by then Asbury Park was in decline, and people had pretty much stopped coming."

"Yeah, a damned sad story," Balenger said. "Are all the sites you explore this well preserved?"

"Don't I wish. Salvagers and vandals often violate buildings before I get to them. The chandelier and the marble plant stands at the entrance, for example. Drug addicts would usually have stolen them long ago. The walls would be covered with obscene graffiti. It's a tribute to Carlisle's precautions that the hotel survived as completely as it has. Look at these photographs."

The group turned toward a wall of framed black-and-white images. Each had a tarnished copper plaque under it: 1910, 1920,

1930, all the way to 1960. Each depicted the lobby and showed festive guests. But although the lobby remained the same in every image, the style and placement of the furniture never varying, the clothing styles changed abruptly, lapels wider or narrower, dresses higher or lower, hair longer or shorter.

"Like time-lapse photography." Cora wandered across the lobby, turning her light this way and that. "But there's no photograph of the guests in the lobby in 1901 when the Paragon was built. I can imagine them around me. Moving calmly, speaking softly. Dresses rustle. The women carry gloves and parasols. The men wouldn't dream of going anywhere without ties and jackets. They have pocket watches on chains attached to their vests. Some have canes. Others have spats over their shoes to protect them from the sand on the boardwalk. As they enter the lobby from outside, they take off their Homburg hats, or maybe they've allowed themselves to be slightly casual at the seashore and their hats are straw. They approach the check-in desk."

Cora did the same.

Meanwhile, Rick went to the double doors at the entrance, inspecting them. "As you said, Professor, the interior doors are metal." He tried to open them, without effect. Proceeding to a window on the right, he pushed away rotted curtains, only to jerk back when another bird erupted, this one from the top of the curtains.

"Damned floor's covered with bird shit," Rick grumbled. He examined a shutter behind the curtain. "Metal." With effort, he freed a bolt. The shutter was mounted on a rail. He tried to push it but wasn't successful. "You mentioned that vandals smashed the windows. Rain and snow must have come in through the holes and rusted the rollers in place. The good thing is, nobody can see our lights."

"And if a security guard happens to pass, he won't hear us, either," Conklin said.

Rick pressed an ear against the shutter. "I can't hear the waves on the beach or the sheet metal clanging in that condo building. We've got the place to ourselves. But how on earth did the birds get in?"

A bell rang.

13

Balenger whirled.

Cora stood behind the check-in counter, her right hand on a dome-shaped bell, the brass of which would once have been shiny. Facing the group, she set her hard hat on the counter, her red hair glistening in their lights. Cobwebbed mail slots occupied the wall behind her. There were pieces of paper in a few of them.

"Welcome to the Paragon Hotel," she said. Her strong beauty was enhanced by the lights directed at her. "I trust your stay will be enjoyable. There is no finer hotel in the world." She reached beneath the counter and took out a wooden box, setting it on the counter, raising dust. "But this is our busiest season. Conventions. Weddings. Family vacations. I do hope you made reservations. Mr. . . . ?" She looked at the professor.

"Conklin. Robert Conklin."

Cora pretended to flip through cards in the box. "Nope. Sorry. Doesn't seem to be a reservation for Conklin. Are you positive you contacted us?"

"Absolutely."

"This is quite irregular. Our reservation department *never* makes a mistake. And what about you, Mr. . . . ?"

"Magill," Rick said.

"Well, there is a reservation for Magill, but it's for a woman only, I'm afraid. The noted historian Cora Magill. I assume you've heard of her. The best people stay here." Cora again reached under the counter and this time set down a thick ledger, raising more dust. She opened it and pretended to read names. "Marilyn Monroe. Arthur Miller. Adlai Stephenson. Grace Kelly. Norman Mailer. Yves Montand. Of course, only well-to-do people can afford to stay here." She picked up a card from next to the bell. "Our rates vary from ten to twenty dollars."

"When twenty dollars was twenty dollars." Rick laughed.

"Actually, you're not wrong about some of those guests," the professor said. "Marilyn Monroe, Arthur Miller, and Yves Montand did stay here. Monroe and the playwright were having domestic difficulties. After Miller checked out in a huff, Montand arrived to console Marilyn. Cole Porter stayed here, as well. So did Zelda and F. Scott Fitzgerald, Pablo Picasso, the Duke and Duchess of Windsor, Maria Callas, Aristotle Onassis, who was having an affair with Callas, and so on. In fact, Onassis tried to buy the hotel. The Paragon attracted a lot of famous and powerful people. And a few who were *in*famous and powerful. Senator Joseph McCarthy, for example. And the gangsters Lucky Luciano and Sam Giancana."

Balenger frowned. "Carlisle let *gangsters* stay here?"

"He was fascinated with their lifestyle. He ate dinner and played cards with them. In fact, he allowed Carmine Danata to keep a permanent suite here, 'a place to roost,' Danata called it, when he wasn't working as an enforcer in Atlantic City, Philadelphia, Jersey City, and New York. Carlisle gave Danata permission to have a vault put in behind a wall in his suite. It was done in the coldest part of the winter of 1935 when the hotel was virtually empty. Nobody knew about it."

"But if nobody knew about it . . ." Cora shook her head from side to side. "This reminds me of what's wrong with *Citizen Kane*."

"There's something wrong with *Citizen Kane*?" Vinnie asked in disbelief. "That's impossible. It's a masterpiece."

"With a big flaw. In the opening scene, Kane's an old man. He's dying in bed in his fabulous mansion. He has a snow globe in his hand."

"Everybody knows that opening," Vinnie said. "You and I once watched that movie together on the classics channel. You never mentioned anything about a flaw."

"I only realized it after you moved to Syracuse. Kane murmurs, 'Rosebud,' then drops the globe, which shatters on the bedroom floor. The noise makes a nurse charge through a door. All of a sudden, the newspapers and the newsreels are filled with the mystery of Kane's last word, 'Rosebud.' Then a reporter sets out to solve the puzzle."

"Yeah? So?"

"Well, if the nurse was out of the room and the door was closed and the bedroom was empty except for Kane when he died, how does anybody know his last word?"

"Oh," Vinnie said. "Shit. Now you've ruined the movie for me."

"The next time you watch it, just skip over that part."

"But what does this have to do with —"

"Professor," Cora said, "how could you know about a secret vault in Danata's room, one that was installed in the winter of 1935 when the Paragon was deserted?"

80

Conklin smiled. "You are indeed my student."

Balenger waited for the answer.

"It turns out that Carlisle kept a diary, not about himself but about the hotel, all the interesting events he observed over the decades. He was especially fascinated by the suicides and other deaths that occurred here. There were three murders, for example. A man shot his business partner for cheating him. A woman poisoned her husband for threatening to leave her for another woman. A thirteen-year-old boy waited until his father fell asleep and then beat him to death with a baseball bat. The father had molested the child for years. It took all of Carlisle's wealth and influence to keep those incidents from being publicized. After he died —"

"How?" Balenger asked. "Old age? Heart failure?"

"Actually, he committed suicide."

The group became still.

"Suicide?" Balenger scribbled a note.

"He used a shotgun to blow the top of his head off."

The group seemed to stop breathing.

"Despair because of ill health?" Balenger asked.

"The autopsy report was among the doc-

81

uments I examined," Conklin said. "Thanks to the strict health regimen and exercise program with which he tried to offset his hemophilia, he was remarkably fit for a man of ninety-two. He didn't leave a note. No one was able to explain why he killed himself."

"His mind must have been as sharp as his body," Rick said. "Otherwise, he wouldn't have been able to hide his intentions from his servants."

"In his last few years, Carlisle didn't have any servants."

"What? He took care of himself in this huge place all alone?" Cora frowned. "Wandering the halls."

"But if he was alone . . . ?" Vinnie sounded puzzled.

"You mean, how was he found?" Conklin said. "For probably the first time in his life, he left the hotel in the middle of the night, went down to the beach, and shot himself there. Even then, Asbury Park was in such decline, it wasn't until noon the next day that someone found him."

"A man with agoraphobia going down to the beach for the first time in his life so he can kill himself?" Balenger shook his head firmly. "That doesn't make sense."

"The police wondered if he'd been mur-

dered," the professor said. "But it had rained earlier in the night. The only footprints on the beach were Carlisle's."

"Eerie," Cora said.

"After his suicide, the old man's personal papers were deposited in the Carlisle family library, which is actually a storage area in the basement of the Manhattan building that used to be the family mansion. Carlisle's trust occupied the building until its funds ran out."

"The papers include the diary?" Balenger asked.

"Yes. When I chose the Paragon for this year's expedition, I did my usual research and discovered the existence of the storage area. The man who oversees the trust allowed me to examine the materials. He was trying to get various universities to bid on them. Evidently, he thought I had my university's authority to participate in the auction. I was given a day with the papers. That's when I discovered the diary."

"You weren't just repeating a rumor? There really *is* a vault in Danata's suite?" Balenger asked.

"All I can tell you is, there's no record of its having been removed."

"Hell, this is going to be more interesting than usual." Vinnie rubbed his hands together. "Of course, we still have to figure out which suite Danata had."

"Six-ten," Conklin said. "According to the diary, it has the best view in the hotel."

"Not the penthouse?"

"Because of Carlisle's agoraphobia, he couldn't bear large windows. A full view of the ocean would have terrified him. But he had other ways of looking. When I told you earlier that Aristotle Onassis wanted to buy the Paragon, I didn't add that Carlisle couldn't have sold it even if he'd been tempted. Without major reconstruction, almost tearing the hotel to the ground, Carlisle would have been publicly embarrassed and probably arrested."

"Arrested?" Rick asked in surprise.

"Because of his curiosity. The building has hidden corridors that allowed him to watch his guests without their knowledge."

"Peepholes? Two-way mirrors?" Balenger wrote hurriedly.

"Carlisle was diseased in more ways than his hemophilia. He allowed his diary to survive because he believed it served a social purpose. He thought of himself as a cross between a sociologist and a historian."

"Who else knows about this?"

"No one," the professor said. "Carlisle left no heirs. The man who administers the trust has remarkably little curiosity about his dead client. He's a blank-faced, bureaucratic type. The sort that does nothing but think about retirement when he's in his fifties. Does his work by rote. No expression in his eyes. Reminds me of my dean at Buffalo. I hid the diary at the bottom of Carlisle's papers. He'll never notice. But if a university buys those documents, eventually many people will learn what I just told you. Of course, it won't make a difference. The hotel will be a vacant lot by then. That's why this is the most important building we've ever infiltrated. The chance to verify and document the Paragon's history has all kinds of cultural implications begging to be included in a book."

"One that you'll write, I hope," Vinnie said.

"My final project." The professor looked pleased.

Cora glanced at her watch. "Then we'd better get going. The night's flying by."

Balenger tilted his headlamp toward his watch, surprised to see that almost an hour had passed from when they'd left the motel. Like the air in the tunnels, time felt compressed.

Cora glanced at the message slots and reached into one of the few that contained something. The paper was brittle. "Mmm, Mr. Ali Karim's credit card doesn't seem valid. The manager wishes to speak with him. Well, don't be embarrassed, Mr. Karim. I've had that happen a few times myself." Putting on her hard hat, she joined them in front of the counter.

"Too bad the elevators don't work," Vinnie said. "We've got a lot of stairs to climb. Can you do it, Professor?"

"Try to keep up with me."

Balenger warily studied dark corners as he and the others crossed the lobby.

"There's the ballroom." Conklin's head-lamp indicated open doors to their right, an empty oak-floored space beyond.

"Can I have this dance, Cora?" Rick asked.

"Gosh, my dance card's all filled. But the only thing that matters is who I go home with."

Rick glanced into the ballroom, smiled, and disappeared. A moment later, an out-of-tune piano began playing "Moon River."

"My favorite song," Cora said to the group.

"A little old-fashioned for someone your age, isn't it?" the professor teased.

"Rick and I love watching those old movies Henry Mancini and Johnny Mercer

86

wrote songs for. The romantic ones. *Dear Heart. Charade.* 'Moon River' in *Breakfast at Tiffany's.*"

Balenger imagined how Vinnie felt about that.

Blank spaces interrupted the notes, some of the keys not working. The tinny music reverberated in the huge space. It put Balenger on edge. Not that Rick was pounding away. The off-key melody wasn't much louder than their voices. Someone outside wouldn't be able to hear it. All the same, it felt like a violation.

The piano stopped. Rick showed his sheepish face around the corner. "Couldn't resist. Sorry."

"I'm sure if there were any more rats around here, you got rid of them," Vinnie said.

Rick laughed and rejoined the group.

They reached the grand staircase. Between magnificent banisters the marble steps rose, then divided, curving higher toward shadows on the right and left. But that wasn't where the group focused its lights. Instead, they stared at swaths of discoloration on the stairs.

"Dried water. Probably from holes in the roof." Vinnie's shoes crunched on shattered glass so covered with grime that the shards didn't glint from the reflection of his head-lamp. "The water flowed all the way down to here. Look at all the dirt it brought along."

"As we go higher, watch your footing," the professor warned Balenger. "There'll be rotted wood."

11:00 p.m.

14

They reached the division in the staircase. Other swaths of discoloration filled the right and left continuations of the steps.

"A lot of water," Rick said. "Years of it. When there's a strong storm, it must really pour down."

"Be careful," the professor said. "It could still be slippery."

They ascended the left curve of the stairs, probing shadows. At the top, they found a row of elegant doors with tarnished brass numbers on them. Murky wood-paneled walls were covered with dust. At intervals, corridors disappeared into darkness. The smell of mold and age was powerful. Balenger peered down at rotted Persian carpeting, its intricate pattern faded and flecked with mildew.

They turned left and followed a balcony. Every dozen paces, a narrow table was positioned against the wall. Some had vases with desiccated flowers, their petals looking as if the slightest touch would make them crumble. Then the group angled left again and came to more stairs. These were made of finely crafted wood, but Balenger couldn't be sure what kind because of the water damage they'd sustained. He peered up.

Vinnie did the same. "My God. The stairs keep following a central open column all the way to the top of the building. Hard to know for sure, but I think I see a glass roof. Moonlight. Clouds moving."

"A huge skylight occupies the top of the roof's pyramid," Conklin said. "The column rises through the middle of what used to be Carlisle's living quarters. He could walk from room to room and look down at the guests on the stairs and those in the part of the lobby that was visible to him."

"Wouldn't the guests have thought his behavior a little weird?" Cora asked.

"The walls of his rooms blocked him. People couldn't see him looking down. He used peepholes."

"The skylight must be broken. That's where the water's coming from. That's how the birds got in," Balenger said.

Abruptly, wood creaked under him. His heart lurched. He grabbed the banister.

Everyone paused.

"I don't feel the stairs moving," Rick tried to assure him. "It's just normal settling."

"Sure." Balenger wasn't convinced. He tested the next step.

"I need more light." Cora pulled her flashlight from her belt.

The others drew theirs, also. The shifting rays gave the shadows vitality, making it seem as if guests had just entered their rooms and were closing the doors.

The water stains became more pronounced as Balenger eased higher.

"What's that line William Shatner says at the beginning of every *Star Trek* episode? 'Space — the final frontier'?" Vinnie asked. "Good old Captain Kirk. But as far as I'm concerned, *this* is the final frontier. Sometimes, when I explore like this, I feel like I'm on Mars or someplace, discovering things I never thought I'd see."

"Like *this?*" Cora aimed her flashlight toward the steps above. "What is it? More mold?"

Green tendrils projected from debris on the stairs.

"No way. It's some kind of weed," Rick said. "Can you imagine? During the day, there must be just enough sun coming through the skylight to allow it to grow. The damned things take root anywhere." He looked at Balenger. "We once found dandelions growing from an old carpet near a broken window in a hospital scheduled to be torn down."

The wood creaked again.

Balenger kept his grip on the banister.

"I still don't feel anything shifting," Rick said. "We're fine."

"Sure. Right."

The group reached the fourth level and kept going.

But the professor hesitated. A dark corridor stretched ahead of him. He pressed his hand against a wall, then leaned against it, catching his breath.

"Always test a wall before putting weight against it," Cora warned Balenger. "On one of our expeditions in Buffalo, Rick leaned against one. He went right through. Then part of the ceiling collapsed. If he hadn't been wearing a hard hat —"

15

"Professor?" Vinnie frowned. "Are you okay?"

The overweight man breathed hard. Through glasses fogged with exertion, he waved away their concerns. "All these flights of stairs. I can tell some of you feel it, too."

Balenger raised a hand. "Guilty."

Conklin drew a water bottle from a slot on the side of his knapsack, untwisted the cap, and drank.

"I'll join you," Balenger said, taking a bottle from his knapsack. "To tell the truth, I wish I had some scotch in this."

"By popular demand, I don't touch the stuff anymore," Conklin said.

Cora offered a bag of granola. "Anybody want an hors d'oeuvre?"

Silhouetted by darkness, Rick and Vinnie each took a handful. Balenger heard the crunch of it in their mouths.

The professor swallowed more water waited, and finally put away his bottle. "Okay, I'm ready."

"You're certain?"

"Absolutely."

"Take a little more time," Vinnie said. "I wonder what the rooms look like." He tested a door, pleased when it opened. As his lights pierced the gloom, he nodded. "This room's got a metal shutter, too."

Balenger walked cautiously over. Stale air drifted past him, carrying a bitter undercurrent. Their scanning lights revealed that the room had a standard layout: a closet on the right, a bathroom on the left, and a bedroom area beyond a short corridor.

Cora glanced into the bathroom. "A marble countertop. The dust makes it difficult to tell, but those fixtures look as if they're —"

"Gold-plated," Conklin said.

"Wow."

There were two small beds, each with four posts and a dusty, floral-patterned bedspread. A Victorian sofa, table, and bureau contrasted with a television set. Apart from cobwebs, grime, and peeling wallpaper, the room presumably remained as it had looked in 1971 or earlier.

Vinnie walked toward the television. "No color-adjustment knobs. It's an old black-and-white. The screen has rounded corners. And look at this phone. The old-fashioned

rotary kind. I've seen them in movies, but despite all the buildings we've explored, I've never come across a dial phone until now. Imagine the eternity it took to make a call."

"That metal shutter." Rick pointed. "What's it covering? We're in the core of the building. There must be several rooms between here and the outside. There's no point in having a window. There's nothing to see."

"Actually," the professor said, "Carlisle put a window in every room. Each quadrant of the hotel has an air shaft. At one time, there were flower gardens, shrubs, and trees for guests to look down at. Some rooms next to the shafts even have doors leading onto balconies. The shafts end at the fifth level. The sixth level and the penthouse don't need them because, at the top of the pyramid, they have direct views of the outside."

"Until Carlisle installed the metal shutters," Cora said. "Was the old man so paranoid that he thought rioters would scale the air shafts?"

"The rampage. The fires. The gutted buildings. For him, it must have seemed like the end of the world." Vinnie looked at the professor. "Did he say anything about it in his diary?"

"No. The diary ends in 1968, the year he closed the hotel to guests."

"Three years before he died." Balenger looked around. "No explanation why he stopped writing it or why he closed the hotel?"

"None."

"Maybe life stopped being interesting," Cora said.

"Or maybe it was *too* interesting," Conklin said. "From the first World War to the Cuban missile crisis, from the Depression to the threat of nuclear annihilation, he'd seen the twentieth century get worse and worse."

"1968. What happened that year?" Balenger asked.

"The assassinations of Martin Luther King and Robert Kennedy two months apart."

The group became silent.

"What's on the bed?" Balenger pointed.

"Where? I don't see anything."

"There."

Balenger's lights centered on the first bed and a flat object on the pillows.

A suitcase.

"Why would anybody leave a hotel and not take a suitcase?" Cora wondered.

"Maybe somebody couldn't pay the bill and snuck out. Let's see what's in it." Vinnie

set down his flashlight and pressed two levers, one on each side of the suitcase's handle. "Locked."

Balenger unclipped his knife from his pocket. He opened it and pried at one of the locks.

"No," Rick insisted. "We look but don't touch."

"But we've been touching a *lot* of things."

" 'Don't touch' means 'don't damage, don't disturb, don't alter.' This is the equivalent of an archaeological site. We don't change the past."

"But then you'll never know what's in the suitcase," Balenger said.

"I suppose there are worse things I won't ever be able to do."

"If I can open it without breaking it, do you have a problem?"

"Not at all. But I don't see how you can manage it."

Balenger pulled out his ballpoint pen. He unscrewed the top and removed the ink cartridge, along with the spring that controlled the tip's in-and-out movement. Humming to disguise his tension, he put the end of the spring into a keyhole in the suitcase. He pressed, twisted, and heard the latch pop free. He did the same to the other lock, although it took him a little longer.

"Handy skill," Rick said.

"Well, I once did a story about a master locksmith, a guy the police send for when they really need to open something and nobody else can do it. He showed me a few easy tricks."

"The next time I lock myself out of my car, I'll give you a call," Vinnie said.

"So who wants to do the honors?" Balenger asked. "Cora?"

She rubbed her arms. "I'll pass."

"Vinnie? How about you? You're the first one who tried to open it."

"Thanks," Vinnie said uneasily, "but since you got it open, *you* should do it"

"Okay, but remember, if this is a monumental discovery, it gets named after me." Balenger lifted the suitcase's lid.

As a bitter smell escaped from the interior, five helmet lights and flashlights blazed on the contents.

16

No one moved.

"I feel like I'm going to be sick," Cora said. "What am I looking at?"

The suitcase was filled with fur. A mummified torso and head. Paws. Hands.

"My God, is it human?" Vinnie asked. "A child wrapped in —"

"A monkey," Balenger said. "I think it's a monkey."

"Yeah, welcome to *Wild Kingdom.*"

"Why would anybody . . . do you think somebody put it in there, locked the suitcase, and smothered it?" Rick said.

"Or maybe it was already dead," the professor suggested.

"And somebody was carrying it around for old times' sake?" Cora raised her hands. "This is one of the sickest things I've ever —"

"Maybe it was a pet and somebody tried to smuggle it into the hotel. But it suffocated before the owner could let it out."

"Sick," Cora said. "Sick, sick, sick. If it was such a prized pet, why didn't the owner take it out of here and bury it?"

"Perhaps the owner was overcome with grief," Balenger said.

"Then why lock the suitcase before leaving?"

"I'm afraid I don't have an explanation for that," Balenger said. "In my experience, all the human-interest articles I've written, people are more crazy than they're sane."

"Well, this is crazy, all right."

Balenger reached into the suitcase.

"You're going to *touch* it?" Vinnie said.

"I'm wearing gloves." Balenger nudged the carcass, which felt disturbingly light. The fur scratched along the bottom of the suitcase as he moved it. He found a rubber ball with flecks of red paint on it.

Noticing a flap on the inside of the suitcase's lid, he looked inside. "Here's an envelope."

The paper was yellow with age. He opened it and found a faded black-and-white photograph that showed a man and woman of around forty. They leaned against the railing of a boardwalk. It stretched to the right while the ocean extended behind them. Presumably, the boardwalk was Asbury Park's. Balenger thought he recognized the shape of the casino at the end. The man wore a short-sleeved white shirt, squinted from the sun, and looked to be in emotional pain. The woman wore a frilly dress and smiled desperately. Each wore a wedding ring. They had a monkey between them. It held a ball that looked like the one in the suitcase. It grinned and reached toward the camera as if the photographer were holding up a banana.

Balenger turned the photograph over. "There's a film-processing date. 1965." He looked closer at the envelope. "Something else is in here." He removed a yellowed newspaper clipping. "An obituary. August 22, 1966. A man named Harold Bauman, aged forty-one, died from a brain embolism. An ex-wife named Edna survived him."

" 'Ex'?" Rick asked.

Balenger used his flashlight to study a name tag on the suitcase. "Edna Bauman. Trenton, New Jersey." He took another look at the photograph. "They have wedding rings in 1965. Within a year, they divorced, and the ex-husband — what's his name? Harold? — died."

"A portrait of despair," Vinnie said. His camera flashed.

"Shut the suitcase," Cora demanded. "Lock it. Put it back where it was on the pillows. We shouldn't have disturbed it. Let's get out of this room and close the damned door."

"Reminds me of what I said back at the motel." Vinnie lowered his camera. "Some buildings make the past so vivid, it's like they're batteries. They've stored the energy of everything that happened in them. Then they leak that energy, like the emotion coming from that suitcase."

"Rick?" Cora asked suddenly, continuing to rub her arms.

"What?"

"Do me a favor. Go into the bathroom."

"The bathroom? What on earth for?"

"Go in there, and look in the bathtub. Make sure there's not another body in here, someone who slit her wrists or took pills or . . ."

Rick studied her, then touched her hand. "Sure. Whatever you want."

Balenger watched Rick guide his light back the way they'd come, to the bathroom. The young man went in. A silence lengthened, broken by the scrape of hooks on a shower-curtain rod.

"Rick?" Cora asked.

He remained silent a moment longer.

"Nothing," he finally answered. "Empty."

"Thank God. Sorry, everybody," Cora said. "I'm embarrassed that I let my emotions get carried away. When I was a kid, I had a cat that disappeared just before my family moved from Omaha to Buffalo. Her name was Sandy. She used to spend most of the day sleeping on my bed. The day we moved, I looked everywhere for her. After several hours, my dad said we needed to get in the car and leave. We had two days of driving ahead of us, and he said we couldn't waste any more time — he had a new job in Buffalo and couldn't arrive late. He asked the neighbors to look for Sandy and let us know if they found her. He promised he'd pay them to send the cat to us. Two weeks later, when I was unpacking some of my toys, I found Sandy in a box she'd crawled into. She was dead. You wouldn't believe how dried out her body was. She suffocated in what my dad said would have been the hundred-and-twenty-degree heat that accumulated in the moving van. A month later, my parents told me they were getting a divorce." Cora paused. "When I saw that dead monkey in the suitcase . . . I don't mean to be a . . . I promise I won't get upset again."

"Don't worry about it," Vinnie said. "My imagination got carried away, too. I wish I hadn't brought us in here."

Cora smiled. "Always a gentleman."

17

Outside, after everyone left the room, Vinnie closed the door. Balenger stood across from the group, his headlamp showing Vinnie and Rick next to each other. Vinnie was thin, with slightly rounded shoulders and pleasant but soft features, while Rick had an athlete's solid build and was outright handsome. All things being equal, it was easy to see why Cora had chosen the latter, Balenger thought. It was also easy to see that Vinnie still cared for her. That was no doubt one of the reasons he went on expeditions with them.

As Vinnie and the professor looked toward Cora, Rick stroked her shoulder. He was clearly bothered about what had happened in the room. In the harsh lights, his face was stark, his eyes now darting toward the door.

"The photograph appears to have been taken on the boardwalk outside." Rick's voice was tight as he tried to express what troubled him. "I wonder if the woman came back here to try to revive better memories.

The likely time for her to do that would have been while her grief was strongest, right after her ex-husband's death, not a couple of years later when she wasn't in as much shock."

"A reasonable assumption," the professor said.

"So let's say 1966, or 1967 at the latest."

"Again, that's reasonable."

"Carlisle died in 1971. The suitcase sat on that bed at least four years prior to that. Professor, you said Carlisle had peepholes and hidden corridors that allowed him to see what his guests were doing in private. He must have known about the suitcase. Why the hell didn't he *do* something?"

"Have it removed? I don't know. Maybe he liked the idea of gradually shutting down the hotel, leaving each room the way it was when its final guest checked out, wanting every room to have a memento that he could visit."

"What a wacko nutjob," Vinnie said.

"Yeah, we've come a long way from calling him a visionary and a genius." Rick's face remained stark. "How many other rooms have stories to tell?"

Vinnie moved toward a door farther along. He tested the knob, pushed the door open, and stalked into blackness, the door banging against the interior wall, the noise reverberating.

The others followed, Cora reluctantly. Balenger heard drawers being opened and closed.

"Nothing," Vinnie said, his light probing the room. "The bed's made. Everything's tidy. Apart from the dust, the place looks ready for its next guest. Nothing in the drawers, not even the customary Bible. Hotel toiletries on the bathroom counter, but nothing else, and nothing in the waste cans. Towels on a rack next to the shower. Everything the way it should be, except for *this*."

Vinnie opened the closet doors wider and showed them a Burberry raincoat, its wide lapels drooping, its tan belt dangling. "Back then, these things were a status symbol even more than they are now. Dustin Hoffman talks about how much he wants one but can't afford it in *Kramer vs. Kramer.* Okay, that movie's more recent than when the hotel closed, but the point's the same. Burberrys were exclusive and damned expensive. So why would somebody not take this?"

"An oversight," the professor suggested. "We've all forgotten something when we're traveling. It happens."

"But this isn't a pair of socks or a T-shirt. This is a very desirable overcoat. Why didn't the owner phone the hotel and ask a staff member to look for it?"

"You've got a point." Rick looked troubled. "But I'm not sure where you're going with it."

"What if Carlisle arranged for the owner to be told that the Burberry wasn't here? What if Carlisle made the owner think he'd lost it someplace else?" Vinnie suggested.

After Vinnie took a photograph of the coat, they left the room. On the balcony, it was now Rick who went to the next door. It too wasn't locked. He pushed it open. "For the love of . . ."

The group followed. The room was a mess: a pile of used towels on the bathroom floor, the wastebasket full, the bed unmade, sheets rumpled, bedspread thrown aside, a full ashtray on the nightstand, a glass and an empty bottle of whiskey next to it.

"I guess it was the maid's day off," Balenger said.

The professor read the bottle's label. "Black Diamond bourbon. Never heard of it. Must have gone out of business a long time ago."

Vinnie used a gloved hand to lift a cigarette butt from the ashtray. "A Camel. Unfiltered. Remember how people used to smoke all the time, how awful hotel rooms smelled?"

"Well, *this* room isn't a bouquet of roses." Balenger turned. "What's your theory, Professor?"

"Another room with a story. When Carlisle stopped accepting guests in 1968, he could have made sure the hotel was spotless and sanitized. But it looks as if he stopped renting the rooms one at a time and kept each in a kind of suspended state, each room retaining a hint of life."

"Or death," Cora said, glancing back toward the room where they'd found the suitcase.

"Professor, are you suggesting that after Carlisle closed the hotel, he wandered from room to room, looking in at scenes he'd preserved, absorbing himself in the past?" Balenger asked.

Conklin spread his hands. "Maybe to him it *wasn't* the past. Maybe the riots and his advanced years caused a nervous breakdown. Maybe he imagined the hotel was still in its heyday."

"Jesus," Vinnie said. He took a photograph and left the room. "Let's see what other surprises he created."

His light wavering, Vinnie walked along

the balcony, reached the next door, twisted its knob, and pushed with obvious confidence that the door would open.

18

But it didn't, and its resistance startled him. A DO NOT DISTURB sign hung on it. Vinnie turned the knob with greater force, pressing his shoulder against the door. "The others aren't locked. Why is *this* one?" He rammed against it, the door shuddering.

Conklin restrained him. "You know the rules. We don't disturb anything."

"Then what was that we did to the door in the tunnel? Taking a crowbar to it? That wasn't disturbing anything?" Vinnie slammed his shoulder against the door again.

"Granted," Conklin said, "but an argument can be made that the door in the tunnel wasn't part of the time scheme of the site. What you're doing is wrong."

"What difference does it make if I smash it? They're going to tear the place down in a couple of weeks."

"I can't allow us to become vandals."

"Fine. Okay." Vinnie looked at Balenger. "You know something about locks. Can you get this open?"

Balenger studied the lock, which had an old-fashioned design with a large slot. He unclipped his knife from his pocket, assuring the professor, "Don't worry. I won't damage anything." He opened the blade and tried to slide it past the edge of the door to pry at the bolt. "There's a lip I can't get past."

"Can't you pick the lock?"

"I suppose I could get a coat hanger from one of these rooms, make a hook out of it, and try to —"

"No need," Cora said behind everybody.

They turned, their lights merging on her.

"Downstairs, when I was behind the check-in counter, I noticed keys in the mail slots."

"Keys?" Rick chuckled. "Now *there's* an original idea. What's the door number?"

"Four twenty-eight."

"I'll go down and get the key."

"Are we sure we want to do this?" Conklin asked. "Our objectives were the penthouse and the vault in Danata's suite."

"If the unlocked doors have weird things behind them, I want to know what's behind a *locked* one," Balenger said.

"*Do* we?" Cora asked.

"If we don't," Rick said, "then why are we here?"

The professor sighed. "Very well. If you're

determined. But you can't go alone, Rick. That's always been another rule. We don't explore anywhere alone."

"Then we'll *all* go down," Balenger said.

The elderly man shook his head from side to side. "The stairs were too strenuous for me. I'm afraid I'd take forever to walk down and come back."

"And we don't need any heart attacks," Vinnie said.

"I seriously doubt there's any risk of that, but —"

"I'll go with Rick." Cora glanced again toward the door to the room that contained the suitcase.

"Use your walkie-talkies." Conklin unhooked his from his equipment belt. "Set one to transmit and the other to receive. That way I can hear you go down and come back. At the same time, I can talk to you without pressing buttons all the time and saying 'over.'"

"Fine."

Rick and Cora each unclipped a walkie-talkie from a belt.

"I'm 'transmit,'" Rick said.

"I'm 'receive,'" Cora said.

"We'll do the same," the professor said. "Vinnie, set your walkie-talkie to receive. I'll set mine to transmit."

Rick and Cora went to the top of the staircase and started down, their headlamps and flashlights making arcs in the gloom.

Balenger heard their footsteps echoing as they descended. A distorted version of those sounds came through Vinnie's walkie-talkie.

"We're at level three." Rick's voice reverberated from below while a staticky version came from Vinnie's walkie-talkie.

The footsteps sounded fainter. Balenger peered over the balustrade. Their lights were weak below him.

"Level two," Rick said.

Balenger could barely see or hear them.

Rick's voice crackled. "One. We're starting toward the lobby."

Vinnie's headlamp moved, causing Balenger to look in his direction. Vinnie was inspecting his surroundings. "Hey, there's an elevator in this corridor."

"We're crossing the lobby," Rick's voice said. "While I'm here, maybe I should go into the ballroom and play an encore of 'Moon River.' "

"Please, don't," Cora begged, joking.

"Besides," the professor said into his walkie-talkie, "that music is far too recent for this hotel. Carlisle would never have allowed it. More likely, the tune would have been something like 'On the Banks of the Wabash' or 'My Gal Sal.' "

"Did you know Theodore Dreiser's brother wrote both of those?" Vinnie asked.

"We're approaching the check-in counter," Rick's voice said.

"For God's sake!" Cora exclaimed.

"What's wrong?" Conklin blurted into his walkie-talkie.

"Another rat. I'm so sick of rats."

Balenger heard breathing from Vinnie's walkie-talkie.

"We're at the message slots. They have keys attached to metal discs with 'Paragon Hotel' stamped on them. Almost every mail slot has a key. Except in four twenty-eight."

"What?" Vinnie asked, puzzled.

"There's no key for six-ten, either," Rick's voice said.

"That's Danata's suite," Conklin said.

"Or to three twenty-eight, five twenty-eight, and six twenty-eight."

"Rooms directly above and below this one," the professor said.

"Wait," Rick's voice crackled.

"What's the matter?"

"I heard something."

Balenger, Vinnie, and the professor listened tensely.

"Rick?" Conklin asked.

Something scraped.

"Another damned rat," Cora's voice said. "I think they're having a convention."

"This is bullshit," Vinnie said. Balenger suspected that he was annoyed with himself that he hadn't gone with Cora.

Rick's voice said, "We're looking in the office behind the check-in counter."

Vinnie aimed his flashlight at his watch. "It's already near midnight. At this rate, we'll never finish before dawn."

"No keys," Rick said from the walkie-talkie. "But there are several filing cabinets."

Balenger heard a metallic sound from the walkie-talkie, presumably a cabinet drawer being slid open.

Rick: "Mostly maintenance records. Staff assignments. Bills and receipts of payments."

Cora: "This drawer has a reservation folder. It's empty. There's a folder devoted to which rooms are occupied. That's empty, too. But a lot of other folders are crammed. Guests who used to come here on a yearly basis, any special needs they had, any preferences for particular rooms, flowers, favorite foods. The most recent guest in that category stopped coming in 1961."

"The basic tedious details of trying to run

a business," Rick's voice said. "All the paper that got wasted before computers were invented."

"Hell, we probably waste just as much paper, printing everything out."

"They could be down there forever," Vinnie said. "As long as we're just standing around, why don't we try the next door?"

"We should wait till they come back," the professor said.

But Vinnie was already turning the knob. He pushed. "This one's unlocked." The door swung open. Balenger watched him stare into the darkness.

"Looks like the maid cleaned *this* one. Smells damp, though." Vinnie stepped inside.

And was swallowed.

19

The sound was like wet cardboard being torn. As Vinnie fell, his arms shot up, his flashlight flipping away. He screamed. Something crashed below him.

Balenger charged toward the open door and dove, landing on his stomach at the entrance to the murky room. The impact sent his hard hat clattering along the floor, its light twisting in sickening angles. He grabbed Vinnie's knapsack where it had caught the edge of a jagged hole in the floor.

Vinnie moaned.

The splintered boards collapsed. As Vinnie plummeted, Balenger tightened his grip on the knapsack, the force of Vinnie's fall dragging him toward the hole.

"Cross your arms over your chest!" Balenger shouted. "Tight! The knapsack! Keep the straps from slipping off your shoulders!"

In a frenzy, Vinnie clamped his arms across his chest. Balenger felt him trembling, felt the force with which Vinnie pressed the straps close to him.

Something crashed downward. Vinnie's headlamp pierced the shadows of the room into which he'd stepped. The floor was a rotted, gaping crater. The crash had come from a bureau falling through and smashing on the floor below. In turn, *that* floor gave way, its furniture cascading lower.

The floor under Balenger's chest began to buckle. His body slipped forward. "Bob! Get over here! Grab my legs! I'm sliding in!"

He heard the professor's heavy footsteps rushing toward him. At once, he felt thick fingers squeezing his ankles, trying to hold him.

Vinnie squirmed, his legs flailing, desperate to find something to support his feet. Another board gave way, repeating the dull wet cardboard sound. Vinnie jerked lower, forcing Balenger's arms into the dark, widening hole. A damp, moldy smell rose.

"Stop moving!" Balenger yelled. "For God's sake, keep still!"

"Gonna fall! Gonna fall!"

Now Vinnie's headlamp showed a gloomy four-poster bed moving. The floor buckled, the bed plummeting, crashing into the darkness below.

Vinnie's struggling weight dragged Balenger closer to the widening hole.

"Bob, hold my ankles harder! I feel your hands letting go!"

"Trying! Can't help it!"

"Lie on my legs!"

"What?"

"My legs! Lie on them, damn it! Your weight will keep me from sliding in!"

Balenger felt a crushing impact on his legs. He winced from the pain, but at least he was no longer being dragged into the hole. The light from the professor's headlamp glared past, revealing the crater. Only Vinnie's head showed. Meanwhile, Balenger's own head was almost in the hole.

"Vinnie, listen to me! I can get you out of there!" Balenger said.

"God, I hope."

"Stop squirming! You're making things worse!"

"Stop squirming," Vinnie told himself, trying to calm his frenzy.

"Count from one hundred backward."

"Why would I —"

"Just do it. Concentrate on the numbers. One hundred. Ninety-nine. Ninety-eight. Do it! Ninety-seven."

"Ninety-six. Ninety-five. Ninety-four."

Slowly, breathing hoarsely, Vinnie managed to still his body.

"Good," Balenger said, his arms aching.

"I'm going to twist you around so you're looking up at me."

Balenger shifted his arms to the left, causing Vinnie to turn sideways to him. Balenger's left arm took most of the strain. He had to lean farther into the pit in order to give his right arm the leverage to help. Despite the chill of the hotel, sweat trickled down his face. "That's as far as I can turn you!" The strain on Balenger's muscles made him grit his teeth. His voice echoed into the pit.

"Don't let go," Vinnie said.

"I promise." Balenger couldn't hold his grip on the knapsack much longer. "Can you see my left arm?"

"Yes." Vinnie's voice trembled.

Balenger studied the way Vinnie clamped his arms across his chest to keep the knapsack from slipping off his shoulders. Vinnie's right hand was pressed against his left shoulder.

"Raise your right hand. Grab my left arm. It's just over your shoulder."

"Can't," Vinnie said. "I'll fall."

Balenger struggled to keep his hands from slipping off the knapsack. "No. You won't fall. Let's do this another way." He didn't say "try" to do it. "Try" implied weakness. "Try" suggested possible failure. Every word had to involve a command that left no doubt of a positive outcome. "Keep pressing your right hand against your left shoulder. Release it just enough to slide it farther up your shoulder. Toward your neck. The straps won't slip off."

"Scared," Vinnie said.

"This is almost over. Do what I tell you." Balenger's arms were in agony. He felt the professor's weight on his legs. "Pay attention. Slide your right hand up your shoulder toward your neck."

Vinnie obeyed.

"Do you feel my left arm?"

"Yes." Vinnie's voice quivered.

"Turn your body. Keep sliding your hand until you grab my arm."

"I—"

"Do it! You're almost out of there!"

Balenger felt Vinnie's body turning slowly to the left. The strain on his arms was almost unbearable.

"Got it," Vinnie said breathlessly.

"You're doing great. You're almost out. Now I'm going to shift my left hand up the strap on your knapsack. I have to do it slowly so I can keep my grip on it. Okay?"

Vinnie's voice sounded terribly dry. "Okay."

"At the same time, move your hand down

my arm. At one point, our hands will touch. Grab onto my wrist."

"Wrist."

"You're almost out of there, Vinnie." More sweat dripped from Balenger's face.

"Got it. I've got your wrist."

"Hang on tight. I need to let go of the strap so I can grab *your* wrist."

"Holy Mary, mother of . . ."

Balenger felt Vinnie clutching his left wrist. At once, Balenger released his left hand from the knapsack and grabbed for Vinnie.

For an instant, Vinnie dropped. He moaned. Then Balenger had him, although the sudden movement caused Vinnie to sway.

"No!" Vinnie said.

"It'll stop. It'll stop!" Balenger said. His right hand felt tortured as it continued to grip the knapsack.

Vinnie's body again became still.

"Hold my wrist as hard as you can," Balenger said. His right hand could no longer bear the strain of the awkward angle that Vinnie's position forced on it. "Good. As hard as you can. Now raise your left arm. Not much. Just enough so I can hook my right hand under it. I need to release the knapsack."

"No."

"We can do this, Vinnie. You're almost out. On three, I'm going to release my right hand from the knapsack and grab your left arm. Are you ready?"

"I . . ."

"You'll soon be up here with me. Ready? It's going to happen on three. One. Two."

"Three," Vinnie shouted, and gripped Balenger's wrist with all his might.

Balenger's right hand shot from the knapsack and drove under Vinnie's left arm. The effort pivoted Vinnie so they faced each other.

"Bob!" Balenger yelled. "Can you pull us up?"

The professor tried, breathing heavily. "I . . . No. Not two of you. I don't have the strength."

"Vinnie, try climbing up my arms."

"Can't."

Balenger thought frantically. "Okay, we'll do something else." Keep it positive, he thought. His voice was hoarse. "I'm going to roll sideways to the right. That'll pull up our arms on the left. Get your elbow over the rim of the hole. I'll keep rolling sideways while you squirm up."

"I'll try," Vinnie said.

"No," Balenger said. "You're going to *do* it. You're getting out of there!"

Racked by the effort of holding Vinnie's weight, Balenger rolled slowly from his stomach onto his right side, his left shoulder threatening to pop from its socket.

"Yes," Vinnie said. "My elbow's over the edge."

"Higher." Balenger gasped. "Get your knee over."

"Can't."

Suddenly, headlamps and flashlights charged at them.

"Holy . . ." The voice was Rick's. He grabbed Vinnie's arm.

Thank God, Balenger thought, his heart pounding with relief.

"We heard noises from the walkie-talkie, but we couldn't figure what was happening!" Cora yelled. "We ran up here as fast as we could!" She tugged at Balenger, pulling with the professor's help.

Five seconds later, Vinnie lay on the floor, shaking. "We did it. No, that's wrong. *You* did it," he told Balenger.

"We *all* did," Balenger said.

"Thank you." Vinnie had trouble speaking. "Thank you, everybody." He turned his head, studying the hole, and squirmed farther from it. His chest heaved with emotion.

Balenger continued to lie on the floor, catching his breath. He pulled a water bottle from his knapsack, took a long drink, and handed it to Vinnie.

"My throat's so dry, I don't know if I can swallow." But once Vinnie started drinking, he couldn't stop. Water trickling from his mouth, he finished the entire bottle. "Never tasted anything so delicious."

"What happened?" Rick shifted carefully toward the hole. He gripped Cora's outstretched hand so he'd have support if the hole opened wider. He aimed his flashlight into the crater. "There's a faint light down there."

"My flashlight," Vinnie said. "I dropped it."

"Every floor collapsed," Rick said. "The furniture's in a heap all the way at the bottom. Smells awfully damp."

Rick stooped and pulled a chunk of wood from the edge of the hole. He eased away, returning to the group. "The wood's soft and pulpy." He raised it to his nose. "Smells like an old basement."

"From rot," the professor said. "The roof must have a leak. When it rains or snows, water seeps down through this column of rooms. After more than thirty years, one step from Vinnie was all it took to make the supports give way."

"Maybe it's a good thing we can't get into

the locked room," Cora said. "It's next to *this* room. Maybe the floor in there is rotten, too."

"Still didn't find a key?" Balenger rose to a crouch, then stood. His arms, shoulders, and legs ached.

"No key," Cora said.

"You're a handy guy to have around," Rick told Balenger. "You know about locks."

Balenger started to say "Not really," but Rick continued.

"You have quick reactions. The height didn't bother you."

"Because I couldn't see the bottom. Anyway, when I was a teenager, I did a lot of rock-climbing."

"Me, too. Where'd you go?"

"Wyoming."

"The Tetons?"

Why is he asking so many questions? Balenger thought. Does he suspect I haven't been telling the truth? "They're out of my league. The Grand in particular scares me. No, I took a course from a wilderness survival school. It's in Lander near the Wind River range."

"Sorry, everybody." Vinnie struggled to his feet.

"Sorry about what?" Balenger was glad to

change the subject. "You couldn't have known the floor was rotten."

"What I meant is . . ."

Their lights showed a wide, dark stain on his jeans, all the way from his crotch to his left ankle where he'd urinated on himself.

Embarrassed, Vinnie tried not to look at Cora.

"In your place, I'd have done the same," the professor said.

Vinnie peered down at the floor.

"Speaking of that problem . . ." Balenger took the empty bottle from his knapsack. "In all the excitement, it almost happened to me. If you can bear to be away from me for a while, I'll find some privacy down that corridor."

"Not too far," Conklin said. "We've learned a lesson about separating. Stay close enough so we can see your lights."

"After you're finished, maybe we'd all better do the same thing," Rick said.

Balenger picked up his hard hat, adjusted the light on it, and put it on. He walked to the corridor, scanned his flashlight along it, and proceeded cautiously, testing the floor. Past a tarnished elevator door and a dusty table with a cobwebbed vase on it, he stopped in the darkness and holstered his flashlight on his belt. In the illumination of

his headlamp, he unscrewed the bottle and urinated into it. He knew that the corridor's echo carried the liquid sound he made, but he didn't care if the others heard him.

As he screwed the cap on the bottle, he heard faint conversation from around the corner. Then he heard a slight thump in the opposite direction and aimed his headlamp toward the gloom at the end of the hallway. Doors stretched along each side. The angle of his light created shadows that made the doors seem slightly open. He set down the bottle with his left hand and used his right to lower his Windbreaker's zipper. He reached under the fabric and circled his fingers around a Heckler & Koch .40-caliber pistol in a shoulder holster.

20

No, keep control, Balenger warned himself. You're letting this damned place get to you. Stay focused. You've been through worse than this. He had a sudden sweat-producing memory of a foul-smelling sack tied around his head. No! Don't think about that! Suppose one of the others sees you holding the gun. If they learn you're armed, they'll surely wonder what else they don't know about you.

He waited, studying the shadows. Inhaling through his nose, exhaling through his mouth, holding each breath for three counts, he calmed himself. The sound at the end of the hall was not repeated. It could have been caused by anything — the building settling or the wind outside knocking something against a wall. Around the corner, the faint conversation continued. Nothing to get alarmed about, he thought.

"Everything okay?" Rick asked from the entrance to the corridor.

"Just finishing." Managing not to seem startled, Balenger closed his fly.

"You took a while. We were worried you might be in trouble."

"Enjoying a quiet moment." Balenger zipped up his Windbreaker, then picked up the bottle, its plastic warm from his urine.

"Where do I leave this?" he asked as he came around the corner, seeing the crisscross of headlamps.

"Not in here," the professor said. "Leave no trace, remember?"

"In your knapsack," Rick said. He went around the corner, heading toward where Balenger had been.

"First time for everything." Balenger made sure the lid was tight and shoved it into his pack.

From down the hall, he heard Rick urinating into his bottle. "Well, we're getting to know each other."

"We're talking about whether we should continue," Cora said.

"I'm okay, honestly," Vinnie assured them.

"You looked awfully shaken up a minute ago."

"I'm fine." To Balenger, it seemed that Vinnie was determined not to show weakness in front of Cora. "We traveled a long way to get here. We've all been looking forward to this, not to mention the time and money we put in. I won't let you go back because of me."

"But are you *able?*" Cora asked.

"There's nothing the matter with me," Vinnie insisted.

"Good," Rick said, coming back, zipping his knapsack shut. "I still want to know what's in Carlisle's penthouse and Danata's vault."

"Whose turn next?" Conklin asked. "Cora?"

She looked as if she was trying to avoid the awkward moment but was eager to get it finished.

As she left, Balenger glanced down at an object on the floor. A file folder.

"We found it in the office behind the check-in counter," Rick said. "It had an interesting label so we pulled it out. That's when we heard shouts from the walkie-talkie."

Balenger picked up the file and scanned his flashlight over the label: POLICE REPORTS. "Yeah, that's an attention getter." He flipped through the pages.

"A lot of crimes happen in hotels, mostly theft, but the guests never know about any of it," he said. "Bad for business. Usually, the police keep their investigations discreet. This file starts with the most recent incident and —"

Cora screamed.

Rick was suddenly in motion, charging around the corner, Balenger racing behind him. With Vinnie and the professor next to him, Balenger stared down the corridor. Zigzagging headlamps showed Cora with her back pressed against the wall, her jeans half down. Kleenex was on the floor next to her half-filled bottle. She gaped toward the far end of the corridor.

"Something's down there!" she said.

Rick hurried to get in front of her, blocking any threat. Good man, Balenger thought. In a frenzy, she pulled her jeans up, buckling them, all the while continuing to stare along the corridor.

"See anything?" Conklin asked.

"No," Balenger said, conscious of the gun under his Windbreaker.

"Yes," Vinnie said. "There."

Fierce eyes blazed from the end of the corridor.

Near the floor.

Balenger allowed himself to relax a little. "Another animal."

The converging lights revealed its head glaring around the corner.

"Hell, another albino cat," Rick said.

It bared its teeth, hissing.

"Look how it stands its ground," Vinnie said. "Not afraid of us. Feral. Furious that we're intruding."

"Must weigh twenty pounds," Rick said. "From that banquet of rats downstairs."

"When I was a kid, I spent summers on my grandmother's farm," Vinnie said. "There were a bunch of feral cats in an abandoned barn down the road. They ate every mouse, rabbit, and groundhog for miles. The birds got smart and stayed away. Finally the cats took to killing chickens. Then they graduated to goats and —"

"Thanks, Vinnie," Conklin said. "I believe we get the idea."

"What happened to the cats?" Balenger asked as the white animal hissed again.

"A farmer left poisoned meat. Didn't work. The cats were too smart to touch it. The guy said he counted at least fifty of them and was glad to jump back in his car and get out of there. A neighbor's wife claimed they made a try for her infant daughter. So, finally, about ten farmers got permission from the game warden or the sheriff or whoever and went out there with guns. I remember the shots lasted all afternoon. My grandmother said she heard they killed over a hundred."

"Vinnie," Cora warned.

"Well, this is just one. Scram!" Rick shouted. He took out his water pistol and sprayed vinegar in the cat's direction.

The liquid didn't come close. Even so, the cat gave a final hiss and disappeared around the corner.

"See, it doesn't like us any better then we like *it*."

Balenger noticed that during the commotion Cora put the bottle of urine into her knapsack. She shoved the Kleenex into a plastic bag, sealed it, and stuffed that into her knapsack, also.

"Are you okay?" Rick asked.

"Fine." She sounded apologetic. "It surprised me is all."

"Maybe we *shouldn't* go on."

"Hey, it wasn't anything." Embarrassment made her stand straighter. "We've all had jumpy moments in various buildings. Isn't that some of the point? To get an adrenaline rush. Just because I yell on a roller coaster doesn't mean I don't want to take another ride."

But it seemed to Balenger that she wished they were leaving.

"If that's what you want," Rick said.

He sounded reluctant, also.

"Let's go," Balenger said.

Midnight

21

Like the darkness that seemed to thicken, time felt even more compressed. Balenger noticed Vinnie limping slightly. Had he lied about not being injured? Then Balenger realized that Vinnie's awkward motion came from the wet feel of his pants.

They returned to the balcony.

"I don't have the need," the professor said, "but perhaps this is the best time. I don't want to delay us later." He removed his plastic bottle from his knapsack. "We know the first three rooms we checked are safe. I'll use one of those."

"Safe, if you don't count a dead monkey in a suitcase," Cora said.

"The room I had in mind is the one with the Burberry coat."

"Professor," Vinnie said, "one of us should go with you. Just to be extra cautious."

"Being cautious is good," Conklin agreed.

Balenger watched them open the door. They tested the floor, even though it had supported them earlier. Their lights went into the darkness.

Balenger put a hand against the balcony's wall. Satisfied that it was sturdy, he slid down, sitting with his back against it. Even if he wasn't relaxed, the illusion of resting felt good.

Rick and Cora slid down next to him. They looked as exhausted as he felt. Well, that's what adrenaline does to you, he thought. Eventually, it wears you out.

"Might as well use the time." Balenger reached for the file folder he'd dropped when Cora shouted.

POLICE REPORTS.

"Want some reading material?" He gave pages to Rick and Cora, keeping the most recent one for himself.

It was dated August 31, 1968. As the professor had explained, that was the year the hotel stopped receiving guests. Balenger expected that the file would be dominated by reports about thefts, the most common crime in a hotel, but what he read was far more serious.

An inquiry about a missing person. In August, one week after a woman named Iris McKenzie stayed in the Paragon, a police detective arrived, asking questions about her. No one had seen or heard from her after she paid her bill and left the hotel. Someone who worked for the Paragon made detailed handwritten notes about the conversation with the detective.

Iris McKenzie lived in Baltimore, Maryland, Balenger learned. She was thirty-three, single, a copywriter for an advertising firm that collaborated with big agencies in New York. After a summer business trip to Manhattan, she went to Asbury Park and spent a weekend in the Paragon. At least, the phone reservation she made indicated that she intended to stay for a weekend. Arriving Friday evening. Leaving Monday morning. Instead, she checked out on Saturday morning. Balenger had a suspicion that she realized how misinformed she was — that Asbury Park was no longer the place to go for a peaceful weekend getaway.

The person who took notes about the detective's inquiries (the handwriting seemed masculine) indicated that he showed the detective the reservation card and the receipt that Iris McKenzie had signed when she paid her bill and checked out early. The phone charges to her room showed a 9:37 a.m. long-distance call to a number the detective identified as belonging to Iris's sister in Baltimore. The detective indicated that the sister's seventeen-year-old son answered the phone and told Iris that his mother wouldn't be home until dinnertime. Iris told the boy to tell his mother she'd be returning to Baltimore that night. Iris then took a cab to the train station and got a ticket for Baltimore, but she never arrived at her destination.

Awfully talkative detective, Balenger thought. He volunteered way too much information. Ask questions. Don't provide details. Let the person you're talking to provide the details.

The hotel had no idea what might have happened to Iris after she left, the document indicated. It then went on to note that a month later a private investigator arrived from Baltimore, asking the same questions. The hotel representative who summarized the inquiries gave the impression that he was keeping a record in order to make sure everyone understood the hotel wasn't at fault.

Balenger felt his pulse quicken with the sudden thought that perhaps Carlisle himself had written the document. As darkness hovered beyond the balustrade, he concentrated on faded ink that was almost purple. His flashlight's beam went through the brittle yellow paper and cast a shadow of the handwriting onto Balenger's hand. Was there a hint of age in the handwriting, an imprecise quality in the letters that might have been caused by the arthritic fingers of someone in his late eighties?

Vinnie and the professor returned. As Conklin put the plastic bottle in his knapsack and zipped it shut, Balenger asked, "Was Carlisle's diary handwritten?"

"Yes. Why?"

"See if this looks familiar." Balenger handed the report to him.

The harsh lights made Conklin squint through his spectacles. The degree of his concentration was obvious. "Yes. That's Carlisle's handwriting."

"Let me have a look," Vinnie said. He surveyed the handwriting as if it posed a riddle. Then he passed the document to Rick and Cora.

"Makes me feel a little closer to him," Rick said. "You told us Carlisle had a . . . How did you put it? An arresting physical presence because of the steroids and the exercise. But what was his face like? His manner? Was he attractive or homely? Charming or overbearing?"

"In his prime, he was compared to a matinee idol. His eyes were the color of aquamarine. Sparkling. Charismatic. People felt hypnotized by him."

Rick gave the missing-person report back to Balenger and indicated a yellowed page from a newspaper. "I've got one of the murders. The thirteen-year-old boy who took a baseball bat to his father's head while he was sleeping. Hit him twenty-two times, really bashed his brains in. Happened in 1960. The boy's name was Ronald Whitaker. It turns out his mother was dead and his father sexually abused him for years. His teachers and the kids he went to school with described him as quiet and withdrawn. Moody."

"A common description of sex-abuse victims," Balenger said. "They're in shock. Ashamed. Afraid. They don't know who to trust, so they don't dare talk to anybody for fear they might blurt out what's being done to them. The abuser usually threatens to do something awful — kill a pet, cut off a penis or a nipple — if the victim tells anybody what's going on. At the same time, the abuser tries to make the victim believe that what's happening is the most natural thing in the world. Eventually, some victims feel everybody's an abuser in one way or another, that the world's all about manipulating people and they can't rely on anyone."

Rick pointed at the document. "In this case, the father took Ronald to Asbury Park on the Fourth of July weekend. A so-called summer treat. A child psychiatrist tried for several weeks to get Ronald to talk about what happened next. Eventually, the words came out in a torrent, how Ronald's father accepted money for another man to spend an hour alone with the boy. The stranger gave Ronald a ball, bat, and cheap baseball glove as a bribe. After the man left, the father came back to the room drunk and fell asleep. Ronald found a use for the baseball bat."

"Thirteen years old." Cora was sickened. "What happens to someone like him?"

"Because of his youth, he couldn't have been tried in a regular court," Balenger replied. "If he'd been of age, he'd have probably been found innocent by reason of temporary insanity. But in the case of a minor, a judge likely sent him to a juvenile facility where he received psychiatric counseling. He'd have been released when he was twenty-one. His court and psychiatric records would have been sealed so that no one could learn about his past and use it against him. Then it was up to him to try to move ahead with his life."

"But basically, that life was ruined," Cora said.

"There's always hope, I guess," Balenger said. "Always tomorrow."

"You sure know a lot about this." Rick studied him.

Is he questioning me again? Balenger wondered. "I was a reporter on a couple of cases like this."

"This hotel soaked up a lot of pain," Vinnie said. "Look at *this* report." The aged paper rustled in his hands. "The woman who owned the suitcase with the dead monkey in it. What was the name on the suitcase tag?"

"Edna Bauman," Cora said.

"Yeah, it's the same. Edna Bauman. She committed suicide here."

"What?"

"August 27, 1966. She took a hot bath and slit her wrists."

"Cora, your instincts are finely tuned," the professor said. "Remember you asked Rick to look in the bathtub? You were afraid something might be in there."

Cora shuddered. "Almost forty years earlier."

"August twenty-seventh," Rick said. "When was the date of the obituary for her ex-husband?"

"August twenty-second," Balenger answered.

"Five days. As soon as the funeral was over, she came back here to where she and her then-husband spent their last vacation the previous summer." Vinnie thought a moment. "Maybe that summer was her last happy memory. That's when the photograph of the two of them and the monkey was taken. One year later, her life was in ruins. Surrounded by better memories, she killed herself."

"Yes," Cora said, "this hotel soaked up a lot of pain."

"But wouldn't the police or somebody have removed the suitcase with the dead monkey in it?" Rick wondered. "Why did they leave it behind?"

"Maybe they didn't," Balenger told him.

"I don't understand."

"Maybe Carlisle took it before the police arrived. Later, he returned it."

The group became silent. Balenger thought he heard the wind outside, then realized that the sound came from an upper level.

"The room that has the Burberry coat," Conklin said. "When I was in there, Vinnie thought to search the pockets."

"I found this." Vinnie handed a letter to Rick and Cora.

Cora read the heading and the date. "The Mayo Clinic. February 14, 1967. 'Dear Mr. Tobin: Your recent chest X rays indicate that the primary tumor has spread from the upper lobe of your right lung. A secondary tumor has appeared on your trachea. A new course of aggressive radiation needs to be scheduled at once.' "

"Tobin." Rick sorted through the pages Balenger had given him and found another yellowed newspaper clipping. "Edward Tobin. Philadelphia stockbroker. Age forty-two. Suicide. February 19, 1967."

"Right after he received that letter."

"February?" Vinnie asked. "Even if he was suicidal, winter's an odd time to come to the Jersey shore."

"Not if he intended to walk into the ocean and freeze to death before he drowned." Rick pointed toward the newspaper article. "The guy was wearing only a shirt and trousers when his body was found iced-over where the tide brought him in."

Again, Balenger was conscious of the shriek of wind above him. "Odd to have two rooms next to each other, both associated with a suicide."

"Not if you think about it," Conklin said. "Thousands and thousands of guests stayed here over the Paragon's many years. A changeover in each unit every few days. Decades and decades. Eventually, every single room would have been associated with a tragedy. Heart attacks, miscarriages, strokes. Fatal concussions from falls in bathtubs. Drug overdoses. Alcoholic rages. Beatings. Rape. Sexual abuse. Marital and business betrayals. Financial disasters. Suicides. Murders."

"Cheery," Rick said.

"A small version of the world," Balenger said. "That's why Carlisle was fascinated with his guests."

"A Calvinist God watching the damned, capable of intervening but choosing not to." Cora rubbed her arms in distress.

"If we're going to finish this tonight, we'd better keep moving." Rick gathered the pages they'd been reading. He put everything inside the file and zipped it into a slot on the back of his knapsack.

"We'll need to remember to return it to the file cabinet when we leave," the professor said.

"I don't know what the point would be," Vinnie said. "This hotel will soon be a pile of rubble."

"But that's a rule," Rick told him. "If we break it even once, eventually we'll break others. Then we'll merely be vandals."

"Right." Vinnie's tone became flat. "When we leave, we'll put the file back."

22

Flashing their lights around them, they left the balcony and headed up the stairs.

"Feels solid," Cora said. "But after what happened to Vinnie, to be safe maybe we should go up in single file. That way, there's less pressure on the stairs."

"Excellent idea." The professor was always ready with praise for Cora, Balenger noted. "Keeping a slight distance between each of us would be useful, too."

Forming a line, they climbed higher through the shadows. On occasion, the stairs creaked, making Balenger tense, but the wood remained steady, and he decided the sound wasn't any different from the normal sounds that old stairs made when someone climbed them.

The professor gasped as a bird on an upper banister panicked, bursting into the air, desperate to escape their intrusion. It slammed into a wall and swung away in greater panic. Blinded, it circled their lights, its wings thrashing. At once, it veered down the stairs, disappearing into the darkness.

"Well, *that* certainly got the old heart racing," Conklin said.

Balenger turned toward him. "Are you sure you're okay, Professor?"

"Couldn't be better." The stocky man was out of breath again.

"Only two more levels to go."

"Terrific."

Footsteps echoing, they reached level five.

"Uh!" Rick jumped away.

"What's wrong?" Cora shouted.

"This." Rick pointed. "Something brushed the top of my hat."

They aimed their lights above Rick's head.

"For God's sake, that looks like —"

"Roots," Vinnie said.

What resembled ropes and strings dangled from the floor of the balcony above them. Threads seemed attached to them: smaller roots.

"I've never seen anything like . . . *What's growing up there?"*

They reached the continuation of the stairs. Rick took the lead, then Cora, Vinnie, Balenger, and finally the professor, whose slow pace made it natural for him to be the last.

Balenger now had a chance to study the skylight. It was spacious, perhaps forty feet square, shaped like the tip of a pyramid. Large segments of glass were held in place by crisscrossing copper supports, their metal green with age.

But many segments were missing or broken. After so many years, heavy accumulations of ice and snow had weakened the supports. Balenger remembered the shattered glass at the bottom of the stairwell. Yes, this is how the birds get in, he thought. He saw a half moon disappearing behind clouds. The wind whistled past the gaps in the skylight, the source of one of the sounds he'd earlier heard. The air got colder.

Something's wrong, he realized. "The stairs don't go higher. We're coming to the sixth level. There should be another set of stairs leading up to Carlisle's penthouse on the seventh. But there aren't any. How do we get up to it?"

"Take a look at that." Rick aimed his flashlight at the balcony he climbed toward.

As one, the group imitated him, their lights revealing the area from which the roots dangled.

"Some kind of . . ." Cora paused in astonishment. "For the love of . . . Is that a *tree?*"

Five feet tall, leafless and listing, its scraggly trunk and branches cast shadows from their lights.

"But how the hell . . ."

"A bird brought a seed in," Cora said. "Or the wind did it."

"Yes, but how did it manage to grow?"

Balanger's flashlight revealed a shattered urn. Dirt lay in a pile among the broken pieces. The tree grew out of the dirt. "There's your explanation. Add a little rain from the broken skylight, and it manages to stay alive."

"Barely," Rick said. "It looks like it's trying to feed off the carpet and the wooden floor. That's why the roots are so long. It's desperate to find food."

"The floor will be weak over there." Conklin paused behind Balenger. "Stay away from it."

Ahead, Rick stepped onto the balcony. Cora got there next. Then Vinnie. Balenger left the stairs and looked for a way up to Carlisle's penthouse. He glanced behind him toward where Conklin trudged up.

Creak.

23

The professor stiffened.

"I feel . . ." He exhaled. ". . . the stairs shifting."

Creak.

Hesitant, he took another step upward.

Creak.

"Definitely shifting."

"Don't move." Balenger watched the staircase begin to sway.

"I suddenly feel as if I'm on a boat," Conklin said.

Crack. The staircase swayed more discernibly.

"No!"

"Try to take my hand." Rick braced himself at the top of the stairs and reached down. "Cora. Vinnie." His voice was stark. "Grab me from behind so I don't get pulled onto the stairs."

Crack.

"If I reach up," Conklin said, "that'll shift my weight and make the staircase —"

As if anticipating his next words, the staircase wobbled.

Rick extended his arm farther, straining. "Damn it, I can't quite —"

Crack.

"It sounds like it's going to . . ." Vinnie held Rick tighter. Rick leaned farther down the stairs.

"Even if I stretch my arm, I'm not close enough." Conklin's voice trembled.

Crack.

"We can't just let him . . ." Cora held Rick with all her might.

"The rope," Balenger demanded. "Who's got it?"

"I do," Vinnie said.

Balenger rushed to him, unzipped his pack, and tugged out the rope. It was bundled in a figure eight. Thin. Made of twisted strands of blue nylon. Climber's rope.

Urgent, Balenger made a loop at one end and tied a slipknot. He hurried next to Rick, his headlamp revealing the professor's frightened features.

"I'm going to throw a loop around you," Balenger told him.

Behind his spectacles, Conklin's eyes were huge with apprehension.

"Raise your arms through the loop," Balenger ordered. "Adjust the rope so it's under your arms."

CRACK.

155

The professor flinched as the stairs jerked.

"When the rope's under your arms, tighten the slipknot. Make the rope as secure around your chest as possible."

No reply.

"Professor, do you understand me?"

CRACK.

The stairs swayed out of control.

"No!" Balenger swung the rope above his head and hurled it toward Conklin. It fell past the heavy man's shoulders. He swung the rope again, threw it, and felt his heart speed as the loop dropped over the professor's head, catching on his left shoulder.

"Reach through it!"

Conklin pushed his hands under the loop and enfolded it with his arms.

"Under your arms! The slipknot! Tighten it!"

Barely able to control his movements, the professor obeyed.

"Rick! Cora! Vinnie! Grab the rope! We need to anchor it!"

"This post on the balustrade," Rick said. "Wrap the rope around it."

"Might not hold. Wrap the rope around each of you!" Balenger said. "Lean back! Hang on! There's going to be a hell of a jolt!" He secured the rope around his chest in a belaying position and braced himself. "Professor, try to walk up!"

"Walk?" Conklin tried to keep his balance on the swaying stairs.

"Maybe they'll hold!"

The professor swallowed. He took a step upward.

The stairway collapsed.

24

Balenger was almost jerked off his feet. The noise was overwhelming. He felt most of the force through his legs and arms. Even so, the sudden pressure of the rope around his chest took his breath away. Clutching the rope with his gloves, leaning back against the dropping force of the professor's weight, he groaned. His feet slid.

"Pull!" he shouted to Rick, Cora, and Vinnie.

The pressure around Balenger's chest tightened as the others stopped him from going over the edge. If not for his Windbreaker, he'd have suffered rope burns. Struggling to breathe, he suddenly felt the professor quit falling. The light from a headlamp bobbed below the edge of the fallen staircase. Balenger stared at the rope where it dug tautly into the remnants of broken wood.

"Professor?" Balenger managed to draw a breath.

No answer.

"For God's sake, can you hear me?"

A faint murmur.

"Talk to me," Balenger said. "Are you hurt?"

"Uh."

Sweat slicked Balenger's face. "Professor?"

"Feel . . . suffocated."

"That's the pressure of the rope around your chest."

"Can't breathe."

Christ, is he having a heart attack? Balenger wondered. "Take slow, shallow breaths. Slow," he emphasized. "If you hyperventilate, you'll throw yourself into a panic."

"Panic's an understatement."

The rope creaked.

Balenger looked behind him. "Rick, Cora, keep holding the rope. Vinnie, get over here and help me pull him up."

Vinnie hurried next to him and grabbed the section of rope that led to Conklin.

"Hurt," the professor said as the rope shifted upward.

"We'll soon free your chest."

"Not the rope."

"What?"

"Leg."

Balenger and Vinnie strained to raise him. Conklin's headlamp came into view, a chin strap securing it. Then his anguished face appeared, paler than before. His spectacles were gone. Without them, his eyes looked vulnerable. Fear made them wide.

Balenger and Vinnie pulled him higher.

The professor gasped. "Stuck on something."

Balenger was conscious of Rick and Cora behind him pulling on the rope, preventing him from being dragged over. He heard the effort in their breathing.

"Vinnie." Balenger's voice sounded as if he'd swallowed sand. "Let go of the rope and tug him onto the balcony."

Vinnie gradually released his grip. As soon as the professor's weight was fully transferred to Balenger, Vinnie eased toward the edge. He grabbed the professor's arm and pulled.

The professor winced but didn't move.

"I see it," Vinnie said. "The front of his jacket's caught on a board."

"You know what to do. The knife. That's what you brought it for. Cut the jacket."

Vinnie seemed to suddenly remember that he had it. He unclipped it from the inside of his jeans pocket, opened it, and sliced at Conklin's jacket. For a brief moment, he looked in terror at the abyss into which the stairs had collapsed.

"Done." He rushed back to Balenger and grabbed the rope.

This time, when they pulled, the professor moved. Slowly, painfully, the elderly man was able to help them. Bracing his elbows on the edge of the balcony, he squirmed his right knee over the edge. With an inward shout of triumph, Balenger moved along the rope, grabbed the professor, and helped Vinnie drag him to safety.

Rick and Cora were suddenly with him as well. The professor lay on his back, gasping as Balenger freed the slipknot and pulled the rope from him.

"Can you breathe now?" Balenger frantically checked the professor's pulse.

Conklin's chest heaved as he sucked in air.

Balenger counted a pulse of 140, the equivalent of an athlete's heart rate after running several miles. For an overweight, out-of-condition man, it was far too high. "Does your chest still hurt?"

"Better. It feels better. I can catch my breath."

"Oh, shit," Rick said.

"His left leg." Cora pointed.

Balenger registered the strong smell of copper. Lowering his gaze toward the professor's pantleg, he saw that it was soaked with blood all the way from his thigh to his shoe.

Conklin moaned.

25

"Okay, everybody, listen up," Balenger said.

As the professor's thigh oozed more blood, Cora turned away in horror.

"Forget what you're feeling. Do exactly what I tell you," Balenger ordered.

Rick put a hand to his mouth.

"We don't have time for this," Balenger said. "Everybody, pay attention. Do what I tell you." He unclipped his knife and cut the professor's jeans from the groin to the cuff. He spread the fabric. "Who's got the first-aid kit?"

Conklin squirmed. There was a deep, four-inch-long gash in his thigh, blood spreading from it.

"Who's got the first-aid kit?" Balenger repeated.

Vinnie blinked in shock. "Rick. I think Rick has it."

"Get it out. Now." Balenger tugged the rope around the professor's thigh, tying it above the wound. *"Who's got the hammer?"*

Cora forced herself to look at the blood.

In the headlamps, her red hair contrasted harshly with her pale cheeks. "I do."

"Give it to me!"

Cora forced herself into motion, unholstering the hammer from her equipment belt.

Balenger wedged the handle under the rope and twisted, tightening the rope around Conklin's thigh. The blood stopped flowing. "Hold it like that."

Balenger took the Pro Med kit from Rick. "Your water bottle. Get it out. Rinse the wound. Who's got the duct tape?"

"I do." Vinnie came out of his shock.

"Get it ready."

"Duct tape? We use it for covering the sharp edges of pipes so we don't get cut. How's it going to —"

"Just do what I say."

Balenger unzipped the Pro Med's bag and opened its two compartments. About to reach in, he frowned at his dirty gloves and replaced them with latex ones from the kit. "Cora, your right hand's free. Aim your flashlight toward the kit."

He pulled out packets of alcohol wipes and ripped them open. "Rick, pour water on the wound. Cora, aim your flashlight toward the gash."

Using his jacket sleeve to wipe sweat from

his eyes, Balenger stared at the water rinsing the wound. With the bleeding temporarily stopped, he saw the jagged flesh. "The artery hasn't been cut." He used an alcohol wipe to clean dirt from the edges, then leaned close, staring hard at a piece of wood projecting from the wound. "Who's got the Leatherman tool?"

"I do." Rick freed the snap on its pouch and handed it over.

Balenger opened it to the pliers mode. "Keep rinsing the wound. How are you feeling, Professor?"

"Sore."

"Is the rope cutting into you?"

"Yes."

"If that's your only pain, you're doing well. The rope not only stops the bleeding, the lack of circulation numbs the wound. But we can't keep it like that too long. Swallow these." Balenger tore open two Extra-Strength Tylenol packets and gave him four pills. "They're not Vicodin, but they're better than nothing."

Conklin shoved them into his mouth. Rick gave him a drink of water.

"My flashlight. I dropped it when the stairs collapsed." The professor sounded as if he blamed himself. "Vinnie lost his, also."

"We still have three." Balenger used an alcohol wipe to clean the end of the pliers. He smelled the sharp fumes. "Here we go. Cora, keep your light steady."

Balenger inserted the pliers into the gash and gripped the splinter just above where it was embedded into flesh. As gently as possible, he pulled it out.

The professor gasped.

"The worst part's almost over," Balenger tried to assure him. "Keep aiming the flashlight, Cora. More water, Rick." As blood was rinsed away, Balenger saw another piece of wood, smaller, almost hidden in the flesh.

Working to steady his hand, he probed the pliers into the gash, heard the professor moan, and tugged out the splinter.

He stared into the wound, searching for other debris, then picked up his open knife and cleaned it with an alcohol wipe. He inserted the tip and moved it back and forth over the raw flesh, feeling for any resistance, anything hard within the flesh. He exhaled, then set down the pliers and the knife.

"That wound needs stitches," Cora said. "A lot of them."

"We'll have to make do with what we've got. Rinse it again," Balenger told Rick. He ripped open four packs of triple antibiotic ointment and squeezed their contents into the wound. "Doing okay, Professor?"

"Feel sick."

"I don't doubt it. You're on the verge of shock. Vinnie, get over here and kneel beside me. Good. Now take off your work gloves and put on gloves from the first-aid kit. Excellent. Now squeeze the wound together."

"What?"

"Squeeze the wound together."

"Are you crazy?"

"It's the only way to do this. You need to hold it together while I seal it."

"For God's sake, seal it with *what?*"

"The duct tape."

"You have got to be fucking kidding me."

"Never mind. If you can't do it . . ." Balenger turned. "Rick, get over here, put on latex gloves, and hold the wound together."

"All right, all right, all right," Vinnie said. He squeezed the edges of the wound together.

As ointment and watery blood oozed out, the professor screamed.

"I know this is tough," Balenger told Conklin. "I promise it's almost over. But first, I need to ask you to do something really hard."

"What?"

"Keep your knee straight while Rick lifts your lower leg."

"Yes," Conklin said, "that's going to be hard." He closed his eyes and fought the pain.

"Ready?"

The professor nodded.

"Rick," Balenger said. As Rick lifted Conklin's leg and Vinnie held the wound together, Balenger peeled duct tape from its roll, the silvery strip reflecting the lights. He pressed it over the bottom of the wound and began wrapping it around the professor's thigh. As more of the wound was covered, Vinnie shifted his hands up, still squeezing the edges together. The professor sounded as if he was about to weep from the pain.

Balenger kept winding the tape around the wound. He put on a second layer, then a third, a fourth. "Okay, Rick, you can lower the leg."

The professor shuddered.

"Now let's find out if anything leaks. Cora, untwist the rope."

The group tensed as Cora removed the hammer's handle from the rope, creating slack. Balenger aimed his flashlight at the duct tape. They stared.

"Pins and needles," the professor said.

"That means the circulation's returning."

"Throbs. Hurts. God."

Balenger kept staring at the duct tape and silently prayed. He watched for blood to leak from the edges and the seams. "Looking okay." The tape remained silvery.

He grabbed the professor's wrist and again checked his pulse. One hundred and twenty. Lower than it was. Not good but not terrible, given what the professor had been through. Still no blood seeped past the duct tape. "Yeah, looking okay."

He pulled his cell phone from his jacket.

26

"What are you doing?" Conklin asked.

"Calling 911."

"No." The professor found the strength to raise his voice. "Don't."

"No choice," Balenger said. "You need an ambulance, Bob. A hospital. Stitches, antibiotics, treatment for shock. Maybe an EKG. If that duct tape stays on too long, you'll get gangrene."

"You mustn't call 911."

"But we can't screw around with this. Just because I patched you up doesn't mean you're out of danger."

"No," Conklin said. "Put down the phone."

"But he's right, Professor," Cora said. "We need to get you to a hospital as soon as possible."

"Outside."

"What?"

"Take me outside. *Then* call 911. If ambulance attendants find you in here, they'll alert the police. You'll all be arrested."

"Who the hell cares about being arrested?" Vinnie said.

"*Listen* to me." Conklin drew a breath. "You'll spend months in jail. The legal bills. The fines. What happened to me is exactly why the police don't want us doing this. They'll make an example of you." He shivered. "Vinnie, you'll lose your teaching job. Rick and Cora, no university will hire you. If Frank makes that call, your lives will be ruined."

"He said 'Bob.' " Rick frowned. "What's going on?"

"I don't understand," the professor said.

"A minute ago, Balenger called you 'Bob.' Not 'Professor,' not even 'Robert.' '*Bob.*' I'd never dream of calling you that. At the motel, he introduced himself, but after three hours, for the life of me I couldn't remember his first name. Not you, though, Professor. Just now you called him 'Frank.' My God, the two of you have met before. You know each other."

"You're imagining things," Balenger told him.

"Like hell. You came in here as an observer, and all of a sudden, you're running the show. You saved two of us from getting killed and acted like it was business as usual. Clint Eastwood crossed with Dr. Kildare. Who the hell *are* you?"

"I don't know what you're talking about," Balenger said, his stomach churning.

"There isn't time for this. We need to get the professor to a hospital."

"Get me outside," Conklin said. "*Then* phone 911."

"It took us two and a half hours to go this far."

"Because we dawdled. If you hurry, you can get me outside in a half hour."

"Quicker, if we use the crowbar to pry the front door open," Vinnie said.

"No! You can't leave a sign that you were in here. If the police look around and find a broken door . . ." The professor trembled. "I'll never forgive myself if I ruin your lives. You need to take me back the way we came in — through the tunnel."

"But what about *your* life?" Balenger demanded. "What if you hemorrhage while we're trying to get you out of here?"

"I'll take that risk."

"This is crazy."

"In your experience, does duct tape seal a wound for an acceptable length of time?" Conklin asked.

Balenger didn't answer.

"Who the hell *are* you?" Rick repeated.

"The duct tape," the professor said. "How long?"

"If it's removed within a couple of hours . . ."

"Help me up," Conklin said.

"What do you think you're doing?"

"Get me up. Rick and Vinnie can support me. I can hobble on my good leg."

"But —"

Conklin winced. "I weigh two hundred and ten pounds! It'll take forever if you try to carry me!"

"Calm down," Balenger said. "You don't want to have a heart attack on top of everything else."

"Why is he trembling?" Cora asked.

"Shock."

"We could have been on our way by now," Conklin said. "We're wasting time."

Balenger studied him. "Bob, is this really what you want?"

" 'Bob,' " Rick said again.

"I've lost my professorship."

"Lost your . . . ?" Vinnie looked stunned. "What are you talking about?"

"I've been ordered to leave the university by the end of the term."

"What in God's name happened?"

"The dean found out what I was doing. He's been looking for ways to cut costs, especially tenured positions. He had the faculty senate terminate me for breaking the law and endangering students."

"No," Rick said.

"I'm an old man. I don't have much to lose, but you three are just starting. I'll never forgive myself if I ruin your future. Help me up! Get me out of here!"

"How?" Balenger asked. "The staircase collapsed. What are we supposed to do? Lower you by rope from balcony to balcony?"

"There'll be emergency stairs."

They scanned their lights around.

"Over there. A corridor," Rick said.

"Keep us together. Rick. Vinnie. Help me up."

The professor groaned as he was lifted. With one arm around Rick and the other around Vinnie, he balanced on his good leg. They helped him limp forward.

Balenger headed along the balcony toward the hallway. Cora hurried next to him. Past an elevator, they flashed their lights at a sign: FIRE EXIT.

"Finally, a break," Balenger said.

He opened the door and flinched as something rushed past his legs. Cora shouted. Something hissed, racing toward the balcony. Almost drawing his pistol, Balenger heard Rick yell, "It's another white cat! The place must be lousy with them."

"No," Conklin said. "Not another."

He sounds delirious, Balenger thought.

"The same," Conklin murmured.

"The *same?* You're not making sense."

"Look at its hind legs."

Balenger flashed his light toward the panicked, awkwardly fleeing animal. So did Cora and everyone else. The glare of their beams showed it dashing along the balcony toward the grotesque tree growing through the floor.

But the albino cat was grotesque also.

"Three back legs," Rick whispered. "It's got *three back legs.* Just like the cat we saw in the tunnel."

"Not *just* like," the professor said weakly. "Mutations of that sort aren't common. The odds are against it."

"The *same* cat?" Balenger said.

"The one we saw on level four."

"But that's impossible," Cora said. "We closed the door that led from the tunnel into the utility room. I know we did. I insisted we do it. So how did the cat get in?"

"Maybe the rats chewed holes through the concrete walls, like the professor said," Vinnie suggested.

"Maybe," Balenger said.

"There's no 'maybe' about it," Vinnie said. "That's the only way it could have gotten in."

"No," Balenger said, moving toward the balcony. "There's another way."

"I don't see what."

"Someone could have come in after us and left the door open."

Except for the wind shrieking past the holes in the skylight, the hotel became deathly silent.

Then the silence was interrupted by another high-pitched sound. Slow but rhythmic. Beautiful but mournful.

"Wait a minute," Cora said. "What's *that?*"

Doom, Balenger thought. Through the gaps in the skylight, the wind carried the distant tolling *clang clang clang* from the strip of sheet metal flapping in the abandoned condominium building. But it didn't obscure the sound below him.

Lyrical. Terrifyingly evocative. A mournful tune that summoned lonely images to his mind.

In the dark abyss below them, someone was whistling "Moon River."

27

"Jesus." Cora lurched back from the balcony.

The others followed.

The whistling continued, echoing upward from the darkness. The melody evoked images of dreams and heartbreaks and longing to move on. Right, Balenger thought. What I wouldn't give to move on right now.

"Who?" Rick whispered.

"A security guard?" Vinnie kept his voice low.

"The police?" Cora shut off her headlamp and flashlight.

If only we're that lucky, Balenger thought.

Vinnie and Rick turned off their lights. Cora extinguished the professor's. As the gloom tightened around them, Balenger's headlamp and flashlight were the only illumination.

"Shut your lights off," Rick whispered urgently. "Maybe whoever it is doesn't know we're up here."

But Balenger left them on. At normal volume, his voice was forceful compared to their whispers. "A policeman wouldn't be strolling around, whistling in the dark. And whoever it is definitely knows we're up here. That's the tune you played on the piano."

"Oh." Rick's voice dropped with unease.

"Then who?" the professor asked. His weakness made his voice low.

"All of you change the batteries in your flashlights. Your headlamps will last quite a while, but the flashlights are fading. We need to be ready."

"For what?"

"Just do what I tell you." With the beam from his flashlight narrowing to yellow instead of white, Balenger took fresh batteries from his knapsack, unscrewed the end of his flashlight, and exchanged the old batteries with the new ones. The light blazed again.

He moved to toss the old batteries into a corner.

"No." The professor's voice was feeble. "We don't leave our trash."

With a sigh of impatience, Balenger shoved the old batteries into his knapsack.

The whistling drifted to a stop. Now the only sound was the shriek of the wind through the gaps in the skylight and the distant *clang clang clang* of the flapping sheet metal.

Whoever's down there knows we're here

and took pains to tell us, Balenger thought. It'll look strange if we don't react. Time to find out what we're dealing with.

"Hey!" he yelled down.

The echo of his voice dwindled into silence.

"We work for Jersey City Salvage, the company that's stripping this place next week!" Balenger shouted. "A security guard's with us! We've got every right to be here, which is more than I can say for you! We'll give you a chance to leave before we call the police!"

Again, the echo dwindled into silence.

"Okay, you made your choice!"

A man's voice yelled from below, "Working at night?"

"We work when the boss says! Day or night! Doesn't make a difference! It's pretty much always dark in here anyhow!"

"Must be nice to get the overtime!"

Only one voice. Balenger felt encouraged. "Look, I'm not interested in a conversation! I'm telling you to leave! This place isn't safe!"

"Yeah, what happened to the staircase sure proves that! Leave? Naw, we like it here! You might say we're at home in the dark!"

We? Balenger thought.

"You bet," a second voice said. "We love it."

"And what was all that screaming a minute ago?" the first voice shouted. "Sounded like somebody got a Halloween screw."

Balenger stared down toward the darkness. He heard footsteps scraping, but he didn't see any lights.

He spun toward the group. "Cora, call 911."

"He's right, Professor," Vinnie said, helping to hold Conklin up.

"I don't care if anybody's life gets ruined because of the police," Balenger said. "At this point, I just want to make sure you get to *have* a life."

"You really think — ?" Rick started to ask.

"Cora," Balenger repeated, "make the call."

She already had her phone out and was pressing numbers. Surrounded by shadows, the group watched her.

"A recording." Cora frowned. "A damned recording."

"What?" Balenger took the phone.

"Hey," the first voice yelled from below, "if you're trying to phone 911, you're in for a big surprise!"

Balenger pressed the phone against his

ear. A recording said, *"Due to an unusual amount of calls, all our emergency dispatchers are busy. Please wait and the next available person will speak with you."*

"I guess you don't live around here!" the voice shouted. "Otherwise, you'd know! It was on TV! The local 911 got a new telephone system! It's all messed up! Nobody can get through! Won't be fixed till Monday! Maybe later!"

The message repeated itself. *"Due to an unusual amount of calls . . ."*

"Now the regular police line's jammed all the time!" the second voice yelled. "Takes thirty minutes to get an answer!"

"Progress!" another voice added. "Everything's new and fancy and so damned complicated, I can't figure how anything works!"

Three of them? Balenger thought.

"When it *does* work!" the second voice said. "Back when this old place was in business, they knew how to make things dependable!"

"Built to last!" the first voice said. "Hey, why don't you tell us more about those gold knives and forks we heard you talking about?"

Balenger gave the phone back to Cora. "Everybody, pack your stuff. The Leatherman. The duct tape. The rope. The hammer. The Pro Med kit. We might need all of it." He folded his knife and clipped it inside a pocket. "Got everything? Let's go."

"Where?" The professor wavered in pain, supported between Vinnie and Rick.

"The only place we *can* go. Down. One thing's sure, we can't stay put. Passive is dangerous. Passive means we lose."

28

Balenger led the way. He returned to the corridor and paused at the FIRE EXIT door he'd opened, scanning his lights down a narrow, cobwebbed stairway. As everybody joined him, he tugged down the zipper on his Windbreaker, reached inside, and pulled out the pistol.

"Oh, Christ, a gun," Cora said.

Rick stared at him with deep hostility. "Who *are* you?"

"Your guardian angel," Balenger said. "Now keep quiet. Walk as softly as you can. Don't let them know where you are. For now, the only lights we need are mine."

"Hey!" the first voice yelled from below. "I asked you to tell us more about those gold knives and forks."

Balenger eased down the narrow stairs. He tested each board, fearful that the steps would collapse. Cora came next, then Vinnie and Rick edging down sideways, supporting the professor. Their shoes thumped. Their jackets scraped against the walls. The combined sound of everyone's breathing was amplified in the stairwell.

Balenger reached a closed door at a landing, presumably the entrance to the fifth level. Was anyone hiding behind it? Would someone step out after they passed? Feeling dizzy, as if he dropped from a great height, he shut off his flashlight and holstered it. Then he took off his hard hat and held it away from him at head level. With the light angled toward the door, he stepped back, pressed himself against the wall, tucked the gun under his belt, and used his free hand to open the door a crack. Then he drew the gun and used its barrel to nudge the door the rest of the way open. All anybody would see was the light. Someone on the other side would attack it, thinking it was above his head when actually it was away from him.

Nothing happened.

Balenger's palms were moist. His stomach felt hot. He peered beyond the door, seeing a deserted hallway. Nothing appeared wrong or out of place. With a nod of momentary relief, he put on his hard hat, then followed the downward continuation of the stairs. They seemed darker and narrower, more smothering.

Behind him, the professor groaned, his

good leg barely holding his weight as Vinnie and Rick eased him down the steps. Too loud, Balenger thought. He's making too much noise.

Then he heard other noises, the footfalls of one or more people climbing the stairwell.

"Ssshh," he told the others. Halting, he strained to listen. Yes, someone was climbing toward them, but he didn't see any lights, which meant that whoever made the sounds was still far below. It also meant that his own headlamp was for the moment not visible.

He saw another door. Ten steps below him. Partly open. Suddenly, he realized that this was the door to the fourth level, where Vinnie had fallen through the rotted section and where they'd seen the white cat for the second time. The partly open door was how the cat had gotten onto that level.

Balenger crept down the ten steps, opened the door all the way, and waited tensely for the others to follow him into a hallway. The moment the group entered, he shut the door and guided everyone around the hallway's corner, hiding them on the balcony. When he extinguished his headlamp, nearly absolute darkness enveloped them. The exception came from the skylight three levels higher, faint moonlight filtering past swiftly passing clouds.

"Don't move," he whispered. He concealed most of his body behind the balcony's corner while he aimed along the hallway toward the unseen door. Moments passed. As time lengthened, his mouth became dry, as if someone had rubbed a towel around his tongue, the roof of his mouth, and the inside of his cheeks. The heat in his stomach spread.

He heard wary footsteps, then the rustle of cloth. He saw faint lights beyond the bottom of the door. Now the creak of wood was replaced by the scrape of hinges. The door came open. As lights probed the hallway, Balenger ducked fully behind the balcony's corner.

"Think they're in there?" the first voice whispered.

"Don't see any sign of 'em," the second voice said.

"I'm telling you they're still above us," the third voice said.

"Then what are we waiting for? It's party time."

The footsteps crept higher. The lights dimmed, then disappeared.

29

Balenger peered around the corner. They'd left the door open. From this angle, he could see their receding lights. As soon as he estimated that the three were far enough away, he would take a position on the stairs, aiming upward, providing cover while Vinnie, Rick, and Cora got the professor down the rest of the stairway, into the tunnel, and out of the building. We're almost finished, he told himself. Close. It was awfully close. But in a half hour, this'll be over.

Now, not even the slightest reflection from the lights was visible. Time to get going. He raised his hand to turn on the headlamp, then stiffened. The heat in his stomach was replaced by a surge of ice shooting along his veins, almost paralyzing him. A floorboard made a noise in the darkness. Not from behind him. Not from the group or from his own movement. The sound came from the floor in front of him.

He realized that they hadn't all gone up the stairs. Someone was standing in the darkness before him.

Alarms jangled in his mind. He remembered that he hadn't seen lights when he'd peered over the balustrade and shouted down to the whistler. *At home in the dark. We like it here,* the voice had said. What did that mean?

Again weight shifted on the floor. Balenger aimed at the sound.

Abruptly, a hard object crashed down on his gun hand. The unexpected impact shocked him, the pain making him groan. The gun was twisted from his hand. Something drove into his stomach, doubling him over, breath rushing from his lungs. His feet were kicked from under him. As he landed hard on the side of his head, a shoe rammed into his side. He rolled in the darkness, crashing against a wall.

"I got him!" a voice yelled.

"Who said that?" Cora called.

"And I got something else! A gun!"

Balenger heard the slide being racked, someone making sure a round was in the firing chamber. Damn it, they know how to handle firearms.

"Frank," the professor managed to say. "What happened?" He sounded helpless in the gloom. *"Are you hurt?"*

Footsteps rumbled down the stairs. Two people charged onto the balcony. But as

188

Balenger peered up through pain-blurred eyes, he didn't see any lights. Have I gone blind? he wondered.

"Friggin' smart," a voice said.

"I told you it would work."

"You're ahead of me," a third voice said. "Let me give him a kick to catch up."

"As soon as we know who's who and what's what."

Why can't I see their lights? Balenger thought frantically. What happened to my head? *At home in the dark. We like it here.*

"What do you want?" Rick shouted.

"For you to shut up," the first voice said.

Balenger heard a groan. Someone struck the floor hard. Was it Rick?

"You won't let *me* hit anybody," the third voice said. "But *you* go ahead and whack the shit out of them."

"Okay, okay, the next one who doesn't listen, you get to play catch-up."

Balenger's head ached. He had the confused sense he was spinning in the darkness.

"Uh!" Cora shouted. "Somebody touched me!"

"Only us ghosts."

"I want all of you on the floor," a voice said.

"You heard him! On the floor!"

Vinnie groaned and fell. Then the professor, wailing in pain as he landed, no one there to hold him up.

"Take off your knapsacks," the first voice ordered.

"Stop touching me!" Cora yelled.

"Do what you're told!"

Balenger heard the rustle of knapsacks being removed.

"You, too, hero," the first voice said.

A metal object tapped Balenger's shoulder. Moving as quickly as his injured stomach and side would allow, he slipped off his knapsack.

"Let's see what we got," a voice said.

Balenger heard zippers being opened, objects dumped on the floor.

"Rope, duct tape, a crowbar, a Leatherman tool, equipment belts, a hammer, walkie-talkies, hard hats, headlamps, flashlights, tons of batteries. I have no idea what these meters are for. Hell, a person could open a hardware store with all this stuff," the third voice said.

"A first-aid kit. Candles. Matches. Look, candy bars." The second voice sounded excited.

Look? He said *look*. Balenger began to understand. He heard a wrapper being torn open, a bar being chewed noisily.

"Water bottles. But what's in these other bottles?"

Balenger heard a lid being unscrewed.

"Smells like . . . piss. These dummies are carrying *piss* around in bottles in their knapsacks!"

"Found another gun!" the third voice said. "What kind of . . . This thing's not real. It's a damned water pistol."

Balenger heard someone sniffing.

"Vinegar?" the third voice asked. "Is that what you've got in here? That's as stupid as carrying around piss."

"Piss and vinegar," the first voice said.

"Knives. Got plenty of knives."

Balenger felt a hand at his jeans. Before he could resist, *his* knife was unclipped from his pants pocket. His spare pistol magazine was yanked from a pouch on his belt.

"Yeah, a hardware store," the first voice said. "Or a knife-and-gun store."

Hands pawed and poked him, searching. "Found a cell phone."

"Me, too. They've *all* got one."

"Stop *touching* me!" Cora said.

"Hey, we gotta make sure you don't have weapons."

"In my *underwear?*"

"Leave her alone." Rick suddenly groaned.

"Oh, Jesus, my nose. I think you broke my nose."

"That was the idea," the third voice said. "Anybody else got something to complain about?"

Except for the shriek of the wind far above them, the landing became silent.

"Finally, a little cooperation," the first voice said. "Okay, everybody, put your arms out in front of you."

Balenger heard a few hesitant movements.

"Hey, don't make me say it again!"

The movements became rapid. Balenger put his hands out. His right one hurt where it had been struck, but at least nothing seemed broken.

"Now press your wrists together," the first voice said.

Balenger knew what was coming. He'd suffered through an ordeal like this before, except that the darkness had come from a sack tied around his head. He still had nightmares about it. He wanted to scream, to fight. But he was powerless. Sweat soaking his clothes, he struggled not to hyperventilate.

Footsteps approached. He strained not to wince, anticipating a blow to his head. Instead, he felt duct tape on his wrists, heard the sticky sound of a strip being pulled off a roll. The tape got tighter and tighter.

"That'll hold you for a while," the second voice said.

The footsteps went away.

"What are you doing?" Cora said in alarm.

"Shut up and keep still, or I'll shove my hand in your pants again."

The only sounds became Cora's harsh breathing and the unpeeling of duct tape.

"Who's next? How about buddy boy with the broken nose?"

The tape made a repeated tearing sound.

"Now you, pal."

Balenger didn't know whether that referred to Vinnie or the professor.

"Hey, this old guy passed out," the second voice said.

From the pain when he fell and his leg hit the floor, Balenger thought. His fury helped distract him from his increasing fear, the terrible suffocating impression that he again had a sack tied around his head.

"Banged up as he is, he can't hurt us," the third voice said.

"Tape his wrists together anyway."

The professor moaned.

"Good," the first voice said. "Now let's have some light."

30

Balenger felt air move against his face. A hand reached for his headlamp. Its sudden beam made him squint. He found himself looking at a large belt buckle. A piece of pipe was tucked under the belt. Must be what he hit my arm with, Balenger thought. Dirty black pants. A grimy denim overcoat.

Except for the professor's, the other headlamps came on. Beams zigzagged across the balcony, revealing three young men. As Balenger raised his eyes toward the one before him, he heard Cora gasp. Then he saw what made her do so and felt as if an icy needle touched the back of his neck.

The men wore night-vision goggles, making them resemble characters in a science-fiction thriller: bulky binoculars that seemed to grow from their faces. *At home in the dark. We like it here. Look, candy bars.*

"Surprised?" the first man asked.

Balenger *was* surprised, but by something else. The first man was tall and muscular, a build that reinforced his cyber appearance. His scalp was shaved. It and his face and the portion of his neck that showed above the overcoat were red, blue, purple, and green with tattoos, a swirl of unrecognizable forms.

"What are you staring at?" the first man asked.

"The goggles," Balenger lied.

"Yeah, clever, huh? I hear ten years ago they cost a fortune and the army kept control of them. Now you can buy them cheap in any military-surplus store."

"You can use them to hunt Bambi or spy on your neighbors," the second man said.

Balenger swung his gaze to his left and saw a slightly less muscular guy in dirty dark clothes taking off goggles. His left cheek was covered by the whorls of a burn scar almost as white as the five-legged albino cat. This young man — around twenty, Balenger estimated — had his scalp shaved, also. But no tattoos.

"All things are revealed," the third man said, removing his goggles. They left red marks around his eyes. Standing between Rick and the professor, he was well built and yet seemed almost skinny compared to his companions. He was also shorter than the others, who seemed to be over six feet.

Unlike the others, his scalp showed hair, a close military-style cut. "Lets us own the night."

"Kind of cool. Makes everything look green." The first guy's swirling tattoos extended almost to his eyelids. "Reminds me of that song." He started humming "It's Not Easy Being Green."

"Those were the days," the third guy said. "Watching *Sesame Street*. Not a care in the world."

"When the fuck did you ever watch *Sesame Street*?"

They're talking so fast, are they high on drugs? Balenger wondered. He fought to control his trembling muscles. Like the last time, he thought. If I let fear get the better of me, I'm done. Passive means I lose.

"Time to get acquainted," the first man announced. "So our new friends here can try to bond with us the way it happens in, what do they call it, the Sweden syndrome. Isn't that what they call it?" he asked Balenger on the floor.

"The Stockholm syndrome," Balenger told him.

The first guy kicked his left leg.

Balenger clutched it, groaning.

"Who the fuck asked you?" the first guy said. "I'm sure they called it the Sweden syndrome in that Kevin Spacey movie we watched the other night."

"*The Negotiator*," the second guy said.

"Was that the title? All I remember is the hostages kept trying to make pals with their captor. Or maybe it was another movie that had the Sweden syndrome in it. It *is* the Sweden syndrome, right?"

"Right," Balenger said.

"Sure, it is. So let's get acquainted. My name's Tod. And this is . . ."

"Mack," said the man with the burn scar on his cheek.

"Call me JD," the younger man said, the one with the military haircut. He looked to be about eighteen.

"And *you* are . . . ?" Tod asked Balenger.

"Frank."

Tod looked demandingly at the others.

"Vinnie."

"Rick." Rick's broken nose made him sound like he had a terrible head cold.

"What's *your* name, Sweets?" Mack asked Cora. He rubbed the top of his shaved head as if it gave him erotic pleasure.

"Cora."

"Cute name."

"And the old guy?" JD asked.

"Bob. His name is Bob." Balenger looked with pity at the half-conscious professor, duct tape wrapped around his bare leg, his blood crusting.

"Pleased to meet you. We're so glad you could join our party. Any questions?"

Nobody said anything.

"Come on. I'm sure you've got questions. This is the time. Ask me anything. I don't bite."

Mack and JD snickered.

"Frank," Tod said. "Ask me a question."

"You watched us go down the manhole?"

"Yep. We've been trying to figure how to get into this building. The damned metal doors and shutters won't budge. The walls are so strong, we'd make so much noise chopping through, even people who normally mind their business would notice. The next thing, they'd find any hole we made. They'd break in and steal stuff before *we* could."

"Or that guy who comes around would notice," JD said. Of the three, his was the only face that didn't give Balenger chills.

"Guy?" Vinnie asked.

"Aha, see, the atmosphere's thawing. We've got another question. Yeah, a guy," Tod said, his tattoos rippling.

"Two different nights he came by," Mack said, taking his gaze from Cora.

"What was he doing?" Balenger asked.

198

Keep them talking, he thought. As long as they're talking, they're not hurting us.

"Just walked around the building. Checked the walls and the possible entrances. We used our goggles to watch from the weeds down the street. He seemed to be making sure everything was buttoned up."

"Maybe he's a security guard."

"In the beach area of Asbury Park?" Mack said. "Don't make me laugh."

"But he wasn't like *us*," JD said. "This guy had a suit and tie. Overcoat. Straight as can be."

"Then maybe he works for the salvage company," Balenger said.

"That stupid story was *true*?"

"In a week, this place gets stripped. Then the wrecking ball finishes it off."

"Guess you showed us how to get in here just in time. Any more questions? Now's your chance. Questions? Questions?"

Balenger indicated the professor. "Can I go over and check him?"

"No. What could you do for him anyhow?"

"Well, for starters, if he was having a heart attack, I could give him CPR."

"Blow in his mouth and all that?"

"Yes."

"You're a braver man than me."

"At least, I could make him comfortable. He's lying on his hurt leg."

"Turn him on his back? You think that's the thing to do?"

Balenger didn't reply.

"Hell, if that's all you're worried about . . ." JD went over and rolled the professor onto his back.

The professor moaned. The movement having roused him, he slowly shook his head from side to side. He opened his eyes and squinted at the three men, focusing his perceptions, terrified.

"See, that took care of the problem," Mack said.

"Questions? Questions?" Tod said. "No? Fine. You had your chance. Now it's my turn. Here's my question. Are you ready? It's a tough one. Are you sure you're all ready?"

Silence.

"How are we going to decide which one of you to kill?"

1:00 a.m.

31

Balenger stared at Tod's watch, trying to disassociate, to distance himself from his emotions. It was an athlete's watch, the kind with several dials. Black rubber coated the case. Tilting his head, he was able to see that the time was a little after one. His heart pounded so fiercely, it seemed to fill his chest.

"Who's it gonna be?" Tod asked. "Anybody want to volunteer? No? Then I guess it's up to JD to decide."

"Tough choice," JD said. "Let's see now. Eenie, meenie . . . Moe!"

JD yanked Rick to his feet, jammed a hand behind his neck, clutched the back of Rick's belt, and rushed him toward the balustrade.

"No!" Cora screamed.

Rick wailed. Just as he was about to fly over the railing, JD pulled back hard on Rick's belt, spun him, and threw him onto the floor.

Cora's duct-taped hands were raised to her mouth in terror. Rick's face was ashen. His chest kept heaving as he hyperventilated.

"Did that get everybody's attention?" Mack asked.

The alternating heat and cold in Balenger's stomach made him nauseous.

"If we give you a few simple instructions, do you think you can follow them without making trouble?" JD asked.

Rick nodded weakly, blood dripping from his nose onto his Windbreaker.

"Then here's the drill," Tod said. "All of you are going to come slowly to your feet. No quick moves. Nothing to make us think you're attacking us."

Unable to use their hands to push themselves off the floor, they shifted to their knees, wobbled, raised one foot, then the other, and stood.

Balenger felt dizzy as blood rushed from his head. His stomach, side, leg, and forearm ached.

"You kept talking about a vault," Mack said.

"According to you, a gangster put it in," JD said. "Only three reasons to do that. Money, guns, or drugs."

"Six-ten." Mack rubbed his bald head. "We heard you say that was the number of the gangster's room. Move. We're gonna check it out."

Balenger nodded toward the professor

on the floor. "We need to help him up the stairs."

"No," Tod said. "He's not going anywhere."

JD opened a knife. "Yeah, he's the weak link. He's the guy we kill to keep your attention."

"Wait!" Balenger said, his muscles cramping. "The professor did all kinds of research. He's an expert about this hotel. He can help you get into the vault."

Tod, Mack, and JD exchanged looks.

"What makes you so sure he can do that?" Mack asked.

"Because that's why he asked me to join the group."

Rick, Cora, and Vinnie straightened.

"You're not a reporter?" Rick said, glaring.

Balenger shrugged. "I once watched *All the President's Men*."

"You son of a bitch!" Cora said.

"The professor lost his teaching job. He got to keep his pension but not his health insurance. As you saw, he has heart problems. But there's no way his pension will pay for the treatment he needs. He's desperate. So he asked me to join the group and learn how to get into the hotel and watch how the vault was opened. Later, I was supposed to return on my own, follow the route we took, go back to the vault, and grab what's in there."

"And what exactly's in there?" Mack stepped close.

"If the professor's information is correct?" Balenger hesitated. "Gold coins."

"Gold . . ."

"The professor's been teaching me a lot about history. In particular, about gold coins in the United States. Ten- and twenty-dollar gold pieces designed by . . . let me think a second. Augustus . . ."

"Saint-Gaudens," Vinnie said.

"Yeah. That's the name. The ten-dollar gold coins were called eagles. The twenty-dollar coins were called *double* eagles. Until the Depression, people used them as currency. But then Black Friday happened."

"What the hell was Black Friday?" Tod asked.

"The great stock market collapse of 1929," Cora answered.

Balenger's heart pounded less frantically. That's right. Keep them talking, he thought.

"Get to the point." Mack rubbed the burn scar on his cheek.

"In the early 1930s," Cora told him, "the American economy was in such trouble, the government feared it would collapse. To keep the value of the dollar fluid, the government went off the gold standard."

"Speak English, Sweets."

"Prior to the Depression, the value of a dollar was linked to the value of the gold that the U.S. Treasury had in its reserves," she said. "In theory, you could go to a bank, put down thirty-five dollars, and ask for the equivalent in gold. One ounce of it. But during the Depression, the government wanted to say that the dollar was worth whatever the government decided it was worth, regardless of how much gold the government owned. So we went off the gold standard. That meant gold could no longer be used as currency. Under the Gold Reserve Act of 1934, it became illegal for private citizens to own gold bars or gold coins. Except for jewelry, all gold had to be surrendered to the Treasury."

"The government *stole* the gold?" JD said.

"People who turned in the coins and the bars got receipts that they could apply to their bank accounts," Vinnie said. "Since then, the only way an American can own a gold coin is by treating it as a historical collector's piece. You can look at it. You can hold it in your hand. You can buy and sell it at a rare-coin store. But you can't buy a tank of gasoline with it."

"Certainly, these days, the face value of a twenty-dollar gold coin won't buy a tank of gas," Balenger said. Keep the conversation going, he thought.

"What about the gangster?" Tod fingered the piece of pipe stuck under his belt.

"Carmine Danata was a mobster in the Roaring Twenties," Balenger said. "One of his trademarks was giving gold coins to his favorite hookers. When the Depression hit, he was sure the government was cheating everybody by confiscating the gold coins and gold bars. So he never surrendered his coins. Instead, he started hoarding them. Finally, he had so many hiding places, he couldn't keep track of them all. That's when he had the vault put into his suite in 1935."

"You're saying the gold coins are still in there?" Mack's eyes sparkled.

"Danata died in a gang shootout in Brooklyn in 1940," Balenger answered. "The suite was rented only to him. He paid for it year-round. His 'roosting place,' he called it. After his death, the hotel's owner —"

"Carlisle. We heard you talking about him. A nutjob with more money than he deserved."

"He never rented the suite to anyone else," Balenger said. "From 1940 to 1968 when the hotel closed and Carlisle lived here alone, it remained unoccupied. Carlisle had a thing about spying on people, about living his life through *their* lives. The professor suspected that Carlisle preserved the room the way it was when Danata was alive. The theory is that Carlisle enjoyed the idea of having a secret stash of gold coins in the vault, of looking at them when no one else could. They're supposed to be beautiful: a soaring eagle on one side, Lady Liberty carrying a torch on the other."

"The sick fuck didn't try to smuggle them out of the country and turn them into cash?" Mack asked.

"He had agoraphobia. He was afraid to leave the hotel. Another country would have been like another planet to him. Why try to turn the coins into cash you don't need when you can have the pleasure of owning more gold coins than any private citizen has looked at since 1934? Tonight, when we explored some of the rooms, we discovered Carlisle was obsessed with preserving them the way they looked when the last guests checked out. Maybe he started doing that as early as 1940 when Danata was killed."

"What's gold worth these days?"

"Over four hundred dollars an ounce."

"So we could melt the coins down and —"

"That would cost you. A double eagle, less than an ounce of gold, is worth almost seven hundred dollars on the collectors' market."

"Jesus."

"But listen to this," Balenger continued. "The 1933 double eagle was minted just before the U.S. government went off the gold standard. Before the coins could be released, they were declared illegal and had to be destroyed. Most of them. Several were stolen. Recently, one of the stolen coins was found by the government and put up for auction at Sotheby's. The winning bid was almost seven million dollars."

"Seven . . . ?"

"Million dollars. The theory is, Danata got his hands on five of the coins."

Tod's eyes reflected the headlamps. He gestured for everybody to move. "I can't wait to see this vault."

32

"Help me with the professor," Balenger told Vinnie.

Vinnie glared, furious at him for lying. Nonetheless, the threat and his affection for the professor made him come over. It quickly became clear how their taped wrists limited them. By process of trial and error, they discovered that the only way they could lift the professor was by shoving their hands under his arms. Because his wrists were taped also, he couldn't help. With effort, they raised him.

Conklin moaned but managed to steady himself on his good leg.

"How bad do you feel?" Balenger asked.

"I'm still alive." The professor drew a pained breath. "Hey, under the circumstances, I'm not about to complain."

"Is it true?" Vinnie demanded. "You and this guy were going to take the gold coins?"

"I'm not perfect," Conklin said. "That's something you have to realize about your teachers. But as I listened to all of you explain about the Gold Reserve Act of 1934

. . . Saint-Gaudens, Vinnie. You actually remember Saint-Gaudens."

"And you were going to split the money?
Just the two of you?"

The elderly man looked ashamed. "Would
you have agreed to be part of it? All along
we've insisted on taking nothing but photographs. Now we wouldn't just have broken
that rule. We'd have been committing a serious crime. Would you have risked going to
prison for the rest of your life, or would you
have told the authorities?"

"But *you* were ready to risk prison."

"At the moment, I don't have a lot to
lose."

Mack and JD shoved the equipment into
the knapsacks, cramming in so much that
they needed only three knapsacks instead of
five. The urine bottles were all they left behind.

Mack put the water pistol in his belt. "It's
been a while since I had a toy." He picked up
one of the knapsacks, JD the second, Tod
the third. Their night-vision goggles hung
around their necks.

"The way this works," Tod said, adjusting
the knapsack straps with one hand while
holding Balenger's pistol, "is I go up first,
moving backward, aiming at you. Mack and
JD come after you, but they keep a distance.

That way, you can't bump against them and try to push them down the stairs. If you try anything, Mack and JD will drop flat on the stairs. Then I'll start shooting. I don't care what anybody knows about the vault — if you fuck with us, I'll shoot you first and then piss on you for making me mad."

Tod left the balcony, passed through the door at the end of the hallway, reached the fire stairs, and started climbing them backward. Headlamps wavering, Balenger and Vinnie came next, their taped hands under the professor's arms, awkwardly helping him. Rick and Cora came after that, then Mack and JD. Their footsteps were loud in the confined space.

"Now that you know I'm not a reporter," Balenger told Vinnie, easing the professor up the stairs, "I've got a question."

"What is it?"

"You were talking about the composer who wrote 'On the Banks of the Wabash' and 'My Gal Sal.' You said he was Theodore Dreiser's brother as if that was a big deal. Who the hell was Theodore Dreiser?"

"He wrote *Sister Carrie*."

"*Sister* who?" Keep talking, Balenger urged himself. Establish a bond with them.

"It's one of the first gritty American novels." Vinnie seemed to understand what

Balenger was trying to do. "It's set in the slums of Chicago. The plot's about a woman who's forced to sleep around to survive."

"Sounds like real life to me," Mack said in the darkness down the stairs.

Vinnie kept the conversation going. "The theme is pessimistic determinism. No matter what we do, our bodies and our surroundings doom us."

"Yeah, definitely real life," Mack said.

It's working, Balenger thought. Moving upward, he felt the professor wince.

"The novel was published in 1900, a year before this hotel was built," Vinnie continued. "Before then, a lot of American novels were about working hard and succeeding, what William Dean Howells called 'the smiling aspects of American life.' "

"I'll wait to ask you who Howells was," Balenger said, helping the professor steady himself.

"But Dreiser grew up in terrible poverty. He saw enough suffering to decide the American dream was a fraud. To make his point, he called one of his other novels *An American Tragedy*. Doubleday was the company that published *Sister Carrie*, but when Doubleday's wife read the book, she was so shocked she insisted her husband

214

keep all the copies in the warehouse, banning it. It wasn't until several years later when the novel was republished that it became a classic."

"Guess I'll have to read it," Balenger said.

"Like I believe that," Vinnie said. "The story's powerful, but the writing's terrible. Dreiser's idea of polished prose was to call a bar 'a truly swell saloon.' "

Below them, JD laughed.

Slowed by Conklin, they reached the fifth level and trudged higher. Balenger worried about the professor's labored breathing. He debated whether to lunge up the stairs and try to grab the pistol from Tod. But Tod was too far above him. The stairs were too confining. Tod would start shooting, or maybe Mack and JD would use their knives on the rest of the group, who couldn't run anywhere. It would be a massacre. No, he decided, this wasn't the time.

"This *Sister Carrie* reminds me of the chick in that movie Sweets here mentioned." Mack referred to Cora, Balenger knew. His rage grew. "The one 'Moon River' is in. What's it called, Sweets?"

"Stop touching me."

"What's the movie called?"

"*Breakfast at Tiffany's.*"

"Yeah. Hell, before I saw it on TV one night, I thought it was a restaurant movie like *My Dinner with Fucking Andre.* But no, it's about this screwed-up chick. What's her name, Sweets?"

"Holly Golightly."

"Even her name's screwed up. Holly the Cock Tease. That should have been her name. She made guys take her to fancy restaurants. Naturally they expected to get in her pants. But after she ate a fabulous dinner, she asked them for money so she could go to the bathroom. Never been to a bathroom where I had to pay to get in, but I guess rich people put up with that stuff. Then she snuck out of the restaurant, and they never got what they paid for. She didn't sleep with them, but as far as I'm concerned, she was still a whore."

They reached the sixth level.

"Where's six-ten?" Tod asked.

Their headlamps showed doors with tarnished numbers.

"Six twenty-two's on the right." JD aimed his light toward the tree growing into the floor.

"Then six-ten's the other way." Tod motioned with his pistol for the group to proceed toward the darkness on the left.

"And that stupid ending," Mack said.

"The hero's supposed to be a smart writer. He knows the twat gets paid to take messages to a gangster in prison. He knows she's gonna marry a South American millionaire to get her hands on the money. But the dumb hero still falls in love with her. In the end, they're in this alley in the rain, looking for a cat she threw away, and they find the cat, and they're kissing, and the music gets all weepy, and I'm thinking, You stupid fuck, run! Get away from that whore as fast as you can! She'll break your heart and dump you the first time a guy with cash comes along!"

"Apart from that, how did you like the movie?" JD laughed.

"Damn it," Vinnie suddenly shouted at Balenger, "I'd have gone along with you!" He was so furious, he couldn't restrain himself. "All the professor needed to do was ask me, and I've have gone along! You think I don't need the money? I make a shit salary in a school where the students beat teachers for giving them homework. I don't have rich parents like Rick has. Hell, my father's dying from emphysema. He doesn't have health insurance. All I do is pay for his damned medical bills! If you'd asked me, I'd have gone!"

"Now there's a guy who knows cash is

king," Mack said. "If you've got dough, you not only pay your old man's doctor bills. You get Holly the Cock Tease."

"I'm sure I care," Tod said. "Here's sixten."

33

A sign indicated DO NOT DISTURB.

Tod twisted the doorknob and pushed. "Locked."

"I'm not surprised." Balenger worked to keep the conversation alive.

"Tell me about it."

"Cora and Rick couldn't find a key for it or for a handful of other rooms. The missing keys must belong to the few doors that are locked."

"Well, in case you wonder why you and your friends are still alive, one reason is *you're* going to do the heavy lifting while *we* take it easy."

"But that's not the only reason," Mack said, looking at Cora.

"Plus, the old man's gonna help us get into the vault," JD said. "Put him down on the floor."

Balenger and Vinnie obeyed, making the professor as comfortable as possible. Balenger felt relieved to be able to stand on his own. He wished his hands were free to massage his arms.

"Now get that door open." Tod switched on a flashlight.

"How?"

Tod aimed the pistol. His flashlight made Balenger squint. "I really hate it when you disagree with me."

"Rick. Vinnie. Give me a hand."

Rick's nose, caked with dried blood, was twice its normal size. He and Vinnie joined Balenger in front of the door.

Although his wrists were taped together, Vinnie managed to twist the knob and test the door. No result. "I'll keep the knob turned while you try to force the door open."

Mack laughed. "Sounds even. They work while you stand there."

Balenger and Rick pounded their shoulders against the door. The wall shook. They stepped back and charged, crashing. The door didn't budge.

"Feels like it has a metal core." Balenger's shoulder pulsed.

"I don't care if it's kryptonite. Get it open."

"My turn to keep the knob turned," Rick said, shoving Vinnie out of the way.

Vinnie joined Balenger. They stepped back and charged, hitting the door with their full weight.

"We could ram it all day," Balenger said. "It isn't going to budge."

"Well, you'd better think of how to open it," Tod said, "because I'm getting impatient, and when I'm impatient —"

"The crowbar."

"Ah. The crowbar."

"It's the only way. Or maybe the hammer."

"The hammer," Mack said. "Maybe you'd like some knives to cut through the wall. Or the gun to shoot the lock."

"I don't think that would do any good."

"Glad to hear that," JD said. "For a second there, it sounded like you wanted us to give you weapons."

"Just a crowbar if you want to get this door open."

"Oh, we want to get the door open. Definitely. Who's got the crowbar?"

"Me," Mack said. His shaved head cast a reflection from Balenger's headlamp.

"Get it out."

"You bet."

Mack pulled the crowbar from his knapsack. "Now you guys wouldn't be thinking of trying to use this against us, would you?"

"We just want to do what you say."

" 'Cause if you do try to use this crowbar

against us, you know what'll happen, don't you?"

"Yes."

"No, I don't think you do," JD said. "I think I should demonstrate."

JD approached the group. Suddenly, he used one hand to grab Rick behind the neck and shoved his other hand under Rick's belt at his spine.

"Hey, what are you —"

But JD was already running, pushing Rick toward the balustrade.

"No!" Balenger shouted.

This time, when JD reached the edge, he didn't shove Rick the other way to safety. Instead, he increased speed, abruptly stopped, and hurtled Rick over the balustrade.

34

"Noooooo!"

Plummeting, Rick disappeared into the darkness. His wail faded.

Silence.

A muted crash echoed from far below. The echo died.

Balenger's heart seemed to stop. He felt suspended in the space between pulses. He couldn't move.

The stillness was broken by JD, who peered down toward the lobby six levels below. "What do you know? I can see a little pinpoint of light glowing down there. His headlamp survived the crash."

"What's the old joke?" Tod said. "The fall isn't what kills you. It's landing."

"Well, Sweets, I guess it'll be me making music with you now," Mack said.

Cora slid to the floor. Her lips moved in a murmur. "No."

Balenger could barely hear her. In the beam from his headlamp, he noted how frantic her eyes were.

"No," she whispered.

Her eyes bulged. The tendons in her neck stood out like ropes. Her shriek filled the sixth level, stronger than the wind that whistled through the gaps in the skylight a level above.

"NO."

"All right, all right, okay, we get the idea!" Tod aimed his flashlight straight into her eyes. "You miss him! Get used to it and shut up, or *you'll* go over the railing next!"

"Not until I'm done with her," Mack said.

"NO!"

"Somebody shut her up," Tod warned. "I'm not kidding. If she doesn't stop —"

Balenger went over to where she slumped on the floor. "Cora."

She kept screaming.

"Cora." He put his taped hands on her left shoulder. "Stop."

"NO!"

"Cora." Balenger nudged her. "Stop right now."

Tears streamed down her face. As she wailed, snot dripped from her nose. Saliva leaked from her open mouth.

"Cora." Balenger managed to grasp her arm. He shook her, shook harder. Her body was like a rag doll's. Her head flopped forward and back. He slapped her, and abruptly, she became silent.

224

Her cheek was red. She looked stunned. Her eyes remained wide, but she hardly blinked, just sank back against a wall and whimpered.

"You didn't need to hit her so hard," Vinnie said bitterly.

"It shut her up, didn't it?" Tod said. "I swear, she was going over the railing."

The professor lay on the floor, horrified.

Mack tapped the crowbar across one of his hands. "So now you know what'll happen if you try to use this against us. Get that door open."

He set the crowbar on the floor and backed away.

Balenger tried to control his emotions. His hands trembled when he picked up the crowbar and wedged it into the doorframe. He braced himself and tugged. Wood splintered.

"No," the professor moaned. "We don't destroy the past."

"Just steal from it. Right, Pops?" JD asked.

"Vinnie, give me some help," Balenger said.

In shock, Vinnie joined him. He put his hands next to Balenger's, who felt them tremble just as his did. The two of them yanked. Crack. Splinter.

Crack. The wood broke almost as loudly as a gunshot. Balenger's ears rang as the door flew open. Darkness beckoned.

"Put down the crowbar and step away from it," Tod warned.

Balenger did what he was told. He watched Mack retrieve the crowbar and return it to his knapsack.

"Now let's find the vault," Tod said.

Balenger and Vinnie lifted the professor to his good leg.

"Cora." Vinnie's voice was unsteady. "We need to go."

But Cora didn't move. She just remained slumped against the wall. Her head was down. The beam from her lamp illuminated her knees. It bobbed as her chest and shoulders heaved with quiet sobs.

"*I'll* get her inside," Mack said. He pulled her up. With an arm around her waist, close to a breast, he walked toward the open door.

"Don't touch me." She struggled.

As Mack forced her into the darkness, Balenger shouted, "The floor!"

"What?"

"You need to test the floor first! Some of the rooms have rotten wood! That's what happened to the staircase!"

Mack lurched back.

"The three of you go first," JD said.

"Yeah, if it's rotten, the fat old guy'll drop through," Tod said.

They shuffled over. Weighed down by the professor, Balenger put a shoe across the threshold and pressed down. The wood felt secure. He applied more weight and still detected no weakness.

"Ready?" he asked Vinnie.

"Why not?" Vinnie's voice quavered. "The way this is going, if we don't get killed one way, it'll soon happen another."

35

The beams of their headlamps pierced the darkness, showing Balenger that the room was larger than those they'd already explored. Numbed by Rick's death and the near certainty of his own, he turned his hard hat to the right and left, seeing vague shapes of furniture. They were in the living room of a suite.

Mack brought in Cora. JD and Tod followed. Their flashlights and the four remaining headlamps were the only illumination, revealing chairs, couches, and tables, an odd array of black, red, and gray.

"They're going to need more light to find the vault," Tod said. "Candles. Somebody mentioned finding candles."

"I did." Mack let go of Cora, who remained in place, leaning one way and then another, almost catatonic from grief.

He took off his knapsack and brought out a plastic bag of candles with a waterproof container of matches inside. He lit a candle and put it in a chrome tubular holder on a table against a wall. The flame wavered, then grew steady. He went about the room, lighting more candles, finding other holders or else dripping wax on the tables and sticking the base of the candles into it. The flames made Balenger feel he was in a desecrated church.

The room had the modest depth of the other rooms Balenger had seen, but it was three times as wide. An expansive shutter, a door, and another shutter — all dusty metal — occupied the wall across from him. He imagined Danata gazing past the wide windows toward the boardwalk, the beach, and the ocean. Carlisle stood in this room after Danata's death, he realized, enjoying Danata's view, filling Danata's space. But only at night. A full view during daylight would have terrified him.

Footsteps made Balenger turn to where JD came back from checking behind two doors on the left. "Closet and bedroom," JD said. "Bathroom's through the bedroom. Nothing to worry us."

They scanned their lights around the room, filling the shadows between candles.

"No TV in the old days," Mack said. "What did he do with the time? He must've been bored to death."

"That." Balenger pointed toward a felt-topped card table that occupied a corner.

Keep the damned conversation going, he reminded himself.

"And that." Vinnie worked to follow Balenger's example, indicating an odd-looking object: a flat rectangle with a semicircle rising from it. Its surface was black with red trim.

"What is it?"

"A radio."

"They sure disguised it. What's that shiny stuff it's made of?"

"Bakelite," Vinnie said. "An early form of plastic."

"Check these magazines lying open, as if Danata just went to take a leak," JD said. "*Esquire. The Saturday Evening Post.* Never heard of it."

Mack went over to a bookcase that had ascending levels in the shape of a skyscraper. Again, the colors were black with red trim. "*Gone with the Wind. How to Win Friends & Influence People.* Yeah, Danata influenced people, all right. With a gun to their head."

Balenger kept staring at the candle-lit room. He couldn't get over what he saw. Another time capsule, he thought. The terror of Rick's falling scream reverberated in his memory.

"Somebody tell me what kind of furniture this is," Tod said.

230

"Art deco," the professor murmured. Tired of waiting for permission, Balenger and Vinnie eased him onto a sofa that had black vinyl cushions, black lacquered wooden arms, and a five-inch strip of chrome along the bottom. The dusty chrome was the gray Balenger had first glimpsed. The cushions had red piping.

"It's a style of architecture and furniture from the 1920s and 1930s," Vinnie resignedly explained. His voice had little energy. Nonetheless, he forced himself to continue, seeming to realize that as long as he was useful, his captors would allow him to remain alive. "The name comes from an art exposition in Paris in 1925. The *Exposition International des Arts Decoratifs Industriels et Modernes*."

"Speak English."

Vinnie breathed with difficulty. "It means the International Exposition of Industrial and Modern Art Decorations. Art Decorations was shortened to art deco. Industry and art. Put simply, it tried to make a living room look like a cross between a factory and an art gallery."

"The materials are industrial." The professor leaned wearily back on the sofa. He too seemed to realize that if he didn't make himself useful, he'd be dead soon. "Glass, steel, chrome, nickel, vinyl, lacquer, hard rubber."

"Not normally attractive," Vinnie pressed on. "But they were given a lustrous veneer and the shapes they were formed into tended to be curved and sensuous. Look at that chair. A strip of lacquered wood, black with red trim, molded into a reclining S that looks like a body rippling. Or look at the tubular steel legs on the glass coffee table over there. You want to stroke them."

No, Balenger thought, quit talking that way. Don't reinforce Mack's obsession with sex.

"Or that lamp" — Vinnie pointed — "which has three nickel tubes holding up a frosted-glass shade with three circles forming a lip on top of a lip on top of a lip."

The candles and flashlights showed furniture that worshiped geometry made seductive: circles, ovals, squares, triangles, pentagons.

"Sometimes, the furniture doesn't look sensuous, even though it is," Vinnie said. "The sofa the professor is on. The lacquer makes the back look hard and uncomfortable. So do the stiff edges on the wooden arms. They're designed as a deception because the deep vinyl cushions are in fact comfortable. Surprisingly so. Isn't that true, Professor?"

"Carmine Danata could have happily napped here."

"But *you're* not going to," JD said. "I looked in all the rooms. *Where's the vault?*"

Conklin's mouth opened and closed.

"He lost a lot of blood," Balenger said. "He's dehydrated."

JD took a bottle of water from his knapsack and tossed it to Balenger. "Lubricate him."

Mack snickered.

Balenger twisted off the cap and offered it to the professor, but Conklin didn't seem to notice it, so Balenger raised the bottle to the injured man's lips and helped him drink. If Conklin didn't get to an emergency room in the next couple of hours, gangrene would set in, he knew. Water trickled from the professor's mouth and into his beard.

Use the opportunity, Balenger warned himself. He raised the bottle to his mouth, gulping the tepid water.

"Where's the vault?" Mack demanded.

An eerie whisper made them turn.

"Moon . . . ," Cora sang to herself. "River." She swayed from side to side, as if hearing private music, ghostly refrains of the melody her dead husband had played for her.

"Wide . . ." Her raw red eyes were huge, but she seemed to see nothing in front of her. "Drifting . . ." As she shifted her weight from one foot to another, Balenger had the disturbing impression that she danced with someone, slowly, chest to chest, cheek to cheek, never leaving the spot where she was rooted. "Dream . . ." Tears rolled down her cheeks as candlelight wavered over her. "Heartbreak."

"She's *your* date," Tod told Mack. "Do something to shut her up."

Conklin gathered the strength to interrupt. Balenger gave the injured man credit for trying to distract attention from Cora. "The vault was hidden. That was the whole idea." The professor leaned back on the sofa, his eyes closed. "If people knew there was a vault, they'd wonder what was inside."

"Hidden *where?*" Tod asked.

Conklin didn't answer.

"If you don't know, why the hell did we bring you?"

"We'll find it. Vinnie, give me a hand." Balenger sensed lethal impatience building in his captors. He'd been there before, felt it before, from beneath a sack tied around his head. *We need to keep making them think we're useful.*

He pivoted toward Mack. "Give me the crowbar."

"Don't think so."

Cora kept singing faintly, swaying as if on drugs or dancing with a ghost. Her blank eyes saw nothing. "Cross . . ." Her throat sounded raw, her voice breaking.

"That bitch is getting on my nerves," JD said.

"No crowbar?" Balenger said to draw their attention. "All right, damn it, I'll improvise." He grabbed a stainless steel ashtray from a glass-and-chrome table, clamped it between his taped hands, and went to the wall on the right. In a fury, he pushed away the bookcase and pounded the ashtray's edge against the wall, the noise blocking Cora's lament. A stylized painting of a woman in a streamlined 1920s roadster, her long hair flying in the wind, fell from the wall.

"No," the professor murmured.

Balenger shifted along the wall, continuing to hammer with the ashtray. Plaster cracked. Another painting crashed.

"Forget the gold coins!" Vinnie told JD, raising his voice to be heard above the noise. "That ashtray he's destroying was in mint condition. You could have sold it for a thousand dollars on eBay. And those two paintings that fell."

"A thousand dollars?"

"Probably more. And then there's the chrome candleholder and the frosted green glass vases and the stainless-steel cigarette case."

Mack picked the case off a table and opened it. "It still has cigarettes." He pulled one out. Paper and tobacco crumbled in his fingers.

"The lamps, the chairs, the glass tables, the lacquered sofa. Perfect condition," Vinnie emphasized. "All told, you're looking at a quarter-million dollars, probably higher, and you don't need to worry about the government coming after you for trying to sell gold coins stolen from the mint. Easy job. Rent a truck. We'll help you load it. We'll smile and wave as you drive away. Just leave us alone. I swear to God, I'll never tell anybody about you."

"A thousand dollars?" Tod repeated. "For an ashtray?"

"But not anymore. Now it's junk."

Balenger overturned a glass table and whacked the ashtray against the continuation of the wall. The table shattered.

"There goes twenty thousand dollars," Vinnie said.

"Hey!" Mack told Balenger. "Stop!"

"But you ordered us to find the vault!"

"How's pounding the wall going to —"

"Aren't you listening? The wall's hollow from bare spaces between the joists!" Balenger's hands throbbed from the force of his hammering. His chest heaved from the frenzy of his exertion. "We need to keep pounding till we find a section that sounds solid. That's where the vault is."

"Then why are you just standing there?" Mack told Vinnie. "Give him a hand!"

Vinnie grabbed a stainless-steel vase and headed toward the wall.

"How much is *that* worth?"

"Probably five thousand."

"Put it down. Use *this*." Mack hurled the crowbar toward Vinnie's feet.

"Try to hit us with it," Tod said, "and I'll shoot your eyes out."

Vinnie grabbed the crowbar between his taped hands and walloped it against the wall. It smashed a huge hole in the plaster.

"Now we're getting somewhere," JD said.

"Mighty nice gun. Heckler and Koch P2000, it says here on the side. Forty caliber," Tod emphasized.

Balenger and Vinnie kept pounding.

"More powerful than a nine millimeter. Less powerful than a forty-five. Like Goldilocks and the three bears. Not too much. Not too little. Just right. A forty caliber's a police load, right?"

Balenger kept slamming the ashtray against the wall.

"Hey, hero, I asked you a question," Tod said. "I'm talking to you. Stop and look at me."

Balenger turned. He breathed deeply.

"A forty caliber's a police load," Tod said.

"I'm not a cop."

"Right."

"Far from it."

"Sure. The more I look at this gun, the fancier it is. It's got a slide release lever on both sides so you can reload with either hand if one of your arms is wounded. It's got a magazine release lever behind the trigger guard where either hand can reach it if one of your arms takes a bullet."

"Mostly, those features are for left-handed shooters."

"Of course, of course, why didn't I think of that? What's your name again?"

"Frank."

"Well, Frank, while your buddy works and gives you a rest, why don't you tell us about yourself?"

"Yeah," Mack said, "convince us you're not a cop."

Vinnie paused.

"Hey, Big Ears, nobody told you to quit," JD said.

Blank-faced, Cora sobbed and sang.

Vinnie whacked the crowbar against the wall.

"Frank, maybe you're not taking us seriously," Tod said.

"Believe me, I am."

"Then talk to us," Mack said. "Convince us you're not a cop."

"Yeah," Tod said. "Convince us not to shoot you."

36

Slowly, carefully, Balenger set down the ash-tray. He didn't want to tell them what they wanted to know, but he didn't see an alternative. Maybe this would help him bond with them. "I'm former military."

"And how come you know the professor?" Tod asked.

"I took a class from him."

"I don't get the connection."

"I was in Iraq."

"I still don't get the connection."

"The first Gulf War. Desert Storm. 1991. I was a Ranger."

"Hi, yo, Tonto," JD said.

"After I came back home to Buffalo, I got sick. Aches. Fever."

"Hey, I didn't ask for your medical history. What I want to know is —"

Vinnie pounded another hole in the wall.

"The VA hospital in Buffalo kept telling me I had a stubborn case of the flu. Then I heard that a lot of other veterans were sick, and finally the newspapers and TV started calling it Gulf War syndrome. The military

240

said Saddam Hussein might have used chemical or biological weapons on us."

"If you don't answer the question . . ."

"Or maybe it was caused by a disease spread by sand fleas. The desert has a lot of insects."

"I ask you to prove you're not a cop, and I get your life story."

"But the more I read about it, the more I suspected what made me sick was the depleted uranium in our artillery shells. The uranium hardens them and makes it easy for the explosive heads to go through enemy tanks."

"Uranium?" Vinnie frowned.

"Hey, Big Ears," Tod said. "A little less listening and a little more pounding on that wall. You're too close to that candle. Move it away before you have an accident."

"The military claims depleted uranium is safe." Balenger shook his head in fierce disagreement. "But I hear it makes a Geiger counter click. We fired an awful lot of artillery shells in Desert Storm. The wind blew a lot of smoke and dust in our direction. It took years before I felt normal again. It ended my military career."

"That's when you became a cop?"

"I'm telling you, I'm not a cop. I drifted from job to job, mostly driving trucks. Then the *second* Iraq war happened." Balenger paused. He was getting close to his previous nightmare. Sweating, he wondered if he could make himself talk about it. No choice. I've got to, he thought. "Our military got overextended. Corporations trying to rebuild Iraq hired civilian guards for their convoys. Former special-operations personnel. The need was so great, they even accepted guys like me who'd been out of the service for a while. And the pay was fabulous. One hundred and twenty-five thousand dollars a year to make sure supply trucks didn't get ambushed."

"One hundred and twenty-five thousand?" Tod was impressed.

"A year. Then conditions deteriorated, and more convoys got hit, and the pay got even better: twenty thousand a *month*."

"Shit, you're rich."

"Not hardly. The companies paid by the month because not a lot of guys were willing to make themselves targets. You needed to have not much going for you at home. Bad job prospects. Nobody close to you. Like me. I mean, it was really crazy over there. Snipers and booby traps all along the road. Most guys didn't last long. Either they got killed, or they said 'To hell with *this*' and quit. In my case . . ." Balenger paused, listening to Vinnie pound with the crowbar. "I got a chance to collect only one paycheck."

"Only one? Shit, what happened?"

Finally, I've got them, Balenger thought. "I was guarding a convoy. We were attacked. An explosion knocked me unconscious." He rushed through it, not wanting to remember the pain and gunfire and screams. "The next thing I knew, I was tied to a chair in a filthy-smelling room. Most of the smell came from a sack tied around my head."

Tod, Mack, and JD stared.

"And?" JD said.

"An Iraqi insurgent told me he was going to cut off my head."

37

Vinnie stopped pounding and looked at him.

In the silence, Cora sank to the floor, hugging her knees. Her eyes were vacant.

"Cut off your head?" Tod frowned.

"After hours of keeping me tied to that chair, a sack around my head, that's what they told me. I was sore from bruises and cuts. My bladder was full. I held it as long as I could. I pissed my pants. I sat in my urine and then my shit."

The memory seized him. He feared he'd throw up. He had the sense that he was talking faster and faster. "Cut off my head. But first they had to brag that they'd caught me. So they set up a video camera, and then of course, they had to prove who I was, so they took the sack off my head. After I quit blinking and squinting, I saw I was in a battered concrete-block room with a half-dozen men next to me. They were wearing hoods with holes for the eyes and mouth. The guy who threatened me — he was the only one who spoke English — had his hand stuck through a gap in his robe. He was holding something under there, and it didn't take a lot of thinking to know it was a sword. The video camera was on a tripod in front of me. It had a red light that kept winking, and the guy ordered me to say my name and who I worked for. He told me to beg all Americans to leave Iraq or else what was going to happen to me would happen to them."

Balenger knew he was talking too fast, but he couldn't control himself, just kept spewing out the words. "I don't know how long I'd been unconscious from the explosion, how long it had been since I'd had anything to eat and drink. Name, rank, and serial number. That's what they taught us in the Rangers. I sure as hell wasn't going to beg Americans to leave the country, but there was nothing wrong with buying time and saying my name. When I tried to speak, though, my voice made a croaking sound. They realized they needed to give me water before I could say anything. Somebody shoved a bottle to my lips. I swallowed. I felt water dripping off my chin. I swallowed some more. Then the bottle was yanked away, and the guy ordered me to say my name to the camera. I tried again, and they gave me more water, and the third time I tried to speak and couldn't, the guy who spoke English pulled out the sword. Seconds. Tick, tick, tick. No past. No future. Just now. Just that sword. I swore to myself that I'd make now last as long as possible. The guy drew back the sword."

Balenger told his story the way he always did, the same words, the same torrent, the way the psychiatrist always heard it for what might have been the hundredth time. "I don't know how, but I managed to say my name. He held back the sword and ordered me to say who I worked for. That was the same as rank and serial number. No harm in it. So I told the camera the company I worked for: Blackwater. Now. I kept making now last as long as possible. Then he ordered me to beg for my life. I thought, what's the harm in pleading? I knew it wouldn't do any good, but at least it kept now lasting longer. I couldn't do it, though."

Faster and faster. "Fear made my voice break. I was sobbing, and they had to give me more water, but I still couldn't force the words out, so the guy drew back the sword, and now was almost over, and suddenly the walls shook. The room filled with dust. Concrete blocks tumbled. My ears were ringing. The guys wearing hoods were shouting at each other. They yanked a door open. Sunlight blinded me. There was another explosion outside. Some grabbed rifles. Two of them threw me in another room, small, a dirt floor. They locked the door. I heard them running away. I heard another explosion. Gunfire. I was still tied to the chair when they threw me into the room. The chair broke when I landed. I twisted away from the shattered wood. Piss and shit were all over me. My hands were still tied behind me. But I could move, and as soon as I squirmed away from the chair, I forced my tied hands down under my hips and legs. Dislocated my right shoulder, but I got my hands in front of me. Like this." In the flashlights and the wavering candlelight, Balenger raised the hands secured with duct tape.

"And?" JD asked.

Balenger rushed on. "The gunfire and the explosions got worse. The room had a closed wooden shutter. I pulled at it, but it was secured from outside, so I grabbed the chair seat, and I pounded. I can't tell you how hard I pounded. Finally, I broke through the shutter. I squirmed through and fell on my dislocated shoulder. I didn't allow myself to faint from pain. I had to keep going. I had to keep now lasting longer.

People were running in panic from the shots and the explosions, and the next explosion lifted me off my feet. It was shockingly close behind me. This time, I did pass out, and when I regained consciousness, I realized that the explosion came from the building where I was kept prisoner. A mortar round hit it and leveled it."

"And?" Tod asked.

"An American Ranger patrol found me. The company I worked for, Blackwater, arranged for me to have medical attention. I'd been in Iraq only two weeks. They gave me the full month of wages. They paid for me to fly home. I had an insurance policy they'd gotten for me. Fifty thousand if I was killed. Twenty-five thousand if I was injured. Twenty-five thousand. That's what I've been living on. The Veterans Hospital psychiatrist I go to says I have post-traumatic stress disorder. No shit. 'Stress' is right. The world's a waking nightmare. There's plenty of stress, especially if you try not to think about a guy wearing a hood who wants to cut off your head."

Balenger was aware of switching from "I" to "you." The psychiatrist called it disassociation. His voice shook. His heart beat so fast, pressure swelled the veins in his neck. "So now you know I'm not a cop."

"Do we? How did you and the professor get together?"

"I told you I took a course from him." Balenger's clothes were soaked with sweat. "When you live a waking nightmare, how do you get away from the world? Iraq. It's everywhere. How do you get away from fucking Iraq? The past. All I wanted to do was escape into the past. My psychiatrist thought it would help to read old novels, books that made me feel I was in the past. I tried Dickens. I tried Tolstoy. I tried Alexandre Dumas. But that chapter in *The Count of Monte Cristo*, where the hero's in a sack and gets thrown over a wall into the ocean, was too much like reality to me. So I started reading history books. Biographies about Benjamin Franklin and Wordsworth and the founding of the House of Rothschild. I didn't give a shit about Franklin or Wordsworth or the House of Rothschild, but it was in the safe, unthreatening past. Anything before the twentieth century. Big fat books that almost gave me a hernia. The thicker, the better. The more details, the better. Footnotes. How I love footnotes. The only modern novels I read were by Jack Finney and Richard Matheson. *Time and Again. Bid Time Return.* Characters who wanted desperately to leave the present.

They concentrated so hard they went into the past. If only. I went to the State University at Buffalo and pretended I was a student and took as many history classes as I could sneak into. When the professor realized I wasn't enrolled, we had a conference in his office. I told him about myself. He let me go to more of his classes. We talked more, and a month ago, after he got fired, he asked if I'd help him. He said we'd have so much money, we'd never have to worry about the present."

A faint rumble shifted through the building.

"Sack over your head, huh?" Tod asked.

Balenger nodded.

"All that time in darkness," Mack added.

"Yes."

"And you made yourself go through those tunnels into this hotel, and you made yourself come all the way up here through the darkness," JD said. "You must have been reminded a lot of what happened to you in Iraq."

"A couple of times," Balenger said flatly.

The rumble sounded again.

"You're tough."

"I don't think so."

"Sure, you are. You saved Big Ears over there. You saved the professor."

But God help me, I couldn't save Rick, Balenger thought.

"Yeah, a hero," Tod said.

The rumble was a little louder.

"But if you try to be a hero again . . ." Tod raised the pistol, aimed at Balenger, and fired.

38

The bullet snapped past Balenger's head. He felt the shock of air it displaced, heard it slam into the wall behind him.

"Jesus!" Vinnie said.

"It didn't come anywhere close," Tod said.

"My ears!" Mack put his hands over them. "For God's sake, why didn't you warn me? They're ringing like crazy!"

So were Balenger's, but not so much that he didn't hear another rumble.

"Don't try to be a hero," Tod said. "Otherwise, that 'now' thing you talked about won't last much longer."

"All I want is to walk out of here."

"We'll see how this goes. So far you've been useless. Where's the vault?"

"What's that noise?" Mack asked.

"The ringing in your ears."

"No," JD said. "I heard it, too. A rumble."

"Thunder," Balenger said.

They stared toward the ceiling.

"Thunder?" Vinnie shook his head. "There aren't any thunderstorms predicted.

Only showers around dawn. The professor said . . ." Vinnie's voice dropped. "Professor?"

No answer.

"Professor?" Vinnie started toward the sofa.

"The crowbar!" Tod warned, aiming. "Put it down before you come near us!"

Vinnie dropped it and crossed the room. He passed Cora, who continued to hum in shock, and reached the professor, whose head was back, his eyes closed.

Vinnie nudged him. "You told us the weather report was for showers around dawn."

Conklin's eyes remained closed.

"You told us —"

"I lied," Conklin said wearily.

"What?"

"Next week, the salvagers are coming. I needed all of you to help me scout the building tonight." Conklin breathed. "Tomorrow night, after we showed Frank how to get into the building and into the vault . . ." Conklin took another breath. "He was supposed to return and take as many coins as he could carry. Tonight and tomorrow night. That's when it needed to happen."

"You prick."

"I estimated that we'd be out of here before the storm arrived." The professor's bearded face was ravaged with regret. "Apparently I was wrong."

"What's the big deal about a storm?" JD wanted to know.

"Getting out of here," Vinnie said in despair. "Depending on how hard it rains, the tunnels might be flooded."

"Right now, you've got bigger problems than worrying about a flooded tunnel," Tod said. "We'll just have to wait and get more acquainted."

"Yeah," Mack said, putting a hand on Cora's shoulder. "We'll just have to find ways to pass the time."

She was on the floor now, sitting bent forward with her arms around her raised knees and her head braced on them. She didn't seem aware of Mack's touch.

"Leave her alone," Vinnie said.

"Make me."

Balenger tried to distract them. "The vault."

"Your great idea didn't work out, smart guy," Tod said. "The wall on that side sounds hollow, too. If this stuff about the vault and the gold coins turns out to be bullshit . . ."

Balenger examined the holes in the wall.

He went over and peered into the dark bedroom, then studied the doorjamb and the space between the rooms. "Looks like five inches wide. Bob, are you sure the diary didn't say it was a wall safe?"

"A vault," the professor murmured through his pain. "That was what Carlisle always called it."

"Then we're wasting our time on this wall. It's too narrow." Balenger stared at the long living room wall, at the metal shutters and the metal door between them. "No room for the vault there, either."

He tugged open the closet door and saw coats and suits, all in a style that suggested the 1930s. Their smell was nauseating. He yanked the garments off a wooden rod and hurled them across the living room, then entered the closet and pounded on the wall.

"Normal. That leaves the far bedroom wall, or maybe the bathroom."

"Careful, hero," Tod said.

"I'll need light in the bedroom." Balenger picked up the crowbar. "Vinnie, help me."

With an angry look toward Mack, whose hand remained on Cora's shoulder, Vinnie followed Balenger into the bedroom. Their headlamps revealed a lacquered black dresser with red trim, a chrome strip at the bottom and a circular mirror on top. A reading chair had the same black with red trim.

So did the bed, but Balenger hardly noticed as he and Vinnie shoved it away from the wall. Standing in the doorway, Tod and JD aimed their flashlights as Balenger pounded the hollow-sounding wall.

"Black and red," Tod said. "Who did Danata think he was, the Prince of Darkness?"

"I'm sure all the men he shot believed it," Balenger said.

Vinnie took an ashtray off a nightstand. "I'll check the bathroom."

As Balenger swung the crowbar against the wall, he heard Vinnie pounding the wall in the bathroom. Even at a distance, the hollow sound made it obvious nothing was behind the wall. At last, Balenger ran out of surface. He stepped back, breathing heavily, scanning his headlamp along the holes he'd made. "Nothing."

He started back toward the living room.

"Drop the crowbar!" Tod warned from the doorway.

Throwing it onto a chair, Balenger entered the living room.

"Bob!" He roused the professor. "Try to remember the diary. The vault isn't here.

Did the diary mention any other place the vault might be?"

"All bullshit," JD said.

"Danata's suite," Conklin said. "The ceiling, maybe. The floor. Leg hurts."

Balenger stared at the duct tape around it. The tape remained gray, no blood leaking, but the leg was alarmingly swollen. He should have been in an ambulance a half hour ago, Balenger thought. "Does it throb?"

"Constant pain. Sharp."

Maybe I left a shard in there. Balenger put a hand on the professor's forehead. "He's got a fever."

"Gosh," Tod said.

Mack was still rubbing Cora's shoulders.

"The first-aid kit," Balenger said. "We need to give him more painkillers."

"We?" JD said. "All we care about is —"

"All right, all right, if I can find the vault, will you give him the painkillers?"

"Sounds like a deal to me."

Balenger thought frantically. "The ceiling's out of the question. Danata would have wanted easy access. That leaves the floor. Vinnie, get the crowbar. Maybe there's a trapdoor."

Vinnie didn't answer. He was staring at Mack's hands on Cora's shoulders.

"Vinnie! The crowbar!" Balenger shoved

furniture away, pulled up a rug, and knelt to study the floor. The strips of hardwood showed no obvious gaps. "We need to clear the room, move all the furniture."

Balenger's headlamp swept along the first wall and the holes he and Vinnie had pounded into it. The beam illuminated the darkness behind the holes. He shivered with understanding. "There's a lot of space behind that wall." He aimed his headlamp through the biggest hole. "A *hell* of a lot of space."

He shoved his gloved hands into the hole and tried to pull at the plaster's edge, but with his wrists taped together, he couldn't manage a grip. "The crowbar! Where's —"

Abruptly, Vinnie was next to him, ramming the crowbar into the hole. He pried out a chunk of plaster. "There's something in here!"

"The vault?" JD asked quickly.

Vinnie pried away more plaster.

"No! Not the vault!" Balenger threw debris onto the floor. "It looks like . . ."

"A staircase!" Vinnie said.

"What?" Mack moved away from Cora.

"A circular staircase!" Vinnie pried at the wall. Balenger kept throwing the plaster away. They soon had an opening large enough to squeeze through.

The roar of a shot made Balenger flinch. A bullet slammed the wall to his right.

"Stay," Tod ordered. "Nobody's going in there till that hole's a lot wider and we can see everything that happens. One of you might get tempted to run down that staircase. Bear in mind we've got the professor here and what's her name — Cora."

"Sweets," Mack said.

"I'll shoot them if anybody tries to escape. Do we have an understanding?"

Balenger's voice cracked. "Yes."

"Then open that wall."

Vinnie pounded with the crowbar, enlarging the hole. By angling his taped hands sideways, Balenger was able to grip chunks of plaster and tear them away. Joists were exposed, two-by-fours, a frame onto which plasterboard had been nailed. More and more of the space behind the wall became visible.

"Hell, you could have a party back there," Tod said.

There was a six-foot gap between Danata's living room and the wall for the next room. On the right, close to the balcony wall, a spiral staircase led up and down. It was metal, and reminded Balenger of a gigantic corkscrew.

"Explain it," JD said.

"Carlisle used the staircase to move secretly behind the walls," Balenger told him. "I'll bet the staircase goes all the way to the ground floor."

"And I'll bet there are other staircases," Vinnie said.

"The nutcase that built this hotel was a Peeping Tom?" JD asked.

"He lived through other people. He had to limit contact. He was afraid of injuries. A hemophiliac."

"What's — ?"

"A blood disease. Carlisle's blood didn't have thickening agents. The slightest bump or scratch could cause him to bleed, and stopping it could seem impossible."

"So he got his jollies spying on his guests?" Tod asked.

Balenger's headlamp revealed the wall on the other side of the passageway. Every five feet, what looked like the eyepiece of a microscope protruded from the wall. "With those. The wall on the opposite side probably has tiny holes hidden at the side of a painting or under a light fixture attached to the wall. Lenses on this side magnified the image."

"He could watch people undressing?" Mack said. "Or going to the bathroom or screwing?"

"Or arguing," Balenger said. "Or a man getting drunk and beating his wife, or a woman getting into a warm bath and committing suicide by slitting her wrists and bleeding to death."

"Or a boy using a baseball bat to smash his father's head into jelly," Vinnie said. "All of those things happened here. Eventually, over the life of the hotel, every room had something terrible happen in it."

"That was the whole idea of the Paragon Hotel," Balenger said. "All our emotions, good and bad. Carlisle wanted to see everything humans were capable of, so he built himself a small version of the world."

"Do I look like I care?" Tod demanded. "Where's the damned vault?"

Balenger glanced from the staircase all the way along the exposed passageway. His gaze rested on a section of wall in line with the long wall in Danata's living room, where metal shutters hid windows that once looked out on the boardwalk and the beach. "There's a door between those shutters. Where do you suppose it leads?"

"A balcony?" Vinnie suggested.

"Or maybe a patio. Each of the hotel's levels is set back," Balenger said. "When Danata walked out the original door, he was standing on the roof of the room below him.

I bet he had a patio there. Planters filled with bushes and trees. An outdoor table and chairs. Maybe a sun lounge. Lean back. Have a drink. Watch the girls on the beach. That's how I'd have wanted it. But Danata had a long career as a mob enforcer. He didn't stay alive for decades by being stupid and sitting out in the open. People in the rooms to the right and left would have been able to see him. A guy whose brother got shot by him might be tempted to rent the room next door and blow a hole in Danata's head while he was having a drink and watching the girls."

"So?" Tod asked.

"In Danata's place, I'd have built extensions along both walls of my suite. Extensions that went all the way to the edge of the patio and the roof. Walls that kept people in the other rooms from seeing him."

"So fucking what?"

"Maybe the extension on this side is as wide as this passageway. Maybe the passageway continues all the way to the edge of the roof." Balenger studied the six-foot-wide section of wall at the end of the passageway. At shoulder level, a screw projected from the right and left. Without asking permission, he walked along the corridor and tapped the wall. "Sounds hollow."

Again, he studied the screws. "With my hands taped, I can't pull at these."

"Stand back." Tod aimed the pistol.

When Balenger was an unthreatening distance away, JD stepped between upright two-by-fours and approached the end wall. He gripped the screws on each side and pulled, but nothing happened. "Those screws are in solid."

"Tug harder. I think they're handles."

JD yanked, then stumbled back as a partition broke free. Headlamps and flashlights pierced the dark continuation of the passageway.

"And there's your vault," Balenger said.

39

It was about ten feet farther along, occupying the height and width of the passageway. Its borders were black metal while its door was brass, now tarnished green. Balenger imagined how it had once gleamed. In the middle, the door had a handle and a dial. Imprinted at the top was CORRIGAN SECURITY, the name of what Balenger assumed was a no-longer-existing company.

"We had to tear down the wall to get in here," Vinnie said. "How could Danata have reached this?"

Balenger noticed an alcove to the left. He stepped back to where JD had removed the partition that hid the continuation of the passageway. The partition had been in line with the wall that faced the boardwalk and the beach. A bookcase occupied the right corner of that wall. Balenger hadn't tried to move the bookcase because it seemed obvious that nothing could be behind it.

Now he went back to the room and tugged at the bookcase.

"Vinnie, give me a hand."

But both of them were unable to budge it.

"I'll get the crowbar," Vinnie said.

"Carefully," JD said.

"Wait a second." Hampered by his taped wrists, Balenger shoved aside books on the right of the middle shelf, pawed along the inside of the case, and touched a metal catch. He flipped the catch upward and pulled at the case. It swung open. The space behind it was the alcove Balenger had seen.

"The extension that goes to the edge of the roof must have a box in this corner," he said, "some kind of decorative effect, probably with flowers or shrubs in front, so Danata didn't have to look at just a plain wall when he sat outside. The box and whatever's in front disguise the exterior of the alcove."

Balenger stepped through the open bookcase, entered the alcove, turned right, reached the passageway, and turned left to face the vault.

"Okay, that explains how Danata went from his living room to the vault," Tod said. "But it doesn't explain the staircase. Wouldn't it have bugged him? Wouldn't Danata have started wondering what kind of creep Carlisle was that he needed a hidden staircase?"

"I don't think Danata knew about the staircase," Balenger said. "All the construction was outside on the patio. The workers didn't have a reason to break into the interior wall."

"All I care about is the vault," Tod said. "Open it."

Balenger pushed down on the handle and pulled. The door didn't move. His spirit sank. "Locked."

"You begged us not to kill the old guy. You said he knew how to get into the vault."

Now we come to it, Balenger thought. The moment for which they kept us alive. In a sweat, he recalled the Iraqi insurgent threatening to cut off his head. The question again insisted: How do I make now last a little longer?

Balenger crossed the room toward the professor, who continued to lean back in pain.

"Bob."

Conklin moaned.

"Bob, do you know the combination?"

"Maybe."

"*Maybe?*" Tod asked. His tattoos seemed like creatures rippling across his cheeks.

"Concentrate, Bob. This is really important. Tell us how to get into the vault."

"A guess."

"A guess?" Tod said angrily.

Conklin breathed with effort. "The diary."

"Yes, tell us about the diary," Balenger said.

"Carlisle used one of his peepholes to watch Danata unlock the vault. Carlisle saw the combination."

"And?" Mack asked. *"What are the numbers?"*

"Carlisle wrote in his diary that Danata used his name for the numbers."

"What's *that* supposed to mean?"

"Bob, was he talking about some kind of alphabet-number transference?" Balenger asked.

"Think so."

" 'Think so' isn't good enough." Tod aimed.

Balenger saw an end table next to the sofa the professor lay upon. He drew a finger along its dusty surface.

"This is the alphabet." He wrote in a fury. "I'll match a number with each letter. A is 1. B's 2. C's 3."

"We get the fucking idea," Mack said.

"Danata, D is 4. A is 1. N is 14. A is 1. T is 20. A is 1. If we put them in a sequence, we get 41141201. That's the combination: 41, 14, 12, 01."

"You'd better be right," JD said.

Balenger rushed into the exposed passageway and reached the vault. Trying to steady his hands, he dialed 41 to the right. "The other numbers! Can't remember. Vinnie, read them to me!"

Vinnie did.

Balenger continued, dialing 14 to the left, 12 to the right, and 1 to the left. Pulse racing, he turned the handle and tugged at the door. It resisted.

No!

"Let's cap 'em all and grab as many of these thousand-dollar ashtrays and candleholders and shit that we can carry," JD said.

"But we don't cap the girl right away," Mack said. "Sweets and I have a date."

"I started in the wrong direction!" Balenger insisted. "I should have started left instead of right!"

He dialed 41 to the left, 14 to the right, 12 to the left, and 1 to the right. Praying, he yanked at the handle, pulling. The door remained solidly in place.

No!

"End of story," Tod said.

"Please! Give me a chance to think! The theory makes sense!" What am I doing wrong? he thought.

The professor murmured something. Balenger only caught the last word. ". . . name."

"What?"

"Wrong name." Conklin strained to speak louder. "Not Danata."

"He's delirious." JD walked over with the crowbar, ready to swing it. The youngest of the group, he craved the most violence, Balenger realized. "Let's put the old bird out of his misery."

"While I show Sweets the bedroom," Mack said.

"First name," Conklin said.

"Carmine!" Balenger said. "Wait!" He moved to another table and wrote CARMINE in the dust. "C is 3. A is 1. R is 18. M is 13. I is 9. N is 14. E is 5. The sequence is 3118139145. *That's* the combination! Five sets of numbers: 31, 18, 13, 91, 45."

"Five sets?" Tod asked. "A little while ago, you were sure there were *four*."

"Just leave the professor alone! He gave us a direction! If this works, he earned the right to live a little longer!"

Balenger's throat cramped. That was all he worked for — the right to live a little longer. But this time, despite the rumble of thunder that sounded so much like approaching explosions, there wouldn't be a Ranger unit to rescue him.

"Show us." Mack's hands slid along Cora's shoulders.

She was oblivious, her eyes staring at infinity.

Balenger ran to the vault and tried to steady his shaking headlamp. "Vinnie, read me the numbers!" This time, he started to the left: 31, right 18, left 13, right 91, left 45.

Flashlights blazed toward him as Tod, Mack, and JD stepped into the passageway. They shoved Vinnie ahead of them.

"Turn the handle, hero. Pull the door," JD said.

Please, God, please, Balenger thought, and pulled.

Suddenly, JD screamed.

40

Whirling, Balenger saw a dark specter crash into JD and knock him down.

"Husband. Killed my husband." Cora had an ashtray in her hands, pounding. "Motherfucker killed my husband."

JD groaned.

Lights zigzagged insanely.

"Motherfucker," Cora aimed the ashtray at JD's teeth.

JD raised his arm. Taking the blow on his wrist, he moaned.

"Don't try anything, hero." Tod aimed the pistol at Balenger.

"Furthest thing from my mind."

"She's *your* date," Tod told Mack. "I thought you were watching her. Get the bitch under control."

"Pull her off me!" JD shouted, frantically protecting his face.

"Motherfucker. Motherfucker." Cora plunged the ashtray toward JD's forehead.

JD blocked it.

Mack grabbed her, straining to pull her away, but her fury was more than he expected.

"Get her *off*."

Mack yanked the ashtray out of her hands.

Now she pounded with her fists.

"I sure hate to do this." Mack picked up the crowbar. "A terrible waste."

"No!" Balenger said. "I'll do it! I'll stop her!" He lunged toward Cora, hooking his taped wrists over hers. She struggled to disentangle her arms, but Balenger twisted to the side, the pressure torquing her off JD. He crawled onto her, resisting her efforts to squirm away.

"I guess you're useful for something after all," Tod said.

"You need her. Don't kill her," Balenger said.

"Oh, I need her, all right," Mack said. "But afterward . . ."

JD came to his feet, wiping blood from his lips. "Give me the crowbar."

"No! You need her! You need all of us! The gold coins!"

"Are you still bullshitting about that?" Mack said. "Those gold coins, if they even exist, are worthless — *we can't get into the damned vault*."

"No! I think I heard the tumblers click. I think I unlocked it."

"From the start, all you did is lie!"

272

"If I can open the vault, if I can show you the gold coins, you're going to need all of us."

"For what?"

"To carry the coins! They'll be heavy. You'll need help getting them downstairs and through the tunnels. Otherwise, it'll take twice as long. You won't get out before the storm hits."

"You think there are that many?"

"Why else would Danata have put in a vault that big?"

Tod and Mack looked at each other.

"Do it," Tod told Mack, "while I make sure this bunch doesn't try anything."

Balenger felt pressure inside his rib cage. The force of adrenaline made his chest seem to swell, about to explode.

Still holding the crowbar, Mack put his flashlight under his arm so he could grip the vault's handle.

Tick, tick, tick. No past. No future. Now's almost over, Balenger thought.

Mack shoved down on the handle. He pulled. The vault door moved. Time seemed to stop.

"Fucking amazing," Mack said. He got out of the way as he swung the door outward.

Balenger's headlamp shone inside. So did

273

Vinnie's. And the flashlights that Tod, Mack, and JD aimed. Thunder rumbled through the broken skylight outside the room. The hotel trembled. Then everything became silent. No one seemed to breathe.

The gold coins were in metal trays on shelves all the way up the right side of the vault. More coins than any of them could have imagined. Perfectly preserved. In pristine condition. The absence of dust on them made them seem to absorb the lights aimed into the vault and give off a glow.

But that wasn't what they stared at. It wasn't what made them gape.

"No," Vinnie said.

The stench of piss and shit escaped from the vault. What occupied all their stunned attention was a woman in a dirty, transparent nightgown, which showed her breasts, her nipples, and the triangle of her pubic hair.

For an instant, Balenger was tricked by the shadows. His horror mounting, she appeared to be someone he knew.

The woman's blond hair hung like a rag mop. Frail, haggard, in her late twenties, she cowered, pressing as far back into the vault as possible. A sleeping bag was crumpled at her feet. Candybar wrappers and empty water bottles lay on it. A toilet pail was in a corner. She raised her hands to shield her frightened eyes from the stabbing lights.

Balenger felt his knees weaken. He had the dizzy sensation of dropping through a trapdoor into insanity.

2:00 a.m.

41

"Jesus," Vinnie said.

Mack's voice broke. "What the hell is . . ."

As Balenger rose to his knees, he noticed that even Cora was stunned into submission.

Mack stepped toward the vault's entrance. His flashlight cast a stark shadow of her head. "Lady, how did you get in there?"

She whimpered, cowering with such desperation that it almost seemed possible she could push her way through the vault's back wall.

Mack still had the crowbar in his hand. "What happened?"

"For God's sake, you're scaring her," Tod said. "Give JD the damned crowbar, and get her out of there."

"Is he here? Is he coming?" The woman moaned.

"Is *who* here?"

"Did he send you?"

"Nobody sent us."

"Help me."

Mack stepped into the vault. Headlamps

and flashlights cast his shadow as he reached for her. "Who did this to you?"

The woman gaped at his hand.

"Whoever he is, I'm not him," Mack said.

". . . not him." The woman gaped now at the grotesque night-vision goggles dangling around Mack's neck.

"He didn't send me."

". . . send you."

"But I'd sure like to know who the sick fuck is. Take my hand. Let's get you out of there."

Legs unsteady, the woman stepped across the sleeping bag. She hesitated, sobbed, and took his hand.

"How did she breathe in there?" Tod wanted to know.

Mack peered at the back of the vault. "Holes. Somebody drilled them."

"You need to . . ." The woman almost collapsed. Mack held her up. "Hurry. Get me away from him."

"Don't worry," JD said. "If he shows up, with us here, *he's* the one who'll need to worry."

"Thirsty."

"How long has it been since . . ."

"Don't know. No sense of time."

"Give her some water," Tod said.

She drank greedily, so desperate that she

didn't seem to notice the white burn scar on Mack's cheek.

"Hurry," she pleaded. "Before he comes back."

"What's your name?" Mack took her from the passageway into the candlelight of the living room.

"Amanda." Her voice was raspy from not having been used. "Evert. Are we in Brooklyn? I live in Brooklyn."

"No. This is Asbury Park."

"Asbury . . . ? *New Jersey?*" It was as if she'd been told she was thousands of miles from home. She frowned at the shadowy wreckage. "My God, what *is* this place?"

"The Paragon Hotel. It's abandoned."

Amanda inhaled sharply. In the candle-light, she recoiled from the tattoos rippling across Tod's cheeks.

His hand shot angrily to his face.

"You're not listening," Amanda begged. "We need to get out of here before he comes back."

"Who *is* this guy?" Mack asked.

"Ronnie. That's what he makes me call him."

"No last name?"

Eyes wild, Amanda shook her head desperately from side to side.

"What's he look like?"

"There isn't *time,*" Amanda wailed, tugging at Mack to take her to the door.

"There are three of us," JD said. "Believe me, if we find him, whatever he did to you, the bastard won't be doing it anymore."

"Three? But what about . . ." Amanda turned toward Balenger, Vinnie, and Cora. Her gaze dropped to the duct tape binding their wrists. She moaned.

Thunder rumbled.

"To hell with this," JD said. "We found what we wanted. Let's go before the rain starts. Hey, Big Ears, were you telling the truth that the tunnels might flood?"

"That's part of what they were designed for. To carry away storm water," Vinnie said.

"Empty the knapsacks," Tod ordered. "Load them with as many coins as they'll hold. Stuff your pockets."

"But what about *them?*" JD pointed toward their captives.

Tod raised the pistol.

"Wait," Balenger said. "Something's wrong." A chill sped along his nerves. Through the open door, he heard the shrieking wind. Thunder boomed through the broken skylight. The smell of rain gusted in. He heard water pelting the remaining glass in the skylight, heard it splashing on the balcony and the balustrade.

"Something's wrong for sure. The storm already started." Mack dumped the equipment out of his knapsack and hurried toward the vault.

"Not what I mean." Balenger stared toward the professor leaning back on the sofa.

The light from the professor's headlamp slowly shifted, sinking until it shone on his ample chest. Then it rolled onto his lap, shining up between his legs, as if his hard hat had come loose. But Balenger remembered that Conklin's hard hat had stayed firmly on his head, even when the stairs collapsed, a chin strap holding it in place.

Legs numb, he shuffled toward the professor, not sure if he had the strength to get there. Please, God, let me be wrong. But as he forced himself dizzily closer, the smell of rain gave way to the stench of copper. Blood. The sofa was drenched in blood. So was the professor, and it was more than a hard hat that lay pointing upward in his lap. It was his head.

42

Acid gushed into Balenger's mouth. He clamped a hand to his lips, hoping it would stop him from throwing up. He swung toward Tod, gagging. "Get her away from the sofa."

"What?"

"The woman. Amanda. Get her to the other side of the room."

"What are you talking about?" Tod peered behind Balenger and saw what was on the sofa. "Oh, fuck." He swung as abruptly as Balenger had. "Mack, get a sheet from the bedroom!"

"Why?"

"Just do what you're told!"

"What's wrong?" JD asked. Then he saw the professor's blood-soaked, headless torso on the sofa and groaned.

"Ronnie," Amanda whimpered.

Vinnie and Cora turned away in shock.

"Ronnie's here," Amanda said.

"How?" Tod demanded.

"We were all in the passageway." Balenger fought his dizziness. His arms and legs were numb with mounting panic. Emotions from Iraq threatened to overwhelm him. No! he told himself. If you let it take charge, you die. Passive gets you killed. "We left the door open." Thunder roared. Rain pelted the balcony. "Somebody came in while we were distracted by opening the vault and finding Amanda."

"Ronnie," Amanda said.

"He stood outside in the dark. He listened for a long time." Balenger's voice was unsteady.

"A long time?" Tod stared at the gloom beyond the open door. "How do you know?"

"Twenty minutes ago, I told you about Iraq, about the guy who threatened to cut off my head, and now we find the professor with his head —"

Mack rushed from the bedroom, hurried to the sofa, and threw a sheet over the professor's body. Blood soaked it. The headlamp between the professor's legs shone dully upward through the fabric. "It stinks," Mack said in disgust. "I never realized how much . . ."

"Yeah," Balenger said. "Blood stinks. Mutilated bodies stink."

"Ronnie," Amanda repeated. It seemed the only word she knew.

"He might still be here!" JD scanned his flashlight into every corner.

"Shut the door," Tod ordered. "Lock it."

"Lock it how? The crowbar broke the door frame."

"Cram furniture against it."

JD dragged the bookcase toward the door. "Somebody give me a hand!"

Vinnie helped him. Balenger rushed to a heavy-looking table. Cora was next to him, sobbing, helping him push the table against the door. Mack lifted a chair on top.

"Nobody's coming through there." Mack grabbed the crowbar.

"But what if he's still in the room?" Again, JD scanned his flashlight toward the corners. Its trembling beam made shadows dance.

"Ronnie's here," Amanda said.

"Check the bedroom, the bathroom, and the closet!" Tod shouted. He hurried toward the bedroom, then turned and aimed at Balenger. "Don't go anywhere."

"I'm not planning on it. Right now, I'd sooner be with you." Balenger grabbed a hammer from a pile of equipment dumped from a knapsack. He entered the exposed passageway, turned off his headlamp to hide himself, and stood near the staircase, ready with the hammer, listening for the sound of anyone climbing the stairs. What he heard instead were the pounding of his pulse and thunder rattling the walls.

He became aware of Cora and Vinnie next to him, shutting off their lights, guarding the staircase. Each held a lamp as if it were a club. He glanced toward Amanda, who cowered in the living room, whimpering Ronnie's name. "Cora, maybe you should stay with her. Try to calm her down."

Cora wiped tears from her face. "Do I look like I can calm anybody?" Nonetheless, she went to Amanda.

Balenger watched Cora touch Amanda's arm and talk softly to her. Then he returned his attention to the black mouth of the spiral staircase. For all he knew, someone was down there, watching him.

"He's not in the closet, the bedroom, or the bathroom," Tod said, returning with Mack and JD.

Mack grabbed a water bottle from the floor and drank half of it.

"We might need to ration the rest of the bottles," Balenger said.

"We?" Tod asked.

"I need to . . ." Amanda said.

"What?"

"Relieve my . . ."

"So do I," Cora said.

"What's keeping you?"

"You took away the bottles we use for —"

"Go in the bathroom. You won't have water to flush it, but so what?"

"I don't want to be in there alone."

"I'll go with you." Mack grinned.

"*I* will," Vinnie said. He turned on his headlamp and motioned for the women to follow him into the bedroom. "I'll be right outside the door."

Cora put an arm around Amanda and led her toward the bedroom. Balenger noticed Mack staring toward the back of Amanda's nightgown. The two women and Vinnie disappeared into the darkness.

Watching them leave and then scanning the wreckage of the living room, the broken furniture, the destroyed walls, Balenger thought. Leave nothing but footprints? Take nothing but photographs? There's not much left to ruin.

"What now, hero?" Tod asked. "Any suggestions?"

"Use a cell phone to call the police."

"Don't you remember the local emergency number isn't working? And the regular police number has a long wait."

"Then phone the police in another city."

"Yeah, right. So instead of facing this Ronnie jerkoff, we get charged for killing your pal, not to mention kidnapping the rest of you. Somehow, I think our odds are better against Ronnie."

"Not so far."

"Yeah, well, we weren't organized a little while ago. We didn't know what we were dealing with."

"You still don't."

"We will when the woman comes back and we get some information out of her."

JD took an empty knapsack into the vault. "Man, does it ever stink in here." He threw coins into the knapsack. They made a dull clinking sound.

"Here's another suggestion," Balenger said. Keep making them feel we're together, he thought. "Collectors won't pay seven hundred dollars for coins that are scratched. Those are perfect, and he's ruining them."

"Hey, asshole," Tod called. "Be careful with those. Don't scratch them. Use the trays. Put the coins in, trays and all. I was confused a minute ago," he told Balenger. "Needed to think. But now I've got everything covered. With our goggles, we'll see Ronnie before he sees us."

"Has it occurred to you that he might have goggles, too?"

Tod frowned, his furrowed brow twisting

his tattoos. Footsteps made him turn toward Vinnie, Cora, and Amanda coming back. "Tell us about Ronnie," he demanded.

Amanda's face tightened. Shaken by memories, she took a deep breath. "He . . ." She bit her lip and forced herself to continue. "I work in a bookstore in Manhattan. He came in a couple of times. Friendly." She hugged herself. "He must have followed me home to Brooklyn and figured where to park a car, where to hide. A few days earlier, my boyfriend moved out. I was living alone in an apartment I couldn't afford by myself. I was so worried about paying the rent, I didn't pay attention when I got off the subway and walked home."

"When was this?" Mack asked.

"I have no idea." Amanda shivered. "What date is it?"

"October twenty-fourth."

"Oh." Amanda's voice dropped. She sank into a chair.

"What's wrong?" Balenger asked.

"The night he grabbed me was June fourteenth." Amanda's eyes communicated her dismay and loss. "The store stayed open that night until ten. An author signing. I didn't get home until midnight. He had a cloth with some kind of chemical in it, something that he pressed over my mouth when I passed an alley." She took another deep breath. "When I woke up, I was on the bed upstairs. He was sitting next to me, holding my hand." She closed her eyes, lowered her head, and quivered as if she tasted something disgusting. "That's when he explained the facts of my new life."

"What does he look like?" Tod demanded. "Does he have a gun? If we end up fighting him, what do we need to expect?"

"Old."

"What?"

"Much older than me. Older than you." Amanda looked at Balenger, who was thirty-five.

"How old?" Tod asked.

"I'm no good at judging that. Anybody over forty looks —"

"You think he's over forty?" Balenger asked.

"Yes."

"Is he *real* old? He can't be if he overpowered you."

"Maybe in his fifties. Tall. Thin. *Nervous* thin. He has a neutral expression on his face. Even when he smiles, it's neutral."

"A thin guy in his fifties?" Tod began to look confident. "I think we can handle him just fine."

"He's very strong."

"Stronger than this?" Tod held up the pistol.

"He lifts weights."

"Thin weightlifters don't exactly leave me quaking in my shoes." Tod looked at Mack and JD. "Questions?"

"Yeah," JD said. "What are we hanging around for?"

Mack looked regretfully at Cora, then nodded. "Right. Let's grab the coins and get out of here."

"And *them?*" JD asked.

"We tape them to chairs," Tod said. He took the hammer from Balenger's hand and tossed it onto the pile of equipment. "We let Ronnie take care of them for us. That way, *he'll* get blamed. The cops will probably also blame him for the guy you threw over the railing."

"Please," Amanda said. "Get me out of here."

"Can't."

"Help me!"

"Hey, I'm sorry, but you're the reason he's pissed off. If we try to take you out of here, he'll come after you, which means he'll come after *us*. You can't expect us to be stupid about this."

"You bastard."

"Well, if that's how you're gonna be, get in

that chair." Tod shoved her into it. JD grabbed the duct tape from a pile of equipment on the floor.

"Sweets, get in this chair," Mack told Cora.

"Hero, you get in this one," Tod said. The remaining chair was propped against the door. "And Big Ears, you stand against a two-by-four in the wall."

JD finished taping Amanda to the chair, securing her ankles and shoulders. Then he went to Cora.

"*I'll* do it," Mack said.

Balenger saw him feel Cora's legs and breasts while he worked the tape.

They put on the heavy knapsacks, then went to the vault and stuffed their pockets with coins. The weight made their bulging coats and pants droop.

"I hate to waste the pocket space, but we'd better take walkie-talkies in case we get separated," Tod said.

Moving awkwardly, they returned to the door. While Tod aimed at it, Mack and JD shifted the furniture away. Mack opened the door and stepped back.

Thunder boomed. Rain pelted the balcony. A chill breeze gusted in.

Tod shouted to be heard above the storm. "Ronnie, you don't need to worry! We're not taking your girlfriend! We're leaving her for you! And there's a bonus! We're leaving some new pals of hers, too! They're wrapped up like presents, all ready for you to enjoy! No harm's been done! We'll get out of your way! Maybe you don't know this place is gonna be torn down! The salvagers come next week! You might want to set up shop someplace else! How's that for being helpful? Sorry we barged in! No hard feelings! We're going now! Have fun!"

They put on their goggles and headed for the staircase. Tod hesitated and looked at Balenger. "I'm an artist, do you know that?" He crossed the room and went into the bedroom.

Straining, Balenger turned his head and watched him come out with an object in his hands.

"You need this to complete the picture," Tod said, approaching.

"No," Balenger said. The realization of what was about to happen filled him with despair.

Tod threw Balenger's hard hat away.

"Please, don't." Balenger's voice broke.

The object in Tod's hands was a pillowcase. He tugged it over Balenger's head.

43

It reeked of age and dust. "No," Balenger begged. "Take it off."

"What would be the fun in *that?*"

In panicked sightlessness, Balenger heard Tod cross the room.

"So long, everybody!" Mack said.

"It's been great!" JD said.

Balenger heard them descending the staircase, the sound of their footsteps getting fainter.

In his tortured memory, he sat tied to a wooden chair in a dirty concrete-block building in Iraq, a sack over his head, while the only one of his captors who spoke English threatened to decapitate him. Until this moment, he was certain that nothing more terrifying could ever happen to him.

Now he realized how wrong he'd been. The second time was worse. *This* was worse. Thunder booming. Rain pelting. Unable to see anything through the pillowcase except the faint light of the candles and the dim beam of the professor's headlamp pointing up from between his legs. The lamp's glow barely pierced the sheet that covered the headless body.

Yes, this was worse. Duct-taped to a chair. Breathless under the hood. Knowing that three other people shared the same death sentence. Waiting for Ronnie. Not being able to see when Ronnie arrived. Not being able to hear his footsteps because of the wind, the thunder, and the rain. Ronnie might be standing in front of him right now, about to slash with whatever he used to cut off the professor's head.

Balenger's chest heaved. His breathing was so labored, he didn't believe he could survive. Sweat surged from his body, from every pore, more sweat than he thought could possibly gush from him. It soaked his clothes. He was hot and then suddenly cold. Shivering, he told himself that now had to end sometime. It couldn't be prolonged forever. He'd managed to make it last a year since Iraq. A year was something. A year more than he'd expected. But now was about to end.

Thunder shook the building. Was Ronnie standing silently in front of him, about to use a scythe or a sword or a butcher knife? Will I feel the force of the blow before my throat gushes blood and my brain shuts down?

Hero. That's what Tod called me. Hero. A joke. A putdown. Hero? I toss from the same nightmare every night. I wake up exhausted, afraid to get out of bed. I needed every ounce of my remaining strength to force myself to come to this godawful place. All of it gone. Hero? The son of a bitch. Leaving us to die. The cocksucker. Putting this pillowcase over my head. I won't let him get away with this. I'll find him. I'll track him down. I'll squeeze my hands around his throat. I'll . . .

"Vinnie!" Balenger's voice was muffled under the pillowcase. "Can you hear me!"

"Yes!"

"Can you move at all? Maybe there's a nail or a jagged edge of wood that you can rub the tape against and cut it!"

"Too tight!"

Balenger heard someone sobbing. At first, he thought he was disassociating, hearing his own sobs. Then he realized they came from Amanda.

"Amanda, we haven't been introduced." Under the circumstances, the normal-sounding statement was insane, Balenger knew. But he had to try to calm her. If they were going to get out of this, they wouldn't be able to do it with someone who was hysterical. "My name's Frank. That's Vinnie

297

over there. And Cora's the gal near you. I guess I'm not supposed to say 'gal.' It's not politically correct."

Amanda's sobs changed rhythm, lessening. Balenger sensed she was puzzled. "So now that we're all acquainted, I want you to do something for me. Do you think you can move the duct tape and get out of the chair?"

"Trying."

Balenger waited.

"I . . ."

Balenger sweated and felt time passing.

"No. It's too tight."

"Cora?"

"Can't. While that bastard was feeling me up, he really made the tape secure."

What are we going to do? Balenger wondered. His hot breath accumulated under the pillowcase, threatening to smother him. He strained to remember the room, to identify something that could help them. Glass. Glass on the floor from the table he'd broken.

"Amanda?"

She sniffled. "What?"

"Can you see the broken glass on the floor? Halfway between me and Vinnie."

Pause. "Yes."

"If I can overturn my chair and drag it

with me, do you think you can give me directions toward the glass?"

". . . Yes."

"I really need your help."

The chair was heavy. Balenger shifted his weight from one side to the other, but the chair resisted. When he shifted his weight harder, faster, the chair started rocking. Abruptly, it was off-balance. Unable to see and judge the fall, he couldn't prepare himself as the chair toppled sideways.

The shock of hitting the floor startled him. He rubbed his head along the carpet, hoping to tug off the hood, but sweat stuck the material to his head. It wouldn't come free.

No time! For all Balenger knew, Ronnie was directly outside the open door, smiling that neutral smile Amanda had described, amused by Balenger's pathetic efforts, holding a knife.

Now! Balenger told himself. Crawl! Although the tape was tight around his ankles, he could move his knees by flexing his lower body and pressing his hips forward. He dug his right shoulder and the side of his right knee into the carpet and did his best to shove the chair along. More sweat gushed from his body. Groaning, he felt the chair move a little.

Harder. Try harder, he told himself. His shoulder and knee felt burned by friction against the carpet. The chair moved a little farther. He gasped with effort.

"Amanda, how close am I to the broken glass?" Under the pillowcase, breath vapor beaded his face.

"Twelve feet."

No! It'll take me forever!

Try.

Can't.

Move!

Thunder roared. The walls shook. Then an eerie silence gripped the hotel. Between thunderclaps and rain gusts, Balenger heard something else. Distant. Faint. From the direction of the stairwell. Echoing up.

A shot.

"What was that?" Vinnie said.

"Don't think about it."

Move! Mustering all his strength, Balenger inched the chair forward. Twelve feet away? Too far. Can't make it.

Another shot.

Several more. Rapid.

"God help us," Vinnie said.

Harder. Try harder, Balenger thought. He heard screams now, far below, magnified by the stairwell, drifting upward.

"Please, God, help us," Vinnie said.

Balenger strained, moving the chair three inches.

"Wait," Amanda said.

"What's wrong?"

"You're going to bump into a coffee table. There's a candle. You'll knock it over."

And set fire to the room and get burned alive before Ronnie cuts off our heads, Balenger thought. On the verge of losing his mind, he wanted to shriek until his vocal cords hemorrhaged.

"Where's the table?"

"About ten inches to the side of your chair."

More screams from the stairwell.

"Where's the candle?"

"On the corner nearest you."

I'm never going to reach the broken glass, he thought. On the verge of exhaustion, he budged the chair in a different direction.

"You're going to hit the table," Amanda said.

"Want to."

"What?"

"Need the candle."

The stairwell was now silent. Twelve feet versus ten inches. Balenger groaned, flexed, and shifted the chair. Thunder roared.

"The corner's in front of your face," Amanda said.

Balenger inhaled as best he could, moisture beading his upper lip under the pillowcase. The tape was around his upper arms, but he was able to flex his elbows and move his forearms. He touched the table's smooth metal leg. Wincing from stress in his elbows and shoulders, fearing he would dislocate them, he groped higher, feeling the table's glass corner. Just a little higher, he thought. His elbows and wrists in agony, he reached over the table's corner and sobbed with relief when his gloves touched the candle.

He pulled it from its base and eased it over the table's side. He felt wax drip onto his Windbreaker. Holding the candle horizontally, he shoved its base between his legs. His thighs gripped it firmly. Seen through the pillowcase, the flame was just visible enough for Balenger to guide his taped wrists over it. He felt heat through his gloves and sleeves.

Duct tape doesn't burn. It melts. He imagined it bubbling and shriveling as he concentrated to pull his wrists apart. The heat intensified. In pain, he felt the tape softening, loosening. At once, the tape parted. He jerked his wrists from the flame and twisted them hard, freeing them from the remainder of the tape.

Dizzy from the accumulation of carbon

dioxide, he tugged the sweat-soaked hood off his head and inhaled greedily. It felt glorious to be able to use both hands. He grabbed the candle from between his thighs and drew its flame along his left shoulder, melting the tape that bound his chest to the chair. His Windbreaker started to burn. The heat felt blistering. He transferred the candle to his left hand and used his gloved right hand to stamp out the flames on his chest.

The stench of melted duct tape made him gag, but he stifled the reflex and pulled at the separated tape, freeing his shoulders. Frenzied, he bent toward his ankles and melted the tape that secured them to the chair. He wavered to his feet. Tense, listening for more sounds in the stairwell, he reached down for a shard of glass, only to notice a knife among the equipment that had been dumped from the knapsacks. Sure, he thought, they had more knives than they needed. Somebody wanted to make room for more coins.

A footstep echoed in the stairwell.

Balenger rushed to Vinnie and sliced the tape at his shoulders, wrists, and ankles. He heard another footstep, higher in the stairwell. Vinnie took a shard of glass from the floor and ran to Cora while Balenger ran to

Amanda. The two men hacked at the tape, working to free the women.

Lightning cracked. In its relatively quiet aftermath, the footsteps ascended. Slow and measured, they made Balenger think of someone who walked with painful deliberate care because of alcohol or drugs. Or maybe the sound came from someone so confident of the endgame that he didn't need to hurry.

Cora and Amanda yanked away the last of the tape and lunged from their chairs. Balenger noticed the hammer Tod had dropped on the pile of equipment. He threw it to Vinnie, then held his knife in an attack position.

"Turn off your headlamps." In the candlelight, he focused all his attention on the stairwell's black mouth.

The slow footsteps kept rising. Steady. Patient. A shadow appeared. Balenger prepared to attack. An arm waved up and down. A pistol was at the end of it. But the arm wasn't aiming the pistol. It was moving the pistol the way a blind man would use a cane, testing the area before him. A head appeared. Night-vision goggles. Tattoos. Tod. He emerged from the staircase. He looked dazed. In the light from the candles, Balenger saw that he was covered with blood.

44

"Is it . . . Are you . . ." Tod lowered his goggles, as if convinced they made him see things that weren't real. He didn't seem puzzled that Balenger, Vinnie, Cora, and Amanda were free of their bonds. Nor did he look fearful that all four might be able to overpower him before he could defend himself. What he did look was relieved.

"Thank God." He plodded from the weight of the gold coins in his knapsack and pockets. He backed from the stairwell, gaping at it. "We're gonna need to stick together. Need all the help we can get."

"Are you hurt?" Balenger asked. "There's blood —"

"Not mine." The sound of rain made Tod frown toward the howling darkness beyond the open door. "No. Jesus. Gotta close it. Gotta barricade it again. Hurry. No time. Get it shut. Now. I'll guard the stairs. I'll shoot anybody who comes up the stairs."

But the candlelight revealed that the slide on the pistol was back. Its magazine was empty.

"Give it to me," Balenger said.

"Need it."

"You fired all the rounds in it."

"What?"

"You emptied it."

"Emptied it?"

"Vinnie! Amanda!" Cora shouted. "Help with the door!"

They reclosed it and piled the furniture.

"The spare magazine," Balenger asked Tod. "Where is it?"

Tod kept gazing trancelike toward the stairwell.

"Give me the damned gun." Balenger twisted it from his hand, amazed at how things had changed. A while ago, Tod would have shot him dead for even looking as if he'd try for the gun. Balenger found the spare magazine in Tod's belt. With military expertise, he dropped the empty magazine, shoved in the loaded one, and pressed the gun's release lever so the slide rammed forward and chambered a round. It gave him a moment's confidence to be armed again.

Balenger aimed toward the stairs. "What happened?"

"Not sure," Tod said. He twitched. "Oh, I know what happened all right. I'm just not sure how it was done."

"Where are your buddies?"

"We went down the stairs."

"I know that. Tell me about —"

"We kept going down and down. Around and around. Turning and turning. At each level, there was a passageway like up here. But the passageways got longer."

"Sure. Each level below us gets bigger and wider. For Carlisle to eavesdrop, he had to extend the passageways farther to reach all the rooms."

"Longer and longer," Tod said. "Finally, we reached the bottom."

"Vinnie," Balenger said. "You and Cora and Amanda take off his knapsack. Dump the coins. Fill the knapsack with as much equipment as you can stuff into it. The rest we'll carry."

"But there wasn't a door," Tod said. "We couldn't find a door." His facial tattoos were almost hidden by blood. "No matter how hard we looked, we couldn't find one. We ran all the way to the end of the bottom corridor. It went on forever. We still couldn't find a door. But at the end, we found something else."

"What?"

"A body."

Amanda made a noise in her throat.

"She'd been dead a long time," Tod said.

"She?"

"A dress. The body wore a dress. An old-fashioned dress. But she looked like a mummy. That's how long she'd been dead. All dried up, her eye sockets hollow. Hard to tell with the green from the goggles, but I think her hair was blond. Like hers." Tod indicated Amanda. "The corpse was sitting in a corner, like she'd run there and got tired and sat down to rest and never woke up. She even had her purse in her lap."

Amanda's throat made that noise again.

"We ran back to the staircase. Mack was so panicked, he raised the crowbar to knock a hole in the wall so we could get out. But before he could swing it, somebody pounded on the other side."

"Ronnie," Amanda said.

"I could see where the wall trembled. I fired at it. Then the pounding was somewhere else, and I fired at *that*. Suddenly, the pounding was all along the wall, and I fired and fired. Mack and JD ran up the stairs. I followed. Turning and turning. Around and around. Above me, I heard a scream. Mack. He fell toward me. His legs were split open. His blood sprayed like it came from a hose. He dropped through the space between the stairs and the railing. 'What cut him?' JD yelled. I didn't have a chance to say anything. 'The room with the vault!' JD yelled. 'We know how to get out of *that* room!' He raced up the stairs. All of a sudden, *he* was falling. *His* legs were split open. *His* blood was spraying. I thought I'd lost my mind. I wanted to run, but I warned myself I had to slow down, to find whatever was on the stairs. So I inched up, waving the gun in front of me, and that's when I touched it."

"Touched . . . ?"

"A wire strung across the staircase. Tight. Thin. Even with the goggles, I could hardly see it. I felt it with the gun. Then I touched it with my finger. Jesus, it was so sharp, all I needed was a little nudge for it to cut me."

"Razor wire," Balenger said.

"Maybe I *did* lose my mind. I eased under the wire. I inched up the stairs, waving the gun, searching for other wires."

"You left Mack and JD alive down there?"

"Believe me, the way they were bleeding, they weren't going to live long."

From the stairwell, far below, someone screamed.

"It sounds like one of them lived longer than you expected," Balenger said.

Another scream.

"We've *all* lost our minds," Cora said.

"But how did Ronnie —"

"He followed you down," Balenger said.

"He was *behind* us on the stairs?" Tod looked startled.

"When you reached the bottom, he rigged the wire above you. Then he used a hidden door to enter the main part of the hotel. He pounded on the wall to panic you into running upstairs."

Tod pulled out a cell phone.

"What are you doing?" Vinnie asked.

"Calling my brother in Atlantic City. He'll tell the police. He'll get help."

"You finally decided going to prison was better than facing Ronnie?" Cora asked in disgust.

"My brother'll save me." Tod finished pressing numbers and shoved the phone to his ear. "My brother'll get the police here and . . ." Listening, he moaned. "No. No. No."

"What's wrong?"

Thunder rumbled.

"Out of service!" Tod said. "The fucking storm's interfering with the phone!"

"Guess you should have called a little sooner, huh?" Vinnie said, his face red with fury. "We ought to tape *you* to the chair and let Ronnie do what he wants to you."

"But you won't."

"You're sure of that? You think I'm not pissed off at you enough to —"

310

"You can't afford to. We're pals now," Tod said. "Don't you get it? We need to stick together. You need all the help you can get."

Vinnie told Balenger, "We stuffed as much equipment as we could into the knapsack. What didn't fit we hooked to our belts. The police-report file is still in the slot in the knapsack. I guess they didn't know it was there. Otherwise, they'd have dumped that, also. You want a souvenir?" Vinnie gave him a coin.

Balenger held it, feeling its weight, its thickness, its perfect edges. A magnificent eagle was on one side. On the other, a buxom Lady Liberty carried a torch. The gold seemed to glow. TWENTY DOLLARS. IN GOD WE TRUST. "That's a great word: 'souvenir.' It means we might live to remember this. Here's hoping." Balenger kissed it and put it in a pocket. "Maybe it'll bring us luck."

Cora pointed. "This is the equipment we left for you."

Balenger put on the remaining tool belt. He hooked a walkie-talkie to it, along with the hammer and a half-full water bottle. "Where's the crowbar?"

"I told you Mack had it," Tod said.

"You damned stupid . . ." Balenger studied the air meters and left them. They were luxuries now. "Here's something else we can leave." He held up the water pistol. "Must have thrown it away in favor of carrying more coins."

"Give it to me." Cora raised it to her nostrils, as if hoping it retained her dead husband's scent, but the disgusted shake of her head indicated that all she smelled was vinegar.

Amanda looked frozen.

"Here. Take my Windbreaker." Vinnie put it around her.

She zipped it over her nightgown, looking grateful for the warmth. The Windbreaker was long enough to cover her hips.

"Ready?" Balenger asked.

"For what?" Tod said. "There's nothing we can do."

"We can take the high ground."

"High ground. What are you talking about?"

"The penthouse." Balenger picked up his hard hat where Tod had thrown it. Its light was out. He flicked the switch. Nothing happened. "You piece of shit, you broke the headlamp."

"Penthouse?" Tod said, appalled.

"I can't." Amanda shuddered. "That's where Ronnie takes me."

"There are other hidden staircases. I'm

sure of it," Balenger said, bitterly examining the useless lamp on his hard hat. "They all lead to the penthouse. Ronnie can't guard them all. We might be able to find a staircase that gets us out of here before he realizes we're gone."

"Yeah, and we might pick one that leads us straight to him," Tod said.

"Your way, he knows where we are, and he comes for us."

"We've got a gun."

"With only twelve rounds left, thanks to you. And how do you know Ronnie doesn't have a gun, also?"

Tod looked sick.

"You should dump those coins." Balenger pointed at Tod's bulging pockets. "The weight will slow you down."

"No way am I tossing that much money."

"Vinnie and Cora have headlamps. Where's your flashlight?"

"Lost it."

"Fucking great. Which leaves this one that Mack or JD dropped so he could carry more coins." Vinnie indicated the flashlight holstered to his belt.

"Not much light. We'd better blow out these candles and take them with us," Balenger said. "And something else."

When he was taped to the chair with the

pillowcase over him, waiting for Ronnie to cut off his head, Balenger had told himself that there couldn't be anything more nightmarish he'd be forced to suffer. But the pattern of his life made him realize he was wrong. Things got worse. They always got worse. And what he needed to do now proved it.

He turned toward the professor's headless body on the sofa. Between Conklin's legs, the headlamp continued to glow up through the sheet. Seized by revulsion, Balenger lifted the edge of the blood-soaked sheet and felt under it. His trembling hands touched the professor's beard. With greater revulsion, he pried the chin strap free and tugged the hard hat away, feeling the professor's head tilt. He pulled the hat from under the sheet and almost wept at the blood on it.

"Sorry, Bob," he said. "I'm so sorry."

He put the lamp on his head and felt his muscles cramp. "Let's go."

45

After a cautious look down the stairwell, Balenger climbed toward the penthouse. He heard footsteps on metal below him, the others following. As he was about to press up on a hatch, Amanda said, "There's a switch to the side, behind the two-by-four on the wall to your right. Ronnie always presses it before he lifts the door. I think it shuts off a trap of some kind."

Balenger felt behind the board, touched a switch, and flicked it. He pushed at the hatch. To his relief and then suspicion, it rose smoothly, with none of the creak of hinges he'd heard in the rest of the hotel. What he heard instead was the increased din of the storm. The skylight didn't extend this far. No rain poured through. But the rain did its best to penetrate, pounding relentlessly on the roof.

The light on Balenger's hard hat revealed a dark chamber. A chair. A bureau. A canopied bed. Wallpaper. All were in a lush, Victorian style. His nostrils picked up the smell of strong household cleaners.

Wary, he peered along the floor and noticed a lever that the rising trapdoor had flipped upward. The lever was linked to wires that led to a metal box. He imagined what would have happened if Amanda hadn't remembered to tell him about the switch. "Looks like explosives. I guess Ronnie figured if the wrong person came up here, it was time to make sure the evidence was destroyed."

Continuing to scan his light around the room, Balenger climbed all the way up and aimed his pistol toward the shadows. Tod, Amanda, Cora, and Vinnie followed. Their headlamps and Vinnie's flashlight searched the room.

"No dust, no cobwebs." Cora sounded puzzled.

Amanda's voice shook. "Ronnie keeps it absolutely spotless."

When Vinnie shut the trapdoor, he discovered a bolt on it and rammed it into a metal slot anchored to the floor. "No way to free the bolt from underneath."

Compared to the chill of Danata's suite, Balenger noticed, the penthouse was curiously warm. "Hurry. We need to find the other trapdoors and lock them before Ronnie gets to one of them." He headed toward a door straight ahead.

"No. That's the bathroom," Amanda said.

Balenger shifted toward a door on the left, and suddenly a blazing light filled the room. It was overhead, making him shield his eyes with his left hand while he crouched, ready with the pistol in his right. "How did . . ."

Amanda stood against a wall, her hand on a switch. "The penthouse has electricity."

The information was so surprising, Balenger took a moment to adjust to it. Now he understood why the penthouse felt warm — the heating system was on.

Tod's single word expressed his dismay but also functioned as an unintentional prayer. "Christ."

Balenger ran to the next room, groped for a switch, and flicked it. Another overhead light assaulted his eyes. Blinking, he saw an array of electronic equipment and monitors.

"Ronnie's surveillance system," Amanda explained.

"Turn everything on." Along the wall to his left, Balenger noticed that a metal shutter was smaller than those he'd seen elsewhere in the hotel. But what he concentrated on was a trapdoor in the floor below it. The door was bolted shut. It, too, had a lever with wires attached to a metal box.

The next room's door took him in a new direction. Balenger had a sudden mental image of the penthouse divided into four quadrants, two rooms per quadrant. The interior of each quadrant faced a wall that separated it from the hotel's center column, where the grand staircase had been.

When he flicked the light switch, he saw a library: floor-to-ceiling wooden shelves, countless leather-bound books, two Victorian reading chairs, another locked trapdoor, another lever with wires to a metal box. His unease intensified. A row of shelves along the inside wall had no books. In their place, the eyepieces of small telescopes projected from holes in the wall, another way Carlisle used to monitor what happened in the hotel, a primitive version of Ronnie's surveillance system.

The next room transported Balenger from 1901 to more than a century later. It was a modern media room, with a flat-screen TV, a surround-sound system, a DVD player, a VHS player, racks of DVDs and videotapes, and a sofa on which to enjoy them. Again, wires led from a bolted hatch to a metal box.

The subsequent door led to another quadrant. Balenger faced a kitchen in a 1960s style, the refrigerator and stove the avocado-green color popular during that era. Sure, he thought. Ronnie could carry video and audio equipment in here by himself and not be noticed, but getting a new fridge and stove in here, not to mention the equipment to remodel the kitchen, would have attracted a lot of attention. Even the sink was green. But a gourmet's array of copper pots and pans hung from hooks in the ceiling.

A hatch, the same as the others.

The schizoid pattern continued in the next room, for when Balenger flicked the light switch, he was again in 1901, looking at a Victorian dining room.

Another hatch, no different from the others. More eyepieces in the wall.

Now a door to the right, another quadrant. An overhead light revealed primitive exercise equipment, an early version of a treadmill and a stationary bicycle. Balenger imagined Carlisle laboring on them, trying to build the muscle tone and stamina that, along with steroids and vitamin supplements, helped him combat his bleeding. But the heavy weights in the corner had to be Ronnie's, not Carlisle's. The strain of the weights on Carlisle's body would have caused bleeding in his muscles rather than have helped prevent it.

Where Balenger expected to find a bolted, wired hatch and a small metal shutter, he saw a compartment with a door. A button was next to the door. An elevator. Aiming, he opened the door, finding a brass gate and dark shaft.

He closed the door and pushed several weights against it. Then he hurried to the final quadrant, where Vinnie stood, looking troubled, having come through a door in the bedroom and turned on the light. As Cora, Amanda, and Tod caught up to Balenger, he saw another bolted, wired hatch. But this time, what made him frown was a primitive medical clinic. A glass cabinet filled with medicines. Hypodermics. A doctor's examining table. Stainless-steel poles with hooks from which bottles containing blood transfusions would have been linked to a needle in Carlisle's bruised arm. The desperation was insane. How do you stop a hemophiliac from bleeding after you've stuck a needle in his arm to give him medication to try to *prevent* him from bleeding?

"All the trapdoors are secured," Balenger said.

"We bought some time," Vinnie said, "but we'd better find a way to disconnect those explosives in case Ronnie has a way of setting them off by remote control."

Everyone looked at Balenger for guidance.

He felt helpless. "In the Rangers, explosives weren't my specialty."

"But you must have had some training in them," Amanda said.

"Not enough." Balenger crossed toward the metal box.

Behind him, he heard Tod ask, "How come the shutters on the windows are so small?"

"We told you Carlisle was agoraphobic," Vinnie said. "Open spaces terrified him. He never left the hotel."

Except once, Balenger thought, remembering that the old man shot himself on the beach.

"The only views he could have tolerated," Cora said, "were through small windows."

"What a nutjob." Tod shifted several vials, examining them. "Never heard of some of this stuff."

"They're blood-clotting agents," Vinnie said.

"Not this one. It's morphine. Did he like to shoot up?"

"Carlisle needed it for the pain when blood seeped into his joints."

"Into his joints? Now I've heard everything. The label on the morphine's from 1971." Tod looked tempted to put it in his pocket, then thought better. "Stuff probably doesn't work anymore. It's probably poison by now."

Balenger unzipped his Windbreaker and shoved the pistol into his shoulder holster. Kneeling, he studied the wires connected to the lever hooked over the trapdoor. "You might want to be in another room while I do this."

They didn't move.

Except Tod. "Guess I'm the only one with the brains to take cover." He went into the bedroom.

"If that thing blows up, I have a feeling it won't make a difference *where* we are," Cora said.

Vinnie knelt beside him. "Besides, how can we help if we don't see what you're doing?"

Balenger gave them a look of respect, then held his breath and pulled the wires from plugs on the lever. He exhaled and gently lifted the box's lid.

They peered over his shoulder.

"Plastic explosive." Balenger managed to keep his voice calm. "The detonator's pushed into a block of the stuff."

"The thing that looks like a short pencil, is that the detonator?" Cora asked.

"Yes. There's some kind of electronic device hooked to it. When the trapdoor rises, it flips the lever and brings these wires in contact with another pair of wires. That closes a battery-driven circuit and triggers the detonator."

"Can the electronic device be activated by remote control?" Vinnie asked.

"Don't know. It might also be programmed to blow up if anybody cuts the wires. The simplest tactic . . ." Balenger steadied himself. ". . . is to pull the detonator from the block of explosive."

"Maybe motion also sets it off," Vinnie said.

"Then we're back to where we started, and we wait to see if Ronnie can trigger these bombs from a distance."

"Damned if we do, damned if we don't," Vinnie said.

"We're damned, all right," Amanda said.

Balenger wiped sweat from his brow. He reached into the metal box, then hesitated and took off his gloves. Again, he reached into the box. Thunder made him flinch. Working to control his trembling fingers, he gently pulled the detonator out. He lifted the block of explosive from the box — it felt like putty — and set it a distance away.

Vinnie stepped back. "Isn't that dangerous to move?"

"You mean like nitroglycerin and the

slightest jolt blows it up? No." Balenger
dried his palms on his jeans. "Plastic explosive's stable. You can pound it with a
hammer. You can throw it against a wall.
You can hold a lit match against it. The stuff
won't go off unless there's a preliminary explosion with enough heat to do the job." He
pointed toward the block he'd put aside.
"Right now, that's one of the least dangerous things in this hotel."

"I'm not encouraged," Cora said.

"Six to go," Balenger said with the tone of
someone rolling a boulder up a hill. "If
Ronnie *can* trigger these things by remote
control, once we remove the explosives, only
the detonators will go off. But even *they*
have a kick. Stay away from them."

Urgency accumulating in him, he headed
toward the bedroom to disable the bomb in
there. "There's an elevator in the exercise
room," he said to Amanda. "Does it work?"

"I don't know."

"Cora, you said you couldn't find keys for
some of the rooms."

"Yes. The penthouse, Danata's suite, and
a column of rooms from three twenty-eight
all the way up to six twenty-eight."

"I think we know what's behind the doors
to those rooms. The shaft for Carlisle's private elevator."

"All these lights," Vinnie said. "Maybe they can be seen from outside. Maybe someone will come and help us."

"No," Amanda said. "No one can see the lights. Ronnie bragged that the penthouse was completely blacked out."

Balenger cursed and hurried to the trapdoor in the bedroom.

"I watched what you did," Vinnie told him. "I'll work on some of the other boxes."

"Slow and careful."

"Bet on it."

"Tod?" Balenger shouted.

"I'm in the surveillance room watching the monitors!"

Balenger went to the door on the opposite side of the bedroom and peered inside. An array of screens showed green-tinted night-vision images.

Tod's facial tattoos were rigid with concentration. "Maybe we'll get a look at what this psycho's doing."

The top row of monitors displayed various angles of the hotel's exterior, but the rain was so dense that Balenger had difficulty seeing the outside walls and metal shutters. A lower row of screens revealed parts of the hotel's dark interior: the lobby, the collapsed staircase, the fire stairs, and the utility room, where a hidden camera was aimed toward the door through which they'd entered from the tunnel. The door was open, confirming Balenger's suspicion that Tod's group had failed to shut it after following their quarry into the building.

"So far all I saw were rats, a bird, and a freaky cat with three back legs," Tod said.

"The cat's beginning to seem normal." Balenger didn't recognize one of the interior images: a deserted garage area, where the camera was aimed toward a metal door.

"That must be where Ronnie comes into the hotel," Balenger said. He hurried back to the bedroom, where he disconnected the wires from the trapdoor's lever. He lifted the metal box's lid and separated the detonator from the explosive. "Two down."

"Three," he heard Vinnie say from another room.

"Four," Cora said from farther away.

"This is him," Amanda said.

Balenger wasn't sure what she meant. As rain pounded the roof, he looked up and saw her holding a framed photograph.

"Ronnie," she said, pointing at the photograph. "This is Ronnie."

46

Chilled, Balenger came slowly to his feet, fixated on what Amanda showed him. In the black-and-white photograph, an elderly man wearing a suit stood next to a young man wearing a sweater. The old man's broad shoulders would once have looked strong. His large chest would once have been solid. Despite deep wrinkles, his square-jawed face retained a suggestion of his youthful handsomeness. His full head of white hair reminded Balenger of Billy Graham in his later years. Indeed, everything about the old man, especially his piercing eyes, reminded Balenger of an evangelist.

"Morgan Carlisle," he whispered. "This is how Bob described him. Those hypnotic eyes."

In the photograph, Carlisle smiled, as did the young man next to him, who seemed barely out of his teens. A thin face, a thin body. Even his hair, which was trimmed closely at the sides and was thick on top, emphasized his thinness. Unlike Carlisle's eyes, the young man's were not expressive. Nor was his smile, which seemed entirely on the surface.

"Ronnie," Amanda said in disgust.

Balenger studied the photograph more intensely. A dark, wood-paneled wall in the background matched walls in the hotel. Despite the pleasure in Carlisle's smile, the elderly man kept a slight distance from the young man, his arms at his sides. The young man's sweater was a crew neck, a shirt collar tucked under it in a style Balenger remembered seeing in movies from the sixties. He had a plain face, soft at the cheekbones and the chin.

Amanda pointed. "This other man was Ronnie's father."

"Carlisle? No. He couldn't have been."

"Ronnie insisted that this man was his father."

"There's no record that Carlisle married."

"Which means nothing," Vinnie said from the doorway to the surveillance room. He and Cora had finished disarming the explosives. "The child could have been the result of an affair."

"But Carlisle was a watcher. A romantic fling doesn't seem in his nature."

"Unless one of the women he spied on gave him inspiration." Cora came into the room and looked at the photo. "Carlisle. So finally we get to see him. The monster responsible for the Paragon Hotel. How can anybody so twisted look so attractive? I bet this S.O.B. was irresistible in his prime. Those eyes. Finding a willing partner wouldn't have been difficult."

"Or maybe the partner wasn't willing," Vinnie said.

Balenger shook his head from side to side. "Rape doesn't match his profile. Even drugged, the victim might have fought back. Carlisle would have been terrified of cuts and scratches and not being able to stop his bleeding."

"But if Carlisle had a son, he'd have mentioned it in his diary," Cora insisted.

"Not if the boy was illegitimate," Vinnie said. "He might have wanted to keep the child a secret."

Balenger sounded doubtful. "It still doesn't fit his profile. From what I've read about hemophiliacs, I gather many choose not to have children for fear of passing the disease on."

Amanda pointed emphatically at the photograph. "Ronnie *told* me this was his father."

"How old is the photograph?" Cora asked.

Balenger freed catches at the back of the

frame, pulled off the back, and studied the rear of the photograph. "There's a developer's date: July 31, 1968."

"Carlisle would have been eighty-eight."

Balenger heard the crack of nearby lightning. "Amanda, you said Ronnie's in his fifties. That means . . ."

Vinnie did the math faster. "Thirty-seven years ago. I'm guessing he's in his late teens or early twenties in this picture. Let's say twenty. So that makes him around fifty-seven. Surely to God, five of us can take him."

"He's strong," Amanda said flatly.

"Tod, anything on the surveillance monitors?"

"Just more rats."

"I'm watching the elevator." Vinnie peered through the medical room toward the exercise room.

"Amanda, what else did Ronnie tell you?" Balenger asked.

"He bragged he never had any trouble getting girlfriends. He often recited their names."

"Names?" Balenger's hands felt cold.

"Iris, Alice, Vivian, Joan, Rebecca, Michelle. A lot more. Always in the same order. The list never varied. He repeated it enough for me to remember the names."

Balenger felt pressure building inside him. He worked to control his emotions, his rapid breathing and heartbeat almost overwhelming him. "I want you to think carefully. When he went through the names, did he ever mention someone called Diane?"

"Diane?" Vinnie frowned. "Who is —"

"*Did* he, Amanda?" Balenger put a hand on her shoulder. "Did he ever mention a woman called Diane?"

Amanda didn't answer for a moment. "Near the end of the list."

"Who's Diane?" Cora asked, mystified.

Now it was Balenger's turn to pause. He could barely get out the words. "My wife."

3:00 a.m.

47

"Wife?" Cora whispered in shock.

Balenger looked at Tod in the surveillance room. "What I told you was the truth — I'm not a cop." He hesitated. "But I used to be."

Tod shook his head in disgust. "And that stuff about Iraq and the hood over your head and the guy with the sword?"

"Was true. I was a detective on Asbury Park's police force. My wife and I live . . . lived here. She works . . . worked . . . I have trouble with tenses when I think about her. Two years ago, she disappeared."

They listened so intently that, despite the rain, the bedroom seemed quiet.

"She was blond. Thin. Like Amanda. Thirty-three. But she looked younger, in her twenties. Like Amanda." Balenger stared down at his clenched hands. "When Mack pulled the vault door open and I saw Amanda in there, God help me, at first I thought she was Diane. I thought I'd finally found her, that a miracle had happened and my wife was still alive."

335

Balenger's chest ached as he stared at Amanda, who reminded him so much of his wife. "Diane worked for a real estate developer here in town. The same developer who'll be tearing down this hotel in two weeks. She often went to New York City to negotiate with the Carlisle trust for the land the Paragon sits on. The trust kept refusing. It's a damned cruel joke that the trust eventually had to surrender the land for taxes. But two years ago, it still had control. And on Diane's last trip to Manhattan, she vanished."

Balenger drew a pained breath. "A lot of people disappear in New York. I used to go there on weekends and unofficially help the missing persons bureau. Leg work. Shoe leather. Finally the case got so cold, I was the only person doing anything. I kept asking for more time off work to look for Diane, until my boss suggested it would be better if I resigned and took all the time I wanted. I ran out of money. Then an ex-Ranger buddy told me about the quick cash to be earned in Iraq guarding convoys, provided I didn't mind dodging booby traps and snipers. Hell, at that point, I didn't much care if I lived or died. What I *did* care about was the twenty thousand dollars I'd earn for one month's work, so I could get back to trying to find out what happened to my wife."

Balenger forced himself to continue. "After a year, I didn't have much hope she was still alive. But I needed to keep trying. It gives you an idea how desperate I was that I went to Iraq again. Diane had gotten me back on my feet after the first time. Damned Gulf War syndrome. She never tired of nursing me. It was her idea that I use my military experience and apply for a job with the Asbury Park police. Nothing demanding. A way to feel useful. Fucking Iraq. I told you how the second time turned out. But with the cash I got, I made myself keep searching. I followed every lead, every sex criminal who might have come in contact with her, every mugger who was known to work in the areas where she went. Double- and triple-checked. In the end, all I had was the feeling I'd had from the start but couldn't prove, that Diane's disappearance had something to do with the negotiations for the hotel. No, not the negotiations exactly. Something to do with the hotel *itself.* I asked permission to go inside, but the trust refused. Safety reasons. I did my best to break in, but the Paragon's a damned fortress."

Balenger's voice tightened. "Three

months ago, I read a newspaper article about urban explorers, how their expeditions are like special-ops missions and how some of them have a genius for infiltrating buildings that are supposedly impregnable. I checked urban-explorer Web sites and approached a group, but I made the mistake of telling the first group why I needed their help getting in. They treated me like I was an undercover agent wearing a wire. With the next group, I tried to convince them to take me into the hotel because it was a fascinating old building. But they didn't trust an outsider any more than the first group did. Plus, there were plenty of old buildings they already had plans to explore. So I used the professor's Web site next and arranged to meet him. This time, I tried the greed motive. I showed him copies of old newspaper articles from when Danata was killed — rumors about gold coins the gangster supposedly hoarded in a secret vault. Bob was polite. He said he'd look into it. I figured he was brushing me off. But it turned out he'd just been fired, and a week later, he phoned and said he'd help me on one condition."

"That you'd get some of the coins for him," Vinnie said.

"Yes. He admired you and Cora and Rick so much, he was certain you wouldn't agree to take the coins. He was afraid about his health and how he'd pay for his heart treatments. He was angry about losing his professorship. You can't imagine how angry. So the deal was, you'd unknowingly help me search the hotel for some clue about what happened to Diane. Then I'd come back the next night and get the coins for the professor. Of course, once I knew how to get in, I also planned to do a lot more searching."

"I know Ronnie kept at least one other woman here," Amanda said.

"What makes you sure?"

"In the dark, in the vault, the first time he locked me in, I touched something on the floor. About a half-inch long and wide. One end was smooth, the other jagged. I didn't want to admit to myself what it was. A broken fingernail."

Rain lashed the building.

Amanda pulled the Windbreaker around her. "You need to understand what it was like. We had candlelight dinners Ronnie made me watch him prepare. Elaborate gourmet menus. The best wine. CDs of Bach or Handel or Brahms playing in the background." Amanda grimaced. "We spent hours reading in the library. Often, he read to me out loud. Philosophy. History.

Literary novels. He's especially fond of Proust. *In Search of Lost Time.* Lost time." Her voice wavered. "He made me discuss what we read. I think that's one of the reasons he kidnapped me — because I worked in a bookstore. We watched movies. Always art movies. Most were foreign, with subtitles. Cocteau's *Beauty and the Beast.* Bergman's *The Seventh Seal.* Renoir's *The Rules of the Game.* All about the past. He never let me watch regular television. He never let me have any idea of what was going on in the world or how long I'd been here. With the shutters closed, I didn't have any sense of whether it was day or night. There weren't any clocks. I couldn't tell hours from days. I had no way of calculating weeks. I couldn't depend on my body rhythms to give me a sense of time. For some meals, Ronnie made me eat when I wasn't the least bit hungry. For other meals, he made me wait till I was starving. In the vault, I couldn't tell if I was dozing for a few minutes or sleeping for hours."

"He must have slept, also," Cora said. "How did he stop you from getting away from him?"

"Except for the first time, when I woke in that damned bed, the only place he ever let me sleep was the vault. When I was with him, he never turned his back on me. He kept a metal belt locked to my waist. The belt had a box on it, like the ones by the trapdoors. He said, if I tried to escape, he could blow me in half, even if I was a mile away. He said the charge was shaped to blow inward so that even if he was in the room with me, he wouldn't be injured."

"Where's the belt?" Balenger asked.

Amanda made a futile gesture. "I don't know."

"We've got to find it." His nerves on fire, Balenger pulled out bureau drawers, searching them. He heard Cora going through the closet. Vinnie looked under the bed.

"Nothing," Cora said. "I'll check the medical room."

"And I'll take the exercise room," Balenger said. "Vinnie, you take the —"

"Wait a minute." Vinnie stared upward. He grabbed a post on the bed and used it for support while he stepped up onto the ornate bedspread. He stretched and peered over the canopy's top. "There it is. Got it."

Amanda looked sick when he stepped down with a metal belt that had a box attached to it.

Balenger tugged at the lid, but it wouldn't come off. "Sealed. I can't disarm the . . ."

"I see him," Tod said.

341

"What?" Balenger whirled toward the surveillance room.

"The son of a bitch is waving at me on one of the screens."

48

Balenger charged into the surveillance room. The others followed. On the bottom right monitor, tinted green by a night-vision camera, a tall, thin, plain-faced man waved at them, silently saying either hello or good-bye. Amanda began to weep.

At least, it *seemed* that he was plain-faced. Hard to be sure when the man's eyes were covered with what Balenger had feared he would have: night-vision goggles. Unlike the ones that dangled around Tod's neck, these were streamlined, almost elegant, the latest high-tech version.

He had a weak chin. His thin nose was a counterpart to his thin lips. The baby-soft look of his skin made the wrinkles on his brow and around his mouth seem painted on. His salt-and-pepper hair was receding. He wore a dark suit, a white shirt, and a conservative striped tie.

"He always dresses that way," Amanda said. "Never takes his coat off. Never loosens his tie."

"Never?" Vinnie asked. "But how did —"

"I recognize him," Balenger said.

"What?"

He turned toward Cora and Vinnie. "The professor described him for us. Remember? A blank-faced, bureaucratic type. In his fifties. No expression."

"The guy in charge of Carlisle's trust?" Vinnie looked startled.

"I spoke with him several times after my wife disappeared. The son of a bitch said Diane spent an hour in his office the day it happened. He showed me her name in his appointment book. Eleven in the morning. After their meeting, he said, he had a lunch appointment, and he had no idea where she went. But he doesn't call himself Ronnie. The name he uses is Walter Harrigan."

"Not Walter *Carlisle?*" Cora asked. "So much for his claim that he's Carlisle's son."

"But why does he use different names?" Vinnie asked. "Who is he?"

On the monitor, Ronnie pointed toward something behind him. When he moved, Balenger saw that Ronnie was in the utility room, that the door to the tunnel was now shut. *More than shut,* Balenger realized.

"Jesus, what's he done to it?" Cora asked.

A metal bar seemed to hang in mid-air in

front of the door. No, Balenger thought in dismay. Not in front of the door. *On* the door.

Ronnie pointed toward something next to it.

"What the hell is *that?*" Tod said.

A metal cylinder resembled the kind of tank that scuba divers used. The tank was on a cart. A slender hose was attached to the tank. A short pole with a handle was attached to the other end of the hose. A mask with thick glass was propped against the cart.

Balenger felt nauseous.

Vinnie answered, "Welder's tools. God help us, he welded a bar across the door. There's no way out."

Balenger stared down at the metal box in his hands. All the time he watched the monitor, he tugged fiercely at the lid, but the seal held firm. He feared that at any moment Ronnie would press a remote detonator. "Need to get rid of this."

He rushed to the trapdoor in the surveillance room. "Cora, free the bolt!"

Holding the belt with his left hand, he drew his pistol with his right. "Open the trapdoor. Maybe this is a trick. Maybe we're watching a video. Maybe Ronnie's actually waiting under this trapdoor." Balenger aimed. "If he is, I'll blow him to hell. Vinnie, shine your flashlight at the opening. Ready? Cora, do it. Open the trapdoor!"

Cora pulled it up. Vinnie's flashlight blazed into the darkness of another spiral staircase. Balenger reached under the curved handrail and dropped the belt and the box. They plummeted, clattering off metal.

Cora slammed the trapdoor shut. While she locked it and Balenger darted back, Tod said, "The bastard's doing something else."

Balenger whirled toward the monitor. There, Ronnie continued to display his neutral smile as he pointed toward something indistinct on a wall to the side.

"What's that on the floor?" Vinnie asked.

"It's moving," Tod said.

"Water from the storm," Cora realized.

Ronnie stepped sideways through the rippling water and reached the object on the wall. It was so far to the side that the camera hardly showed it. The object had a handle.

"No!" Amanda said, realizing what it was: an electrical transformer.

Looking surreal in his goggles, suit, and tie amid the water rippling in the utility room, Ronnie waved again, almost looking enthusiastic now, definitely communicating good-bye. He pulled down the lever.

The lights went out. The monitors became blank. The rain pounding the roof seemed to get louder as the group found itself for the first time in absolute darkness. Not even the skylight was available to show flashes from the storm. To Balenger, the darkness seemed to have density and weight, compressing around him, squeezing.

Cora gasped.

Fabric rustled, the sound of Vinnie's arm moving as he turned his headlamp on. So did Balenger and Cora, the beams darting around the surveillance room.

"Give me the flashlight," Tod told Vinnie.

It gleamed. For the previous four and a half hours, Balenger had been in semi-darkness. He had almost gotten used to it. By contrast, the bright lights of the penthouse had at first seemed unnatural, paining him. But how quickly he had adjusted to them. And now how quickly the semi-darkness was hateful.

"Amanda?" Cora asked.

"I'm okay. Fine." But she didn't sound fine at all. "I can handle this. I can handle this," she said unconvincingly.

Unseen lightning cracked.

"I've been through worse." She spoke rapidly. "Being in the vault was worse. Being alone was worse."

"Alone?" Vinnie said, puzzled. "But —"

"Now's our chance," Tod said.

"Chance?" Balenger asked. "What do you mean?"

"He's down in the basement. We can use one of these staircases to get to the ground floor."

"I hate to agree with this creep," Vinnie said, "but he's right. We've got seven staircases to choose from. Ronnie can be in only one at a time."

"But which staircase?" Cora asked. "You said you couldn't find an exit down there."

"And *he* said" — Tod indicated Balenger — "there must be secret doors."

"Which staircase?" Cora repeated. "The one we already used is too obvious."

"Or maybe it's so obvious, Ronnie won't think of it," Tod said.

"I'm not going down *that* one." Vinnie pointed toward the trapdoor where Balenger had thrown the metal box. "All Ronnie needs to do is press a remote detonator and —"

"That sound. What is it?" Amanda said.

"Just the storm. It's bugging *my* nerves, too."

"Something else. From in *there*." Amanda pointed toward the bedroom.

"I hear it, too." Cora turned.

"Not the bedroom. The exercise room," Balenger said.

"The elevator!" Tod blurted.

Lights zigzagging, they ran toward the medical room, where they stared through the doorway into the exercise room. Despite the pounding of the rain, Balenger heard the whir of cables and gears. The whir got louder.

Behind the closed door, the elevator rose.

49

"If Ronnie's in the elevator, he can't stop us from going down the stairs," Tod said.

Vinnie scowled at the closed door. "How do we know he's in there?"

"He's gotta be. Somebody's gotta be in there to run the controls."

"But what if the elevator works like a dumbwaiter?" Balenger asked. "What if Carlisle arranged for outside controls so his meals could be sent up without a waiter intruding on him?"

"Well, if that jerkoff isn't in the elevator, who *is*?"

"Or *what* is? I'm not sure I want to hang around and find out," Vinnie said.

The elevator stopped below them. Although the rain persisted, the absence of the *whir* made the room seem tensely quiet.

Then the *whir* began again, the elevator rising.

"Must be on a separate electrical circuit," Cora murmured.

"When it gets here, shoot the door," Tod urged. "It's wood. The bullets will —"

"I don't shoot what I can't see," Balenger told him. "There might be a policeman behind that door."

"You want to open it and find out?"

The group stared at the door, concentrating on the stillness behind it. Then the stillness changed to the rattle of the interior gate being pushed aside.

"Shoot!" Tod yelled.

"You in the elevator!" Balenger aimed. "Identify yourself!"

"Pussy! Give me that gun!" Tod grabbed for it, but Balenger whacked the barrel against his forehead, knocking him to the floor.

Balenger whirled and realigned his aim as something thumped against the door. He motioned everyone into the medical room. Then he pushed the weights from the door and took cover behind the treadmill.

The door budged outward.

He tensed his finger on the trigger as the door opened slightly, revealing a portion of what seemed to be an empty compartment.

Tod groaned on the floor.

The door opened farther.

Balenger saw motion. Tod's flashlight remained in his hand, gleaming across the floor. It revealed rats scurrying from the elevator, three, eight, a dozen, some with open sores, others with no ears or two tails or only one eye. Squealing in the lights from the headlamps, some leapt under the stationary bike or onto the treadmill, veering when they saw Balenger, following others that scrambled into the other rooms.

Cora screamed. But not because of the rats. A figure stumbled from the elevator.

Balenger almost fired but suddenly recognized the bloody jeans and Windbreaker, the muscular torso bent forward in pain, the blood, so much blood, a wooden spike sticking into the figure's chest.

"Rick!" Cora ran to him.

"Wait!" Balenger said.

But his warning was too late. Rick tripped over Tod's squirming body, lurched into Cora, and knocked both of them to the floor. Cora's hard hat clattered away.

Balenger rushed to the empty compartment. Aiming, he shouldered the door all the way open. As his headlamp dispelled the shadows, he studied the ceiling but didn't see a trapdoor through which Ronnie could have squeezed up and hidden himself. He now realized that the compartment wasn't totally empty, though. On the floor, in a corner, mocking him, were the five bottles of urine that had been abandoned on the fourth level.

"Vinnie, use the weights to keep this door and the gate from closing! As long as they're open, the elevator can't go down." Balenger turned toward Cora and Rick. Rick was on top of her, gasping from pain. She struggled to get free. Balenger turned Rick over and saw that the fall had rammed the spike deeper into his chest. Rick's lung made a whistling sound. His front teeth were broken away. His lower left arm projected at a right angle to his side.

"Jesus," Cora said. "Rick." She wiped his blood-smeared forehead. "Baby."

Vinnie hurried to prop a weight against the elevator door.

Cora stroked Rick's face. His eyes were unfocused. His chest heaved, continuing to whistle.

Balenger looked over his shoulder toward the medical room. "Help me get him on the exam table."

Together, he, Amanda, and Cora lifted him. Rick moaned. Cora pressed his shoulders down to keep him from rolling off the table.

Amanda propped the flashlight on the counter. "We'll need more light. I'll get the candles from Vinnie's knapsack."

Balenger used his knife to cut open Rick's Windbreaker, sweater, and shirt. As

Amanda and Vinnie lit candles, the increased illumination showed an alarming amount of blood streaming from Rick's chest.

"The spike's all the way through," Balenger said.

"Hang on, baby," Cora told Rick, stroking his brow. "Hang on."

But Rick didn't seem to hear.

"If I take out the spike, he might hemorrhage worse than he is now. But if I don't . . ."

Rick's groan communicated his agony.

"Can't we at least help him with the pain?" Cora begged. "The morphine."

"No. It'll kill him," Balenger said.

"Surely just a little —"

"Morphine depresses heart rate and blood pressure." Balenger felt Rick's wrist. "I can hardly find a pulse as it is."

"Pull the spike out. Use duct tape to stop the bleeding the way you did with the professor."

Balenger couldn't think of an alternative. "See if there's rubbing alcohol in that cabinet."

Vinnie yanked open the glass door.

"Wait," Balenger said.

"But —"

"Never mind," Balenger said.

Rick's lung stopped wheezing. His chest became still.

"No," Cora said. Frantic, she stared into Rick's eyes, searching for a sign of consciousness. She opened his mouth and breathed into it. In horror, she stopped when the air whistled past the spike in his chest.

"Twice." She sobbed. "Oh, baby. Oh, Jesus, twice." Weeping uncontrollably, she held Rick's head against her chest. "Twice."

Amanda put an arm around her.

Thunder rumbled. In its aftermath, they heard the crackle of static. Balenger frowned toward his equipment belt and then toward Vinnie's.

More static.

"What the —" Vinnie stared down.

It came from the remaining two walkie-talkies. Balenger's mind swirled. With a sense that he shifted deeper into madness, he raised his unit to his mouth and pressed the transmit button.

50

"You took a walkie-talkie from one of the men you killed," Balenger said.

"As you'll learn, I'm resourceful." The voice was smooth, calm, neutral, in the tenor range, its pronunciation precise, with a hint of an elitist accent. It made Amanda jerk a hand to her mouth. "Your friend didn't drop all the way to the lobby. I found him in a pile of wreckage two levels down. He actually had the strength to help me put him in the elevator. Remarkable. How is he progressing?"

"He isn't," Balenger said into the walkie-talkie."

"Ah," the voice said.

Static.

"You're violating my home," the voice said.

"It's not as if you had any No Trespassing signs around the place. The only good thing is, if we hadn't come in, we never would have been able to rescue Amanda."

Cora raised her tear-streaked face from Rick's body.

"Amanda has no need of being rescued," the voice said. "I treat her with the greatest respect. Many women would envy her."

"Except for being molested."

"I never touched her that way *ever*." For the first time, the voice contained a hint of emotion. "If she told you I did, she lied."

Balenger frowned. He remembered several puzzled questions Vinnie had tried to ask her. Was Ronnie telling the truth?

"What about your other girlfriends?" Balenger asked into the walkie-talkie. "What are their names? Iris, Alice, Vivian." Abruptly, something about the list troubled him. The names. Something about the names. But so much was happening, he didn't have time to figure out what bothered him.

"I've been honored with an abundance of female companionship."

"Is that one of them dead in the downstairs corridor?"

Static.

Dreading the answer, Balenger forced himself to ask, "What did you do with my wife?"

Static.

"If you surrender, I promise you won't feel pain," the voice said.

Abruptly, Cora grabbed the walkie-talkie.

Furious, she yelled into it, "You prick, I promise *you* something." Pacing angrily in front of the medicine cabinet, she shouted, "When I get my hands on you, I'll —"

The floor exploded.

Balenger lurched back. Wood disintegrated at Cora's feet. As a shotgun roared from below, blood sprayed from Cora's abdomen. Another roar slammed her against the medicine cabinet, shattering glass. A third blast. A fourth, more wood erupting from the floor, buckshot tearing Cora open.

She dropped to her knees, agonized surprise contorting her face. She toppled to the gaping floor, her blood spreading, dripping through the holes. A candle fell with her, but her blood extinguished it.

The startling moment lengthened. As the smell of burnt gunpowder drifted up through the holes, Balenger's reflexes took control. He tugged Amanda and Vinnie to the outside wall, his frenzied heartbeat making him light-headed. "He's on the balcony below us," he whispered. "Cora shouted so loud, he heard where she was."

From below, through the holes in the floor, Balenger heard a shotgun being reloaded. Cora's headlamp lay on the floor. He stretched to reach it, then gave it to

Amanda. He raised a finger to his lips, urging her and Vinnie to be silent. He motioned for them to follow him into the bedroom. His muscles contracted, anticipating more shotgun blasts through the floor.

He reached the bedroom, his headlamp crisscrossing the darkness. Something else was wrong. Tod. Where was . . . The last Balenger remembered, Tod was groaning on the floor, holding his head where Balenger struck him with the pistol. Now Balenger turned and scanned with his headlamp. *Tod was gone.*

As Balenger looked at Vinnie to warn him, the longing on Vinnie's face made him pause. Staring toward Cora's body, Vinnie was devastated, tears streaming down his cheeks, the woman he loved gone forever. Vinnie's anguish intensified Balenger's own grief. To lose the person you loved. He understood all too sharply the hell Vinnie suffered.

Balenger tugged Vinnie's sleeve, urging him to move. For her part, Amanda seemed to have passed through an emotional frenzy, incapable of anything except a desperation to survive. She followed Balenger's lead as they crept through the surveillance room and into the library. They'd been forced to abandon the flashlight that Amanda set on the counter next to the examination table. Now all they had were three headlamps.

The lights converged on the library's trapdoor, which to Balenger's surprise was open. Tod must have hurried down the staircase while Ronnie was distracted, Balenger realized. A further thought gave him hope — maybe Tod can be a distraction for us. Maybe he'll make enough noise to lead Ronnie away.

Balenger locked the trapdoor and moved softly into the kitchen. He drew his pistol and aimed toward the trapdoor there. Vinnie lifted it. But the only thing their headlamps revealed was another empty staircase.

51

Balenger descended first. He had to move slowly, probing the air with his pistol to test for razor wire. They crept downward, constantly turning. The revolving flash of headlamps was dizzying. The stairwell amplified the noise from the storm. Approaching the fifth level, Balenger heard water streaming, then realized that the sound didn't come from the rain outside but from something in the stairwell. His headlamp reflected off a torrent rushing along a hidden corridor.

A flash of lightning revealed a huge hole in the roof, the water on the upper levels channeling into it. The crash of water cascading down the stairwell reminded Balenger of a cistern being filled. At once, his headlamp showed an object floating along the corridor. A corpse. Amanda gasped when she saw it. A desiccated woman. Dressed. Holding a purse. Blond. Diane? Balenger wondered in dismay. But before he had a chance to see more, the stream carried the corpse into the stairwell, and it disappeared into the roaring darkness.

We can't get out this way, Balenger realized. For all he knew, Ronnie was on the
opposite side of the wall, about to blast a
hole with his shotgun. He motioned for
Amanda and Vinnie to retreat to the penthouse. They didn't need encouragement,
and he followed them as they scrambled
through the hatch. In shadows, breathing
hoarsely, they sank to the kitchen's floor.

"We'll try another staircase," Amanda
murmured.

"Maybe," Vinnie said without conviction.
He raised his head slowly. "Or maybe we
don't need to do a thing."

"What do you mean?" Balenger asked in
confusion.

"The professor left a note with a colleague. When the professor doesn't call him
by nine this morning, the colleague's supposed to open the note and tell the police
where to send help."

They were so close to the outside wall that
the pounding of the rain cloaked their
muted voices.

"No," Balenger said. "Bob didn't leave a
note."

"But . . ."

"When Bob got fired, he stopped trusting
people in his department. He assumed the
colleague would open the note and show it

to the dean to get brownie points. Bob was afraid we'd all get arrested."

Vinnie tried another plan. "How about *this?* The salvagers come on Monday. They'll rescue us. All we need to do is wait for a day."

"Ronnie can arrange plenty of surprises if we give him that much time. I told you before, if we're passive, we'll lose."

"Then what are we going to do?"

Static crackled from the walkie-talkies.

"He's trying to get me to talk." Balenger spoke softly. "He's hoping he'll hear my voice and have something to shoot at."

"That could work the other way around," Amanda murmured. "If you hear *him* talking, you can shoot at *his* voice."

Balenger debated. "Tell me more about this bastard. Was he lying when . . ."

"He never touched me." Amanda shuddered. "He always treated me with terrifying politeness. I had the sense that something was building in him, that he struggled against it. The last time I saw him, when he brought me the nightgown, he stopped being polite. He yelled. He threw things. He called me a bitch and a whore. It was like he hated me because he felt aroused."

From the walkie-talkie, more static taunted Balenger.

He shut off Vinnie's unit, then lowered the volume on his own, put it to his lips, and pressed the transmit button, keeping his voice down. "I don't understand why you use different names, Ronnie. Why do you call yourself 'Walter'?"

Static.

"Is your last name really Harrigan?" Balenger didn't dare remain in one spot too long. He shifted into the dining room. Again, he whispered into the walkie-talkie. "Ronnie, what's your last name?"

No answer.

"What's your last —"

"Carlisle," the voice said.

Amanda and Vinnie crouched, trying to determine where the voice was below them.

"That's not true," Balenger whispered. "Carlisle didn't have children."

"He's my father."

Continuing to move, Balenger eased into the exercise room, where weights propped open the elevator's door.

"No," Balenger said. "He's not your father."

"He acted like one."

"That's not the same thing."

"Sometimes, it's all there is."

"What about you?" Balenger asked. "Did *you* act like a good son?"

Balenger shut off his headlamp before shifting into the candlelit medical room. Amanda and Vinnie did the same. Otherwise, their lights would show through the holes in the floor. The sight of the two bodies made him feel cold.

"You're moving cautiously," the voice said, "but the candles react to the air you displace. Through the holes, I see them flicker."

Abruptly, Balenger realized that Ronnie stood directly below him. He barely had a chance to step back before a shotgun blast tore through the part of the floor where he'd been.

Balenger aimed toward the fresh hole, about to shoot, only to decide Ronnie wanted him to do that, to waste ammunition on a phantom target.

"Did you disarm the explosives up there?" the voice said from the walkie-talkie. "I assume a former Ranger has the ability to do that."

Balenger forced himself to stay quiet.

"You wonder how I know your background?" the voice asked. "It's not just because I heard you talking to the others. The first time you came to my office and questioned me, I knew you were trouble. When you showed up the next time, I had a stack of information about you. A shame about that Gulf War syndrome. At least you had someone to take care of you. Your wife made clear how devoted she was."

The reference to Diane struck Balenger like a punch in the stomach. His emotion bent him forward. At once, rage took the place of pain and loss. He aimed toward where he thought the voice was below him. With all his heart, he wanted to shoot. No! he warned himself. Not till you're sure. Don't let him goad you into making mistakes.

Desperation crept over him. Our lights, he thought. We shut them off so Ronnie can't see them through the holes in the floor. But we can't get out of here without using them. And he has night-vision goggles.

Reluctantly, he understood what needed to be done. What he didn't want to do.

Drawing Amanda and Vinnie to another room, he kept his voice low. "You need to distract him for me. Vinnie, have you ever fired a gun?"

"No."

"Hold it with both hands. Like this." Balenger curled Vinnie's right fingers around the grip. Then he curved the left fingers over the opposite side, the tips overlapping. "Aim along the top of the barrel.

Keep your fingers tight on the grip. There's a kick. When you shoot, you don't want to get startled and drop the gun."

"When I shoot?"

"Go back to the medical room. Count to fifty. Then turn on your walkie-talkie. Increase its volume. Set it on the floor and back away. My voice will distract him. When he shoots, shoot back. You won't hit him, but we don't care about that. Just make sure he doesn't hit *you*."

"But what about —"

"I'm going to try to get the other night-vision goggles."

Vinnie nodded, but Balenger couldn't tell if it was in hope or despair.

"Amanda, lock the hatch behind me." Balenger spoke with desperate softness. "Don't open it unless you hear two taps, then three, then one. Can you remember that? Two, three, one?"

"I'll remember."

"Vinnie, fifty seconds after your first shot, throw something on the floor of the exercise room. Make sure you're a distance away. Try to make him shoot again. Then shoot back and move to another room. Keep distracting him. But don't use more than one shot each time. We need the ammunition. Can you do this?"

"Don't have a choice."

"If I can get those night-vision goggles, we'll have a *lot* of choices." Balenger hoped he sounded convincing.

Far from the holes in the medical room's floor, they could safely switch on their headlamps. Balenger moved quietly through the kitchen, the library, and the surveillance room, finally coming to the bedroom. He stared at the locked trapdoor. In theory, the door to Danata's suite remained barricaded, so Ronnie couldn't get in and shoot at anyone coming down the staircase.

In theory.

Balenger took the pistol from Vinnie, then motioned for Amanda to unlock and open the trapdoor. He aimed as his headlamp pierced the darkness of the stairwell. No one. Breathing slightly easier, he gave the gun back.

"Start counting to fifty." He climbed into the stairwell and motioned for Amanda to close it. As he heard her lock the hatch over his head, he had the terrible sense of descending into hell.

52

The coppery odor of the professor's blood filled the exposed passageway and Danata's living room. Balenger counted the seconds just as Vinnie did: three, four, five. Guided by only one source of light, feeling the darkness crowd him, Balenger crept lower. The furniture remained piled in front of the door, giving him slight encouragement. He unholstered the hammer from his utility belt and descended from the sixth level toward the fifth and its secret corridor, waving the hammer in front of him, testing for razor wire. He listened for water streaming into the stairwell but didn't hear it, the roofs in this section of the hotel evidently remaining intact.

He aimed his headlamp along the darkness of the fifth corridor. Something seemed to be in there, something seated motionless that filled him with suspicion, but he didn't have time to investigate. He kept counting: eighteen, nineteen, twenty. The air felt colder as he reached the fourth level and went lower.

Static crackled from his walkie-talkie, Ronnie taunting him again. No doubt, Ronnie hoped to hear a response and use it as a target. But Balenger was too far away now.

He kept counting. Twenty-five. Twenty-six.

He pressed the pulse button on his walkie-talkie. Ronnie would hear a similar buzz of static, Balenger knew.

"So you're still alive," the voice said. Although Balenger's walkie-talkie was at minimum volume, the stairwell's echo amplified the words. "I wondered if I'd hit you."

The light from his headlamp turning dizzily on the spiral staircase, Balenger reached the third level and continued to wave the hammer into the shadows before him.

Static.

Balenger pressed the transmit button and put the walkie-talkie directly against his mouth, cupping a hand around his lips, working to shut out the stairwell's echo. "Carlisle had agoraphobia. I kept asking myself why a man terrified of the outdoors would leave the hotel and shoot himself on the beach."

Forty-seven. Forty-eight.

"It didn't make sense. But now I understand. Something else terrified him more."

Balenger was certain the count was past fifty. Vinnie, for God's sake, do what I told you!

"I didn't hurt him," the voice said.

"You weren't a good son."

"Your voice sounds different."

Balenger imagined Vinnie following directions, turning up the volume on his walkie-talkie, and setting it on the floor. He imagined Ronnie peering up toward Balenger's suddenly amplified voice. Abruptly, he heard a shotgun blast from his walkie-talkie. He listened fiercely for the distant sound of a handgun firing in response. But thunder rumbled through the hotel, vibrating through the stairwell, and he heard nothing else, not even static from his walkie-talkie.

Breath froze in his chest as his hammer probed the air and felt resistance. He knelt, saw blood on the stairs, and scanned his headlamp. There it was — the tautly strung wire. The dark blood on it made it almost indistinguishable from the shadows.

He sank onto his back and squirmed under the wire. Straightening, he heard another burst of static from his walkie-talkie, but he ignored it and waved the hammer in front of him, searching for more wire while descending toward the darkness at the bottom of the stairs.

Now he allowed himself to consider a thought he'd been avoiding. What if Ronnie took more than the walkie-talkie? What if he also took the night-vision goggles so that no one else could use them? Then we don't have many options left, he thought. Hell, we might not have any.

Leave, a part of his mind told him. *While Vinnie distracts Ronnie, try to find a way out.*

Abandon them?

Not exactly. Find a way out and go for help.

There isn't *a way out. The only way to end this is to kill him.*

Even if I could *get out, what would I do? On foot? In the middle of the night? In a thunderstorm? A deserted part of the city? It'd take me forever to reach the police station. Vinnie and Amanda could be dead by then.*

This is your chance.

Bullshit. I won't leave them.

He reached the bottom, where the limited space made the smell of death even more pronounced. His single beam of light revealed two corpses, Mack and JD surrounded by blood, their throats slit, their legs almost severed. Balenger saw footprints in the blood. Ronnie had evidently approached them, finished them with a knife, and taken the walkie-talkie. The footprints seemed to come and go through a wall. Presumably, it had one of the secret doors Balenger was sure existed, although how the door could be opened he didn't know.

He crouched, studying the gloom-enshrouded bodies. Each corpse did indeed wear night-vision goggles. He reached, then remembered booby-trapped corpses in Iraq and paused, taking a closer look at the bodies. Something was stuck under Mack's left side.

JD, too, had something under him. Not obvious. Not unless you'd been seasoned in the hell of Iraq and you knew not to trust anything at any time. Explosives of some sort. The pressure of the bodies armed the detonators. If Balenger moved the bodies, the triggers would be released and the bombs would explode.

He shifted around to their heads, knelt in blood, and reached under Mack's skull, guiding his fingers toward the strap on Mack's goggles. Do it gently, he warned himself.

Static buzzed from his walkie-talkie.

Balenger eased the strap over Mack's skull, the shaved head providing no resistance. He lifted the goggles from Mack's sightless eyes and attached them to his equipment belt. Then he took a breath, leaning toward JD and the strap on *his* goggles.

In the distance, he thought he heard a shotgun blast. He removed JD's goggles and put them on. He shut off his headlamp.

In place of the shadows that fought his headlamp, he now saw a green twilight that made everything faintly visible. His breathlessness and the sound of the storm created the feeling he was underwater. With increased vision, he saw a long dark object. The crowbar. He picked it up.

He whirled toward the stairs, desperate to hurry back to the penthouse. But he hesitated and faced the narrow corridor. Despite his apprehension, he entered it. The enhanced light that the goggles provided made it possible to see all the way to the end.

All the way to what Tod had described finding: the corpse of a fully clothed woman seated against the back wall. Shrunken like a mummy. Despite the green of the goggles, it was obvious she had blond hair. She held a purse in her lap and seemed to be waiting patiently to go on a journey. Balenger hated to imagine the terror she must have endured. Her old-style clothes told him that she wasn't Diane, but that knowledge didn't console him. He now took for granted that his beloved wife was dead, and yet he longed to be with her, even if she was lifeless. Amid a sea of green, he stooped and tried to determine how the woman had died.

No signs of violence. Wrong, he thought, focusing on her neck. The larynx and windpipe projected inward, the bones broken. She'd been strangled. He felt paralyzed until static from the walkie-talkie jabbed him into motion. About to hurry back to Amanda and Vinnie, he nevertheless set down the crowbar and reached for the corpse's purse. Its fabric was grimy and dust-covered. He set down the walkie-talkie, using both hands now to open the purse and take out a wallet.

There was a driver's license inside. A shudder swept through him when he saw the name on it. The name told him almost everything.

Need to get back. His thoughts were frenzied. Need to look in Vinnie's knapsack.

He shoved the license in a Windbreaker pocket, then grabbed the crowbar and the walkie-talkie. As thunder rumbled, he raced toward the staircase.

Watch out for the razor wire.

Poking with the crowbar, he found it. He squirmed under and rushed higher. His arm ached from the crowbar's weight as he thrust it up and down ahead of him in case Ronnie had managed to follow him and rig another trap. He thought he heard a distant shotgun blast and then a pistol. Third level. Fourth.

At the fifth, he halted again, unable to restrain himself from peering into the secret corridor. He remembered thinking he'd seen an object propped against a wall in there. Now his night-vision goggles revealed that he was right. Another corpse of a woman. Blond. Fully clothed, this time in slacks, a turtleneck, and a blazer.

No, Balenger thought.

The clothes were familiar to him.

No.

53

He stumbled toward her. When a rat appeared on her shoulder, he swung the crowbar, smashing it against a wall. Overcome with emotion, he sank to his knees. The woman wasn't as shrunken as the corpse on the bottom level. Her eyes were gone. Chunks had been chewed from her, but the face was nonetheless impossible not to recognize.

Diane.

Grief cramped his chest. It took away his breath. Tears burned like acid on his cheeks. Wracked with sobs, he raised a hand, caressing her leathery face. Her blond hair hung below her shoulders, longer than she preferred it — because it had continued growing after her death. Her expression was a grimace of terror. Like the corpse on the bottom level, her neck bones were cracked inward from having been strangled. His Diane. His wonderful Diane.

He knelt, worshiping her, mourning her. Diane. Eleven years together. She never gave up on him, never tired of taking care of him after he came back sick from his first time in Iraq. He had tried to make it up to her, tried to make her realize how much he loved her. Kind, selfless Diane. Beautiful Diane with holes chewed in her face.

A gunshot brought him back to the moment. Continuing to sob, he opened her purse, took out her wallet, and put it in his Windbreaker. He kissed her parched forehead, picked up the crowbar and the walkie-talkie, and stalked up the stairs.

Fury made him want to rush, but that would be playing Ronnie's game, letting the son of a bitch manipulate him into making mistakes. *I'm coming for you, Ronnie,* he inwardly shouted. Ready with the crowbar, he emerged into the sixth-floor passageway and studied the wreckage of Danata's living room. The furniture still barricaded the entrance.

He climbed to the trapdoor. Beyond it, he heard a commotion, hurried footsteps, a gunshot. Frenzied, he knocked twice, three times, once.

No response. What if they think I'm Ronnie? What if they shoot through the trapdoor?

As he knocked again, he heard the lock being freed. The trapdoor was lifted. A headlamp blazed toward his face, stressing the sensor in his goggles, creating a flare that made him temporarily blind. The headlamp jerked away, allowing his night vision to return. He hurried up and locked the trapdoor behind him.

The smell of burnt gunpowder was everywhere. Vinnie stood in the doorway to the surveillance room, aiming toward two jagged holes in the floor. He saw Balenger and retreated to him. "I did what you said. I counted to fifty. Then I turned up the volume on my walkie-talkie and set it on the floor. He blew it apart."

"How many rounds did you fire?" Balenger took the pistol.

"Three. I hope you don't think I wasted —"

"You did your job. You distracted him. Nine rounds left. We'll need to make them last."

"He's been shooting at random through the floors."

"He can't get into Danata's living room and shoot at us from there. We're safe for a moment. Give me your knapsack."

Balenger raised the walkie-talkie to his lips. "Hey, asshole, guess what?"

Static.

"I asked you a question, jerkoff."

"What am I supposed to guess? Are the vulgarities necessary?"

"When it comes to you? Absolutely. I found my wife, you piece of shit."

Static.

"You strangled her. You strangled them all."

Balenger took the knapsack from Vinnie and pulled the police report from the compartment in back. He reached into his pocket for the driver's license from the corpse on the bottom level.

"Candlelight gourmet dinners," Balenger said into the walkie-talkie. "Soothing classical music. Literary reading sessions. Foreign movies with subtitles. All very proper and formal and intellectual. Need to keep it intellectual. Can't let emotions get in the way. Emotions make you weak. Emotions make you lose control."

He studied the name on the driver's license: Iris McKenzie. When Amanda listed the names of Ronnie's "girlfriends," something had nagged at him. Now he knew what it was. Iris. He flipped through the pages in the police report.

"Found it!" he said to the walkie-talkie. "Iris McKenzie. Age: thirty-three. Residence: Baltimore, Maryland. Occupation: advertising copywriter. Hair: blond. Sound familiar, you bastard? She ought to. If I'm right, she was your first." Balenger scanned the report, which an old man had written with painstaking neatness. "In August of 1968, Iris took a train from Baltimore to New York on business. Coming back, she decided to spend the weekend in Asbury Park at the famous Paragon Hotel. Nobody told her Asbury Park wasn't the jewel it used to be or that the Paragon Hotel was a nightmare. She arrived on Friday. One night in this spooky old pile was enough for her. She checked out the next morning to go to the train station. Nobody saw her again. Except me. *I* saw her, Ronnie. She's sitting downstairs in a corridor with her purse in her lap, still waiting for her train. It's going to be a long time coming."

His mouth dry, his chest aching, Balenger needed to pause. He felt as if his surging emotions could cause his veins to explode.

He raised the walkie-talkie. "Amanda says you treated her with terrifying politeness. Apart from locking her in the vault, of course. But what the hell, nobody's perfect, right? Then you showed up with a sheer nightgown for her to wear. What happened, Ronnie? Did you decide the courtship was finally over? You fed her. You entertained her. You proved what a prince of a guy you were. Now you wanted something for your efforts. You're a man of the world, after all. You know how the game's played. But all of a sudden you got angry. You called her a whore. Did your sexual needs make you feel weak and resentful? I bet you'd soon have hit her. Then you'd have hated yourself for letting your weakness and needs get the better of you. Maybe you hated yourself for wanting her and hated *her* for being a woman you wanted. Or here's an opposite possibility. I like this one better. Maybe you hated yourself because you believed you *ought* to want her but you didn't. Maybe you didn't feel any sexual interest at all, and that really bothered you. You were comfortable cooking gourmet meals, reading Proust, and watching subtitled movies. But when it came to the man-woman stuff, you were numb. 'What's wrong with me?' you wondered. Gotta do something about that. So you made her put on a nightgown. That ought to give you a charge. But it didn't, and now you hated her because she didn't make you feel like a man. You knew where this was going. The same way it went with the others. You couldn't make yourself screw them, so you strangled them to hide your shame and your failure. Maybe the next woman would make you feel like a man. Next time. There was always next time, right?"

Unseen lightning cracked. Amanda and Vinnie watched Balenger, listening in horror.

"So now you're a pop psychologist in addition to being a failed soldier and a mediocre policeman?" the voice asked.

"*Detective,* I was a detective. And I guess all that research you did about me didn't tell you the crimes I investigated. Or maybe you made yourself ignore that because you didn't want to think about your problem. Sex crimes, Ronnie. I investigated sex crimes. I can see into your head, pal, and it's a sewer."

Ronnie. That name, too, kept nagging at Balenger.

"1968," Balenger said into the walkie-talkie. "There's a photograph of you and Carlisle. It has a date on the back: July 31, 1968. A month later, Iris McKenzie disappeared. By the end of the year, Carlisle closed the hotel, dismissed the staff, and lived here alone. Or maybe he *wasn't* alone. Ronnie. Ronnie. Why does that name —"

Balenger flipped through the police file, page after page, remembering something, searching for it. Ronnie. Then he found the page, and the name stared up at him. It made him shudder. "Ronald Whitaker."

"What?" the voice asked.

54

"Ronnie. Ronald. The Fourth of July, 1960. Ronald Whitaker."

"Shut up," the voice said.

Thunder rumbled.

"You're Ronald Whitaker."

"Shut up. Shut up."

Amid the din of the rain, Balenger heard pounding from below. Not from the trapdoor. Farther down. Aiming, he unlocked and opened the trapdoor. His goggles revealed the curved, green-tinted stairs.

"Shut up. Shut up," Ronnie yelled.

As the fierce pounding continued, Balenger eased down the stairs and peered through the demolished wall into Danata's ravaged living room.

The pounding came from the barricaded door, powerful enough to jostle the furniture stacked against it.

"Your mother died," Balenger said into the walkie-talkie. "Your father molested you."

"I'll make you hurt so much, you'll beg me to kill you!" Ronnie shouted from outside the door.

Balenger entered Danata's living room and aimed toward the door. Keeping his voice low, trying to make Ronnie think he was still in the penthouse, he continued speaking into the walkie-talkie. "Then your father thought he'd earn a few dollars out of you, so he brought you here to the Paragon Hotel for the Fourth of July, and he rented you to another pervert."

"I won't listen!"

"The guy tried to bribe you with a baseball, a glove, and a bat. I can't imagine how unspeakable it was. Afterward, your father came back to the room with the money. He was drunk. He fell asleep. You bashed his head twenty-two times with the bat. Ronnie, in your place, I'd have hit him *fifty* times. A hundred. I can't tell you how sorry I feel for that little boy. I'm enraged when I think about what was done to him. My heart breaks for the childhood he lost."

Rain lashed against the building. Thunder shook the walls.

"But I hate everything he became, Ronnie."

"My name's Walter Harrigan!"

Balenger fired toward the voice. Once. Twice. At the door's middle, his bullets plowed through the wood.

Immediately, he shifted position, an instant before part of the wall roared open from two shotgun blasts, pellets spraying toward the noise from his gun.

One of the pellets caught Balenger's arm. Ignoring the pain, he fired to the right and left of the holes in the wall. He veered toward the stairwell as two more holes roared through the wall.

From the darkness beyond the holes, he heard Ronnie reloading the shotgun.

Damn it, I let him trick me! He got me to waste ammunition! Only five rounds left!

Static crackled from his walkie-talkie.

Ronnie's aiming toward the sound! Balenger realized. As the walkie-talkie again crackled, he charged up the stairs. Two roars sent pellets clanging off the metal steps below him.

"The holes don't show the light from your headlamp," the voice said from Balenger's walkie-talkie. "Now I understand. While your friends distracted me, you went down the stairwell to the bodies. You got their night-vision goggles."

Balenger braced himself at the trapdoor's opening. Ronnie couldn't get a shot at him there. "I found the explosives you planted under the bodies," Balenger said into the walkie-talkie.

"Well, there's one you *didn't* find," the voice said.

A rumble shook the building. For a moment, Balenger thought it was another strong burst of thunder. But as the walls trembled, it was obvious that the reverberation came from inside. He had to grip the edge of the trapdoor's opening to steady himself. He felt a shock wave slam his ears.

Above him, Amanda yelled, "Over here! The surveillance room!"

Balenger surged up through the hatch. He ran to the surveillance room and opened its trapdoor. Smoke made him cough. As it cleared, the goggles showed him that the staircase had been blown apart three floors down. The twisted steel remnants vibrated, swaying. Far below, there were flames.

Balenger raised the walkie-talkie. "If you're talking about the metal box you strapped to Amanda, we *did* find it. I threw it down the surveillance room's staircase. A fire's trying to get started down there."

"Tomorrow, I planned to burn this place to the ground anyhow. The coins are worthless to me."

The abrupt change of topic made Balenger uneasy. "The coins?"

"A fortune, but I couldn't use them to pay

the taxes on this place," the voice said bitterly. "I went to different coin dealers in different cities. Never more than a couple of coins at a time. Never the priceless ones. But you need to sell a lot of seven-hundred-dollar coins to try to pay fifty thousand dollars in property taxes. One day, in Philadelphia, a dealer I'd never met looked at what I offered and said, 'So you're the guy with all the double eagles. The other dealers are talking about you.' And that was the last coin I dared try to sell."

Why is he talking so much? Balenger wondered. He's stalling for time. What's he up to?

Abruptly, Balenger recalled what he'd said to Ronnie seconds earlier: *I threw it down the surveillance room's staircase. A fire's trying to get started down there.* Jesus, I told him where I am.

Balenger charged from the open trapdoor, lunging toward the bedroom. Something exploded behind him, but there wasn't any shrapnel. What the blast sent was a flash of heat that filled the surveillance room. The detonator next to the trapdoor, Balenger realized. Ronnie triggered it by remote control. Smoke blossomed.

Amanda and Vinnie rushed ahead of him. But Vinnie's direction made it clear that he didn't understand what caused the small blast.

"Vinnie, get away from —"

In the bedroom, Vinnie stopped and turned.

"The trapdoor!" Balenger shouted. "Get away from —"

Stunned, Vinnie glanced down at where he'd stopped.

The trapdoor.

The detonator.

The blast was small but deafening. It sent a flash up Vinnie's legs. His jeans burst into flames. Screaming, he fell to the floor, swatting at his pants.

Balenger grabbed the bedspread and flailed at Vinnie's legs, desperately smothering the fire. Vinnie's screams continued.

In rapid succession, detonators exploded throughout the penthouse. Balenger saw their flashes, saw flames in the surveillance room and the medical room.

"A fire extinguisher!" Amanda yelled. "The kitchen!" She ran through the surveillance room, dodging the fire.

Balenger grabbed a decorative pitcher from a bureau and hurried into the bathroom. He twisted a knob on the sink, but no water came out. The electricity's off! The pump isn't working! he remembered. He scooped water from the toilet bowl, ran into the medical room, and dumped the pitcher onto the flames. A shotgun blast tore another hole in the floor, but by then Balenger was racing back to the bathroom. He yanked off the toilet-tank lid and scooped water. This time, he didn't enter the medical room but stopped at its entrance, hurling the water onto the flames. The fire hissed and shrank. The toilet tank again. He scooped out all the water he could get and ran to the medical room. Now, when he threw the water, the flames went out.

No more water. How am I going to —

He heard the spray of a fire extinguisher, Amanda attacking the blaze in another room. But she wasn't in the dining room where flames rose also. Water. Need to find more water. He stared at the open elevator in the exercise room. Ignoring the risk of a shotgun blast, he raced to the elevator and scooped up the five urine bottles that Ronnie had tauntingly returned to them.

Wrong move, you son of a bitch, Balenger thought, tossing urine onto the flames. The ammonia stench made him gag. He dumped more urine. The fire sizzled. A third bottle. A fourth. Drenched by piss, the fire retreated. The fifth bottle put it out.

Another shotgun blast tore through the

floor. Running, Balenger felt a chunk of wood sting his face. He found Amanda in the library, where she frantically worked the extinguisher, putting out a blaze. She hurried to the surveillance room, spewed a white cloud onto the flames there, and put them out, also. But an instant later, the cloud stopped, the extinguisher empty.

The floor erupted from another blast, but by then, Balenger tugged Amanda into the bedroom. They crouched next to Vinnie against the outside wall. Theoretically, it was the safest spot — above Danata's living room, the door of which remained barricaded. Smoke drifted around them. Vinnie's charred jeans were stuck to him, the flesh blackened, leaking fluid. Third-degree burns. Balenger had seen plenty of them in Iraq.

"Hurts," Vinnie said.

Balenger knew that Vinnie was going to hurt a lot worse when his nerves recovered from the shock they'd received. Soon, he would be in agony.

"Hurts." Despite the green of Balenger's night-vision goggles, Vinnie's face was ashen.

"I know," Balenger said. "Can you walk?"

"Only one way to find out." Wincing, Vinnie motioned for Balenger to pull him up.

But Vinnie's legs were swollen. His knees refused to bend. Weight on them made him gasp. Balenger feared he'd pass out.

"Okay, not a good idea." Balenger eased him back to the floor. "Amanda." He was surprised to see that she still held the empty fire extinguisher. "Go quietly to the surveillance room and throw the extinguisher as far as possible. Into the library, if you can. But wait until I'm at the door to the medical room."

"What are you going to —"

"Help with the pain."

Balenger went to the right, toward the medical room. Its candles glowed dimly, surrounded by smoke. He nodded to Amanda, who hurled the fire extinguisher in the opposite direction toward the library. As soon as he heard it crash onto the floor, distracting Ronnie, Balenger shifted into the medical room and reached through the broken glass door of the cabinet. He grabbed a syringe and the vial of morphine, then darted back into the bedroom an instant before pellets exploded from the floor.

He knelt beside Vinnie. "I'm giving you only enough to dull the pain, not put you out."

Vinnie nodded, biting his lip. "Just hurry and do it."

Balenger exposed Vinnie's left wrist and gave him the injection.

Vinnie's face remained rigid with pain. Slowly, it relaxed. "Yes."

55

The smoke hovered.

"It's thicker." Amanda coughed. "I thought all the flames were out."

"Not down there." Balenger pointed toward the open trapdoor in the surveillance room. He stepped warily toward it. Three levels below, the flames were stronger. The only thing he could think to do was shut the trapdoor and lock it.

Surprising him, Amanda rushed in with towels she'd soaked in the remaining water in the toilet tank. She pressed them over the edges of the trapdoor, sealing off the smoke.

With the electricity off and the heating system no longer engaged, the penthouse had rapidly cooled. Amanda hugged herself. Glancing down at her bare feet and the nightgown that gave little protection to her legs, Balenger said, "Maybe I can do something about that."

At the door to the medical room, he stared at Cora's body. I'm sorry, he thought. He gripped Cora's hands and pulled. There were so many holes in the floor, Ronnie would surely hear, he worried. But he needed to keep pulling. He eased Cora's body into the bedroom.

"Here," he said, taking off Cora's shoes and socks. Cora's feet had the terrible coldness of death. "You and she are about the same size. These ought to fit you."

Amanda gazed at what he offered. Madness became normalcy. She took the shoes and socks. "But not the pants." They were soaked with blood. "I won't put on the pants."

Balenger understood. Even desperation had its limits.

The walkie-talkie crackled. Balenger thought, Hit back. You can't let him think he's winning.

He pressed the transmit button. "Why blondes, Ronnie?"

No answer.

"Was your mother a blonde?"

No answer.

"Are you trying to replace your mother? Is that why your girlfriends don't put bounce in you?"

"You piece of shit," the voice said.

Got you, Balenger thought. "What were you saying earlier about vulgarity?"

No answer.

"Iris McKenzie disappeared in 1968,"

Balenger said. "Your Fourth of July of horrors happened in 1960. Eight years earlier. What's the connection?" A tingle swept through him. Hours ago, Cora had asked what would happen to someone who'd been through what Ronald Whitaker had suffered. Balenger had answered that the boy would have spent eight years in a juvenile facility, receiving psychiatric counseling until he was —

"You were twenty-one," Balenger said into the walkie-talkie. "That photograph of you and Carlisle — it was taken just after you were released. What happened? Did Carlisle show an interest in you? Did he send you letters while you were being treated? Did he phone you? Did he finally behave like a human being and feel sorry for you? Did he ask you to come and stay here? Maybe he arranged for a psychiatrist to help you face the hell of your past. After all, how could you move on if the past kept its hook in you? That's why he stays a respectful distance from you in the photograph. He knows how sensitive you are about men touching you. Or maybe Carlisle never stopped being a twisted S.O.B. He was never a part of life. He only watched it. Maybe he brought you here so he could see how the rest of the story turned out. And you showed him, didn't you, Ronnie? You showed him the rest of the story."

"Don't talk about him like that."

"Carlisle was a monster."

"No. You don't know anything about my father."

"He's not your father. Maybe he sort of adopted you, but he wasn't your father, although he was almost as sick as your real father was."

"My real father?" the voice said with disgust. "No real father would have treated me like that."

"But no real son would have treated Carlisle the way *you* did," Balenger said. "He suspected what you were doing, but he couldn't prove it, right? He was twisted, but not as twisted as *you*. So he closed the hotel to take away your hunting territory. He hoped you'd stop, and hey, he wasn't sure to begin with, right? As far as he was concerned, closing the hotel was just a precaution. Hedging his doubts. What did you do, gradually make him a prisoner in this hellhole? Did you threaten to cut him, the thing he most feared? Did you force him to sign documents that put you in charge of the trust? When the riots occurred, did you make it seem that *he* ordered the metal shutters and doors installed? That way, you could keep tighter control on him at the same time you hid your secrets. But somewhere along the line, he discovered what you'd been doing — not just once but for years. Isn't that what happened, Ronnie? He found the corpses of some of your girlfriends. He managed the strength to break out of here. Something frightened him more than a cut that could make him bleed to death. More than the paralyzing open beach he forced himself to run toward. Something scared him so much he killed himself. *You,* Ronnie."

"A lot of questions," the voice said.

"You destroyed *two* fathers — the one you hated and the one you wanted."

"Questions that don't have answers."

Balenger peered into the surveillance room. Wisps of smoke squeezed their way past the towels around the trapdoor. I've bought enough time, he thought. The morphine should be working by now. He crouched next to Vinnie. "How's the pain?"

"Better. Floaty."

"Good. Because we need to get you on your feet."

Vinnie's eyes widened.

"No choice," Balenger said. "We can't stay here. The fire will get to us if he doesn't."

Which trapdoor? Balenger thought. If we use the staircase in Danata's suite, Ronnie will see us through the holes in the wall. He'll shoot.

The staircase from the surveillance room was in flames. The one in the kitchen was flooded. Balenger took for granted that the elevator was a death trap. As soon as Ronnie heard its *whir,* he'd shoot through the door and kill everyone in the compartment. Or else he'd shut off the electricity to it, trap his quarry in the shaft, and let the fire take care of them.

Balenger crept to the library. When he raised its trapdoor, he heard water, the equivalent of another cistern being filled. He shut the trapdoor, locked it, and eased through the kitchen into the dining room. Opening the trapdoor there, he exhaled when he didn't hear water.

He moved back to the bedroom. Vinnie's charred legs were more bloated, leaking more fluid.

"Just go along for the ride, Vinnie. Amanda and I will do the heavy lifting." Balenger looked at her. "Ready?"

56

"Always," Amanda said.

Her spirit reminded him so much of Diane's that for a moment, in the smoke haze, he thought he was actually looking at his wife. He shook his head to clear it.

"You're hurt," she said, pointing toward his right arm.

Balenger was surprised to see that his Windbreaker sleeve had blood on it. "Shotgun pellet, I think."

"And your left cheek."

He touched it and felt blood. "Flying wood splinter maybe. Here." He unstrapped the spare night-vision goggles from his belt. "You'll need these."

As she put them on, he told Vinnie, "It'll get dark now."

In pain, Vinnie nodded. "Just do what you need to."

Balenger switched off the lamps on Amanda's and Vinnie's hard hats. He prayed Vinnie had enough strength to keep from panicking in the darkness that would come when they took him from the candlelight. While Amanda adjusted to the green glow of her goggles, Balenger put on the knapsack. He holstered his pistol and shoved the crowbar under his utility belt.

Amanda took Vinnie's left arm, Balenger his right. When they lifted, Vinnie groaned.

"Lean on us," Balenger whispered. "Don't try to walk. Let us carry you."

But the moment they started, Balenger knew it wasn't going to work — Vinnie's shoes scraped along the floor.

They paused.

"Maybe if he puts his arms around our necks," Amanda murmured. "If he helps to lift, we can support him with our arms around his back and our other hands under his thighs."

They tried it, raising Vinnie's hips so that he was now in a kind of chair formed by their hands, his knees bent painfully. Inching ahead, they reached the trapdoor in the dining room and set Vinnie down.

Balenger aimed as Amanda unlocked and opened the hatch. His goggles detected only a green-tinted stairwell. The only sound was the rain outside.

He studied the opening. It wasn't large enough for two people, so he descended the stairs until his head was below the trapdoor. Amanda went to Vinnie's shoulders and pushed him legs-first toward the opening. The pain made Vinnie hiss, but otherwise he had the resolve to keep silent. Balenger gripped Vinnie's belt and pulled him into the staircase, trying to be gentle, aware of what Vinnie suffered.

The stench of scorched flesh made him gag. He set Vinnie's hips on the steps and waited for Amanda to enter the stairwell. Then he turned his back to Vinnie and felt Amanda place Vinnie's arms around his neck. Clutching them, Balenger stood and bent forward so that Vinnie's torso was over his back, the injured legs dangling behind him.

About to descend, Balenger suddenly thought. No, we're doing this wrong. "Squeeze past me," he whispered to Amanda. His voice was almost inaudible, but it made him cringe, as if he were shouting. "Wave the hammer in front of you. Check for wire."

Her goggles hiding whatever apprehension was in her eyes, she took the hammer from his belt and edged past him. Vinnie tensed from the pain. As they moved in a downward circle, Balenger became aware of their hoarse breathing. *Too loud. Ronnie'll hear us.* His stomach hardened. He had to balance himself carefully, lest Vinnie's weight topple him forward.

Ahead, Amanda stopped. They were almost at a corridor on the sixth level, and Balenger stared down past her shoulder. Her hammer tapped on something.

Razor wire.

Balenger saw it tremble.

He leaned back and set Vinnie on the stairs, momentarily grateful to be free of the weight. "Lie on your back," he whispered to Amanda. "Squirm under it. Then I'll slide Vinnie down the steps."

Without hesitation, she proceeded, then turned, and this time did hesitate when she understood that she'd be reaching for Vinnie's charred legs. But the hesitation lasted only for an instant. Readying herself, she waited as Balenger eased Vinnie under the wire.

But Vinnie's body thumped on the stairs. To Balenger, it seemed that the excruciating sound came from a loudspeaker.

He shoved his hands under Vinnie to cushion the impact. Vinnie couldn't see the obstacle and didn't know why it was necessary to slide him. But Balenger gave him credit. Vinnie didn't resist. He followed orders.

Then Vinnie was through, and it was Balenger's turn to go under the wire. Seconds later, he rose beyond it, put

Vinnie's arms around his neck, and stooped forward once more with Vinnie's weight on his back.

Amanda continued downward, using the hammer to check for more wire.

Suddenly, the stairs wavered. Bolts popped from the wall, the staircase pulling loose from its moorings. Balenger swayed. As the bolts clanged onto the lower stairs, he grabbed the unsteady railing. The stairs were a huge bobbing coil anchored at the top but not at the sides, banging against the walls.

Vinnie's legs hit the railing. He screamed. Amplified by the stairwell, the noise seemed to fill the hotel. Ronnie couldn't fail to hear it. Balenger pulled the crowbar from his belt, turned, and swung toward the razor wire. He hit it with all his strength, the wire so taut that it snapped from the impact.

"Upstairs!" he shouted to Amanda. "Now!"

Pellets blasted through the wall. More bolts popped, the staircase wobbling. Sweat dripping from his face, Balenger groped for the trapdoor's opening. Grateful to touch something that was solidly anchored, he scurried up and yanked Vinnie through, trying to ignore his screams. He stopped in the kitchen, hoping for safety against the outside wall. The trapdoor banged shut, and Amanda was suddenly next to him.

57

"We'll try another stairwell," Amanda said, hoping.

"Hardly any left."

Amanda sank wearily, her hips on the floor, her back against the wall. "He has a good chance of finding us."

Balenger slid down next to her, sounding as exhausted as she did. "Probably has traps in them."

"Yes," Amanda said. "Probably." She looked down at Vinnie, whose pain had caused him to pass out. "Any other ideas?"

"Not at the moment."

"Me, neither."

In the surveillance room, smoke drifted past the wet towels that sealed the edges of the trapdoor.

"But there must be *something*," Amanda said. "I won't give up."

Yes, just like Diane, Balenger thought. "That's right. We won't give up."

Static from the walkie-talkie.

"Still alive?" the voice asked.

Balenger pressed the transmit button and

squeezed his elbow against his holstered pistol, trying to draw reassurance from it. "Waiting for you."

"Waiting for the fire," the voice said.

Waiting will get us killed, Balenger thought. We need to do something. We're not going to let ourselves die here. He was conscious of the rain lashing against the metal shutter above him.

Something. There's got to be *something*.

Amanda stared up toward the shutter. With a chill of hope, Balenger realized the thought that came to her. Slowly, they stood and examined the shutter. Like the others in the hotel, it had rollers that rested on a horizontal bar above the window. In theory, a sideways sliding motion was the only thing necessary to open it. At the bottom, a lock secured it.

But unlike the shutters downstairs, the rollers on this one were rust-free. As with everything else in the penthouse, Ronnie kept the shutters scrupulously clean.

Balenger shoved the end of the crowbar under the lock. He started to apply leverage, then worried that Ronnie might hear.

"I'll distract him," he whispered to Amanda, putting her hands on the crowbar.

He eased into the dining room and pressed the transmit button on the walkie-talkie. "Walter Harrigan. Ronald Whitaker. Ronnie. Did your mother call you 'Ronnie'? Is that why you want your girlfriends to call you that? So they'll be like your mother?"

"You're guaranteeing more pain for yourself."

Balenger looked into the kitchen, where Amanda tugged furiously at the crowbar.

"Walter Harrigan. You're Ronald Whitaker, and yet you're . . . Of course." Balenger felt a thrill of understanding. "When you left the juvenile facility, did you change your name? Is that what happened? With a new name, you wouldn't be stalked by your past. No one would connect you with that Fourth of July. No one would know you killed your father. No one would know he abused you."

Balenger watched Amanda. The lock's plate seemed about to separate from the wall.

"Was that it, Ronnie? Was it Carlisle's idea to change your name? Was that another way he helped you?"

"Oh, he helped, all right," the voice said. "He couldn't stop helping."

"Or making excuses? Even when he suspected what you were doing, he still made excuses for you, didn't he? He didn't really believe what you were capable of. Why would —"

Amanda strained against the crowbar. As the lock's plate pulled from the wall, Balenger returned to the kitchen and grabbed the plate before it could strike the floor.

"Why would he make excuses for you, Ronnie?" Balenger felt sick as the answer occurred to him. "He watched through the wall. He saw your father . . . He saw the pervert your father took money from come in and . . . After a lifetime of watching, Carlisle finally got disgusted with being a watcher. He could have done something to stop it, but . . . He was a god who observed without intervening in this hell he created. But when he saw you bash in your father's brains, he finally felt more than curiosity. Maybe because he was alone so much as a child, he identified with you. He felt guilty. He wished he could have stopped what happened. The only thing left was to try to make amends. He spoiled you, and then one night, he discovered the consequences."

"Tonight, *you'll* discover consequences. I see smoke down here," the voice said.

Balenger put the walkie-talkie into his knapsack. He and Amanda pushed at the shutter. He was surprised how smoothly the rollers shifted along their rail.

4:00 a.m.

58

The window gaped. Like the others in the hotel, it was broken, part of the hotel's disguise to make it appear oppressively deserted. Out of the howling darkness, wind and rain struck Balenger's face. He and Amanda took urgent breaths, filling their nostrils, throats, and lungs. Lightning flashed, illuminating the beach seven levels below.

Balenger raised the window frame to avoid being cut by the shards in it. "I'll find a spot to anchor the rope," he told Amanda. "Close the shutter as soon as I'm out. If Ronnie smells the fresh air, he'll know what we're doing."

He climbed through the window. Rain lashed him. In green-tinted darkness, he eased down to the roof. The wind gusted at him, imaginary hands shoving. Moisture pelted his face, entering his mouth. It tasted bitter, a mixture of sweat, dirt, and blood from his cheeks.

The rain on his goggles made it difficult to see. He wiped their lenses, flinched from a nearby lightning strike, and moved cautiously forward.

The roof felt spongy. He shifted to the right, breathing slightly easier when the area under him became solid again. At the roof's edge, he crouched to prevent the wind from pushing him over.

For a moment, he allowed himself to hope, but then he peered down, and despair swept through him. The center of the roof below him was collapsed, water streaming into it. Lightning revealed the lower levels. They were damaged from years of punishing weather and lack of maintenance. Surfaces were peeled back, flapping in the wind. Holes were evident, even from a distance.

Balenger opened his mouth to breathe. Wind filled his throat. No, he thought. No! Lightning struck the beach. The rain strengthened, intensifying the chill of his drenched clothes, but that was nothing compared to the chill that invaded his spirit. He looked for a place to secure the rope that was in his knapsack.

A ventilation pipe. He approached it, his goggles revealing rust. When he pushed a shoe against it, the pipe held. He pushed with greater force. The pipe continued to hold. Wiping rain from his goggles, he headed back to the shutter. Another spongy section of roof threatened to collapse. He skirted it, took three steps, and abruptly, his left shoe broke the surface. He froze, supporting his weight on his other foot. Slowly, he pulled the shoe free. Testing, he continued across the roof.

When he reached to slide the shutter open, it startled him, seeming to move on its own. Amanda's arms came into view, helping him through the window.

Dripping, shivering, he squirmed into the kitchen and closed the shutter. After the fresh air, the penthouse's atmosphere of smoke, pain, and death was overwhelming.

His goggles couldn't hide how depressed he felt.

"What's wrong?" Amanda asked.

"The three of us can't do it."

"Can't?"

"Two of us lifting Vinnie — the roof won't hold our weight. If you go separately, you might make it. But if I carry Vinnie, I'll . . . he and I will go through the roof. We might never stop dropping till we reach the ground floor."

"But . . ."

"Leave," Vinnie whispered in pain.

Balenger was surprised that Vinnie was conscious.

"Holding you back." Vinnie's murmur was distorted with agony. "Leave me. Get help."

"No, I won't leave you." Balenger took off the knapsack and removed the rope. "Amanda, you weigh the least. There's a ventilation pipe. I tested it. It'll hold you. Loop the rope around it. Slide down the wall. Pull the rope down to you. Find another anchor and keep climbing down."

Amanda's face tensed in concentration. "How far to the ground?"

"Seven levels."

"Slide down the rope? It's called 'rappeling,' right?"

"Yes."

"It's not as easy as you make it sound. Even if I manage to reach the bottom, what happens next? Where do I find help?"

"There's nobody in this area. You'll need to go to the police station. I'll give you directions."

"How far?"

"A couple of miles."

The smoke made Amanda cough. "In this storm? As weak as I am from being in that vault? With my legs protected only by this nightgown? I'll collapse from hypothermia before I get there. You go."

"But —"

"You're the strongest. I'll stay with Vinnie."

He studied her. Blond hair. Determined, lovely features. So much like Diane.

The idea abruptly seemed futile. "By the time I bring help, it might be too late," he said.

"Then what are we going to do?"

Balenger listened to the rain against the shutter. "Maybe there's only one chance."

She watched him, trying to control her desperation.

"I need to go after him," Balenger said.

"Yes." The cold made Amanda's lips pale.

An apron hung next to the sink. He wrapped it around her unprotected legs.

Something made her frown toward a corner. When he looked in that direction, he saw a rat. Other rats stared in from the dining room.

"They're attracted to the smell of Vinnie's legs," Amanda said.

More rats appeared at the door to the library. One had a single eye.

Balenger went to the bedroom and took an object from Cora's jacket. When he returned, he showed Amanda what it was.

The water pistol.

"Vinegar." He squirted a rat. It darted away.

She took the pistol.

Static came from the walkie-talkie. "The smoke's thicker down here," Ronnie's voice said.

"Then maybe you should leave the building," Balenger replied.

He turned off the walkie-talkie and put it into his knapsack. He shoved the crowbar in also. Facing Amanda, he promised, "I'll come back as soon as I can."

But he didn't move, couldn't turn away from her. Each felt the same impulse. They put their arms around each other.

Balenger tried to draw strength from her, possibly the last friendly person he would ever see. His chest swelling with emotion, he slid the shutter open. The rain pelted him. Just before he eased onto the roof, he peered back into the kitchen and saw Amanda sink to the floor, where she cradled Vinnie's head on her lap. The green-tinted rats formed a semicircle at the edge of the room. She aimed the water pistol. He settled his weight on the roof and closed the shutter.

59

The wind threatened to suck air from his lungs as he worked his way toward the ventilation pipe. With each step, he feared that his foot would again break the surface. Drenched, he studied rain-swept puddles, deciding that the roof would be weakest where water collected. But the next spongy section he encountered was in a raised area that turned out to be a blister. He stepped back and veered around it.

A crack of lightning struck the tip of the pyramid. It reminded him of an artillery shell exploding. Despite his urge to run, he forced himself to be cautious. Rain obscured the pipe. He looped the rope over it and pulled, again testing. Designed for mountain climbing, the rope had a standard length of 150 feet, reduced now to 75 because it was doubled. Although thin and lightweight, it was exceptionally strong, its polyester sheath protecting a core of silk fibers.

Earlier, Rick had questioned him about his familiarity with heights and rope.

Needing an innocent explanation, Balenger had responded that he was a rock climber. In truth, he knew about heights and rope because of his Ranger training. He knotted the rope about four feet from its tips. The knot would warn him when he was almost at the end. He dropped the doubled rope off the roof. Straddling it, he pulled it up behind him, over his right hip. He looped it across his chest, over his left shoulder, and down his back, making sure the rope was cushioned by his jacket and wouldn't cut into his neck. He used his left hand to grip the forward part of the rope while his right gripped the section behind and below him. The arrangement allowed his body to act as a brake.

Somewhere, somehow, he'd lost his gloves. As a consequence, he risked rope burns on his hands. Straining to be optimistic, he told himself that the gloves would have been slippery in the rain, that under the circumstances exposed skin was safer.

Right. Be positive. Look on the bright side.

In green-tinted darkness.

It keeps getting worse, he thought. Yet his emotions puzzled him. The Gulf War syndrome from his tour of duty in Desert

Storm was suddenly so distant a memory that it seemed not to have happened. The post-traumatic stress disorder from his near-beheading no longer weighed on him. After the hell of the previous six hours, after so many deaths, after discovering the corpse of his beloved wife, a grim rage overtook him. It was so expansive and powerful that it left no room for fear. Vinnie depended on him. The woman who resembled his wife depended on him. *They* mattered. Punishing Ronnie. *That* mattered.

He tested the rope one final time, then stepped backward off the roof. Swaying in chaos, he eased the rope through his right hand behind him while his left hand gripped the forward section. The rope slid around his body. With his shoes pushing against the wall, he walked horizontally backward and downward, approaching the crater in the patio below.

The rope jerked. Had the pipe bent? Friction burning his cold fingers, he eased more rope through his right hand. The rope jerked again. Don't think about it. Keep going. Keep thinking about Amanda and Vinnie. Through rain-streaked goggles, he saw that the surviving edge of the patio was just below him. A moment later, he set down on it, holding the rope around him so he wouldn't drop if the remainder of the patio gave way.

He was braced against a closed, rusted shutter on the sixth level. There was no way inside. To re-enter the hotel, to get to Ronnie, he needed to descend farther. Into the crater of a room on the fifth level. His soaked clothes weighing on him, he walked to the edge of the crater and leaned back, settling into it. Without a wall to brace his feet against, he grimaced from the strain of lowering himself, the rope biting into his hip, chest, and shoulder. Now the moisture falling around him was thicker, not only rain but also water accumulating on the roof. It poured over him. Below, he saw a canopied bed, a bureau, a Victorian table, the basic arrangement he'd found in most of the other rooms. The middle of the floor was another crater, water crashing farther down.

He kicked his legs. The motion started a pendulum effect that he increased by kicking several more times. Swinging, he neared the remainder of the floor across from him, kicked again, and suddenly his breath was taken away as he dropped. The pipe's breaking, he thought. He jerked to a stop.

The rope constricted his chest. Still breathless, he exhaled through his mouth and inhaled through his nostrils, trying for a calming rhythm. Staring up, he saw that the reason the rope had dropped was that it had dug into the crater's edge and broken away a portion of the roof. Six feet of ceiling had crumbled. That was how far he had fallen. Now he hung below the hole, dangling into a fourth-level room. He tried to pull himself up, to lift his legs over the edge.

But the rim of *this* crater now began to disintegrate. As the floor gave way, he sank lower, dangling farther into the fourth-level room. Water fell past him. Then a chair. It brushed past his jacket sleeve.

Jesus, the whole ceiling's collapsing. The furniture's going to —

The table plummeted past him. The bureau tilted toward the widening hole. The bed slid in his direction.

Staring down, he saw that the door to the fourth-level room was open. Nearly all the floor was gone, the entire contents having cascaded, hitting subsequent floors and crashing through. At once, Balenger understood that this was the room from which he'd rescued Vinnie after Vinnie dropped.

More of the crater's rim collapsed. The rope dropped him another two feet. With a *woosh,* the bureau hurtled past. The bed slid nearer. He worked down along the rope. At the same time, he swung his body. His right hand touched the knot that warned him he was near the rope's end. As he swung again, the pressure of the rope made that section of the ceiling give way. The bed plunged toward him. His pendulum's arc sped him toward the open door. His fingers clawed, snagging the jamb. He tightened his grip on the door frame. The bed swooped past him.

The rope held him prisoner, tugging him backward into the chasm while he fought to pull himself around the doorjamb. The bed crashed far below. His right hand released the rope and joined his left hand clinging to the side of the open door. He pulled himself farther through. Although soft, the balcony's floor held. He took another step. Another.

Unwrapping the rope from his hip and shoulder, he freed the knot and tugged one end, trying to pull it down. It snagged on something. Worried that his effort would stress the weak floor, he took a step farther back, then tugged again. The rope refused to budge.

60

The noise, Balenger warned himself. Ronnie can't possibly fail to hear it.

Abandoning the rope, Balenger drew his pistol. But as he aimed along the green-tinted balcony, he became aware of a roar inside the hotel. It came from the storm's vibrations. The sound of the room collapsing was merely part of the larger rumble. It was nothing that Ronnie would have thought suspicious.

Balenger surveyed the hotel's hollow core. Rain from the broken skylight formed a veil. Nonetheless, he was able to see toward the opposite balcony. Flames emerged from the fifth-floor wall over there while smoke wafted from the sixth.

Amanda. Vinnie.

He shifted down the corridor that led to the emergency stairs. The noise of the storm muted any sounds he made climbing the stairs. At the fifth level, he crept to the balcony, hoping to glimpse Ronnie above.

No sign of him.

Something dangled onto Balenger's head.

Roots. The tree that grew through the ceiling. Hours earlier, it had seemed strange. Now, compared to everything that had happened, it felt normal.

He returned to the emergency stairs and went higher. The door was open. He left the stairs and inched along a short corridor. Across from him, the smoldering balcony seemed deserted. The flames would soon reach the penthouse. Despite his increasing urgency, he forced himself to go slowly, to make sure he didn't get careless. At the end of the corridor, he peered onto the balcony. Still no sign of Ronnie. Except for Danata's suite, every door was open. Ronnie could be in any of the rooms, listening for sounds above him.

To the left was the tree. In front of it, smoke drifted from a doorway. Ronnie wasn't listening for sounds above him, Balenger realized. He was starting another fire.

Movement separated the smoke. As a figure backed from the room, Balenger tightened his finger on the trigger. A tall man in a suit wore night-vision goggles and held a pump shotgun. Ronnie! Balenger raged at the memory of his futile conversations with the man two years earlier. *"And that was the last time you saw her?" "Yes.*

When she left my office at noon." But somehow the monster looked different, not as thin as Balenger remembered him or when he'd appeared on the surveillance monitor a while ago.

As Ronnie turned in his direction, Balenger shot twice, hitting him in the chest. The reports coincided with thunder, Ronnie jolting back. Before Balenger could shoot a third time, Ronnie's backward momentum lurched him into the tree. Wood cracked. That part of the balcony, weakened by roots, collapsed. Arms flailing, branches snapping, Ronnie and the tree plummeted through the hole.

Balenger hurried to it. Now he realized why Ronnie wasn't as thin as he ought to be. *He wore a bullet-resistant vest.*

Balenger aimed down through the hole, determined to get a head shot, but the only target was an arm as Ronnie frantically rolled away. Balenger had only three rounds left. He couldn't risk wasting a bullet. He knew that by the time he charged down the emergency stairs to the fifth level, Ronnie would be impossible to find — too many rooms, too many other emergency stairs, too many secret doors.

Balenger acted before he realized what he was doing, jumping through the hole, dropping to the balcony below. Since it hadn't collapsed from Ronnie's impact, he believed it would hold him. He landed, bending his knees to absorb the shock, tucking and rolling the way he'd been taught in jump school. Avoiding the tree, he rose to a crouch and searched for a target. But his unsteady footing alarmed him. The balcony wavered.

Five doors away, he saw Ronnie aim his shotgun. As the balcony swayed, throwing Balenger to his knees, it jerked Ronnie off-balance also. The shotgun roared, pellets whistling over Balenger's head.

Before Ronnie could pump another shell into the chamber, Balenger charged. They collided, crashing to the floor, and at once, Balenger felt his stomach rise, the impact of their combined weights making the balcony drop.

A section tilted, crashing down onto the next level. It formed a slide onto which Balenger and Ronnie tumbled over each other, hitting the bottom. The impact made that balcony waver.

Ronnie's hands found Balenger's throat. He remembered Amanda's insistence on how strong Ronnie was. Ronnie's hands were certainly strong, expertly squeezing Balenger's windpipe, but after all, the monster had years of practice.

The balcony vibrated. Or perhaps Balenger's mind was swaying. As his green-tinted vision turned gray from the effect of strangulation, he tried to shoot, but the only angle available to him was toward Ronnie's chest, toward his bullet-resistant vest.

Balenger pulled the trigger. Although the vest blocked the bullet, it couldn't muffle the shock of the impact. As if struck by a sledge hammer, Ronnie fell back. Balenger dove for the solid floor of a hallway. An instant later, the remainder of the upper balcony collapsed onto this one. Ronnie screamed amid rubble as the balcony fell away, struck the next one, and caused a chain reaction, the rest of the balconies crashing to the lobby, splashing into the water.

From the solid footing of the hallway, Balenger gaped down at the wreckage. Dust rose, only to be flattened by the rain pouring from the open skylight.

Amanda. Vinnie. He holstered his gun and raced for the emergency stairs. One level. Another. Coughing from the smoke, he emerged onto the sixth floor and tried to figure how to get to the penthouse. The door to Danata's suite was barricaded. Were there secret doors in any of the other rooms? Was that how Ronnie got into the stairwells and rigged the traps? Where were the doors?

Choosing a room away from the new fire Ronnie had set, Balenger hurried in. The bureau caught his attention. It would be easy to hide a door behind there. He yanked the bureau down, but all he found was an apparently solid wall. He took the crowbar from his knapsack and whacked it against the wall. He struck again and again, his frenzy mounting, his desperation making him wail. The hole got larger, revealing a gap between two-by-fours, a hidden corridor. He walloped as hard as he could, widening the space. One more fierce blow, and he could squeeze through.

He put the crowbar in his knapsack and entered the corridor. At once, he saw the dangling spiral staircase, its moorings pulled from the wall. My God, I'm under the penthouse dining room. Amanda, Vinnie, and I tried to come down these stairs. They have hardly any support.

He put his weight on the stairs. They wobbled. He eased upward, trying to move smoothly, to keep the staircase steady. Again, it wobbled. Please, he thought. He stepped higher, gripping the curved banister. He felt as if he were on the unsteady deck of a wave-tossed sailboat. Unable to get enough air into his lungs, he reached the trapdoor and pounded. Twice. Three times. Once.

The trapdoor opened, Amanda looking at him in relief. "There's a second fire."

"I know." Balenger crawled from the staircase. The pressure of his shoes pushing him away from the stairs was enough to send them crashing down.

The penthouse was filling with smoke. As they rushed to Vinnie in the kitchen, Amanda said, "I was afraid I'd have to open the shutter and put Vinnie outside, then join him. At least we'd have been able to breathe, even if we got hypothermia or the damned building collapsed."

"Help me get him to the bedroom. We'll take him down to Danata's suite."

"Ronnie. What about —"

"I don't know. Maybe he's dead."

"Maybe?"

"I hope. Can't be sure."

They put Vinnie's arms over their shoulders and dragged him toward the bedroom, no longer caring if they made noise.

They set him down at the bedroom's trapdoor. Then Amanda unlocked and lifted the hatch while Balenger aimed into it. Only two rounds left, he thought. Can't waste them. But all he saw was green-tinted smoke.

The moment he entered the staircase, he hesitated. "Wait a second." He took a step upward and grasped the block of plastic explosive he'd set aside when disarming the bomb.

"What can you do with that?" Amanda asked.

"Don't know."

"You said it was useless without a detonator."

"It is." He stuffed the explosive into his knapsack. Just below the opening, he waited with his back turned. Amanda slid Vinnie onto him. He carried Vinnie down to Danata's living room and again set him on the floor. With effort, he and Amanda tugged the heavy tables and chairs from the door. He aimed as Amanda opened it.

Flames rose on the other side of the hotel's core. They also spread from a room on this side.

"It was dark for so long, I thought I'd give anything if I could see." Vinnie was appalled by what he faced. "Now I wish I couldn't."

"Help me get him on my back," Balenger told Amanda. "Vinnie, hang on to the straps on the knapsack. Can you do that?"

"My legs are messed up, but there's nothing wrong with my hands."

They worked their way into a corridor

and reached the entrance to the emergency stairs. Again, Balenger aimed. Again, there wasn't a target. Bent forward with Vinnie, he climbed down as quickly as he could without losing his balance. Fifth level. Fourth. Third.

"I hear water," Amanda said.

"So many roofs to collect it. So many holes. The place is flooding," Balenger told her.

Second level. First.

They were submerged knee-deep as they tugged a door open. The water chilled them, but not as much as what they saw: the chaos of the lobby. Now Balenger understood why furniture piled up, tangled against columns and doors. The force of the water falling from the upper levels was dismaying, the din overwhelming. Any object that wasn't anchored got swept away.

61

"How do we get out?"

The voice startled Balenger, almost making him pull the trigger. It belonged to a man struggling through the current toward them. The figure wore goggles. He had bulging pockets that weighed him down. Tattoos covered his face.

"I tried the tunnel door!" Tod shouted. "The bastard really did weld it shut! I tried every other door and shutter I could find! We're trapped!"

"We'll use the crowbar! We'll try to wedge a door open!"

The instant Balenger stepped into the current, it almost knocked him over. Twenty feet to his right, a waterfall cascaded.

"This whole damned place is about to come down," Tod said.

"Get rid of the coins. If you fall, they'll hold you under the water."

"Then I'd better not fall."

Balenger saw a chair rush by, carrying a rat. He dodged the chair, only to stagger from Vinnie's weight. Amanda grabbed him, holding him up. They waded past a pillar, where rats teemed on a jumble of furniture.

"What happened to him?" Tod said.

"His legs got burned. Ronnie blew the detonators."

"I'd love to shove a detonator down his throat if I ever get my hands on —" Tod gaped in shock.

"What's the matter?"

"A body just floated past. A woman. The woman I saw in the corridor."

Blond hair disappeared in the current. Balenger was sickened by the thought that it could be any of the other corpses that Ronnie hid in the building. Or maybe it's Diane, he thought.

Objects spattered the water. The roar in the lobby was sufficiently loud that Balenger realized only belatedly that a shotgun had gone off behind him. Fighting the current, he reached a pillar, taking cover behind the furniture caught against it.

"Amanda!"

"Here! Behind you!"

"Where's Tod?"

"There!"

She pointed toward a neighboring pillar.

Balenger gave Vinnie to Amanda, drew his pistol, and peered around the furniture jammed against the pillar. The wreckage of the main staircase faced him. Piled next to it was the twisted debris of the balconies that had collapsed, providing a warren of places in which Ronnie could hide.

Leaning as far out as he dared, Balenger thought he saw movement beneath a tangle of railings. Only two rounds left, he thought. Need to be sure. As the water kept rising, he shifted back behind the furniture and the pillar. Pellets tore a chunk from a table next to him. Hiding, he didn't see the muzzle flash.

Eager for a better sense of Ronnie's location, Balenger took the walkie-talkie from his knapsack. "The rain will eventually put out the fire," he said into it. "You can't possibly destroy all the evidence."

He turned the walkie-talkie to a minimum volume and strained to listen for Ronnie's voice across the way. But the roar of the waterfall made it difficult to distinguish any other sound.

Useless to Balenger, Ronnie's voice came from the walkie-talkie. "The fire and the rain will destroy fingerprints. The rest of the evidence can't be linked to me. No one, except you, knows I come here. The police will think intruders did this."

Balenger cocked his head, focusing on Ronnie's voice. He was almost certain that it came from the right, from a pocket in the tangle of railings. *Get him to say more.*

Ronnie puzzled him by readily talking. "It's just as well the city's forcing me to go. The floods were never this destructive. When a storm came, it used to be all I needed to do was purge the swimming pool. Then the water from the storm would fill it again. The overflow drains would handle the rest."

Yes, definitely from that tangle of railings, Balenger thought. But why is he talking so much? Is he trying to bait me again? Is he shifting his position, hoping I'll waste another shot?

"Do you know the word 'exponential'?" the voice asked.

Balenger decided he had to answer, to encourage Ronnie to keep talking. He spoke into the walkie-talkie. "In the military, I understood it to mean something like a rapidly increasing series of attacks." Immediately, he again reduced the volume.

"Something like that," the voice said across the way.

From the same place. On the right. Among the wreckage. If I don't shoot, will he decide I'm out of ammunition? Balenger wondered. Will he take the risk of coming for me? Can I bait him?

"That's what happened to this hotel. Exponential attacks," the voice said. "By the way, you sound cold."

Balenger did indeed feel cold, shivering in the frigid water.

"You'll soon have muscle cramps. You won't be able to defend yourself."

"You've got the same problem."

"No," the voice said. "I'm high and dry."

"Hey! Ronnie!" Tod yelled from the neighboring pillar, surprising Balenger. "I'll make a deal with you!"

"What possible deal could you make?"

"I can't hear you!" Tod yelled. "I don't have a walkie-talkie!"

Good, make Ronnie shout, Balenger thought. Help me be certain where he is.

"You don't have anything to bargain with!" Ronnie said.

Now the voice seemed to come from a different location. Again, the chaos of noises in the lobby made it difficult for Balenger to judge where Ronnie hid.

"Sure, I do. I'll help you get the others. If I do that, will you let me go?" Tod yelled. "You don't need to be afraid of me."

"I'm afraid of no one."

"I'm not a threat. All I want is to get out of here. I don't have a reason to go to the cops. Not with these coins."

"Ah, yes, the coins."

Balenger's legs were numb. He wondered if he'd be able to move when the time came.

"If I help you get them, do we have a deal?" Tod asked.

"Help is always welcome."

"But do we have a damned deal?"

"I can always use a friend."

What the hell is Tod up to? Balenger wondered. He watched Tod pull something from the water: a long railing that floated by.

"Get ready!" Tod shouted. "Here they come!"

In dismay, Balenger watched Tod poke the railing at the tangle of furniture he, Amanda, and Vinnie hid behind. A table shifted. A chair moved. Tod poked harder. As the wreckage was about to drift away and expose him, Balenger didn't see any choice except to use one of his last two bullets on Tod.

He aimed.

In response, Tod let go of the railing and splashed through the water, taking cover behind a section of stairs jammed against the pillar. Abruptly, something leapt from the wreckage and made him scream. It struck his head, wrapping around his face, claws raking his cheeks and neck. White. With three hind legs. The cat. As blood spurted from his neck, Tod stumbled blindly in the water. Weighed by the coins, desperate to pull the animal from his face, he staggered from the pillar, wailing.

His chest erupted from a shotgun blast. The coins in his pockets provided so much resistance that instead of jerking backward, Tod sank to his knees. He toppled sideways, his face disappearing. In the swirl, the cat surfaced.

Balenger heard wood scraping. The chair Tod had pushed broke free. The table came with it, releasing other debris. All of it swept around the pillar. Balenger holstered his gun. When he turned to help Amanda keep a grip on Vinnie, he lost his footing. Something banged into his legs. He went under. Holding his breath, he struggled to the surface and managed a glimpse of Amanda and Vinnie as the current took all three of them. He thought he heard a shotgun. Then the water shoved him under, thrusting him through the lobby.

He had the sense of cascading down stairs, of streaming along a corridor, of speeding through parted doors. He grabbed for something, anything, to stop him, but all his fingers clutched was a chunk of wood. Fighting to the surface again, he saw Amanda and Vinnie ahead of him. He sucked in air and saw a blur of tiled walls. The swimming pool area.

The current tugged him through an open door. He slammed against a gigantic metal storage tank. The utility room.

He strained to breathe. "Amanda!"

"Here!"

The flood was above his waist. Shivering violently, he swam toward her. "Vinnie? Where's —"

Facedown, Vinnie floated away. Balenger and Amanda grabbed him, bracing his head above water. Vinnie coughed. Around them, the surface was covered by panicked rats squealing to reach pipes and claw their way up. The white cat struggled past. Light-colored objects surged by, and Balenger realized he was seeing hair. The blond hair on Ronnie's victims.

Something in his mind seemed to tilt. He feared he had gone insane.

"Need to get out, or we'll drown." Amanda's voice quavered.

Balenger couldn't bring himself to tell her that even if they managed to fight their way back up to the lobby, their chilled muscles would render them helpless in the water, unable to prevent Ronnie from shooting them.

For a dismaying instant, Amanda's lovely

441

cheeks and blond hair made him think he was looking at . . .

"Diane?"

"What did you call me?"

He took her arm and worked to guide her and Vinnie toward the swimming pool. But he managed only one step before the relentless current pushed them back against the metal tank.

Cold. So cold.

Balenger's hands felt stiff.

The water rose to his sternum.

Finally found her. Can't let her die. Damn it, how do we get out? If that bastard hadn't welded the door shut . . .

Letting the current pull him from the tank, he waded toward the door. The welds, he thought. Maybe they're not strong. Maybe I can use the crowbar to break them.

With all this water pushing against the door? Tons of it? Even if the door wasn't welded shut, I could never get it open.

Welds. Something jogged his memory. Something important that he couldn't quite identify. Something . . .

Balenger remembered that when Ronnie appeared on the surveillance monitor, when he motioned toward the pipe he'd welded across the door, there was a welder's tank to the left of the door. Now Balenger waded in that direction. Praying that Ronnie hadn't moved the tank, he groped in the water but couldn't find it. He groped lower, his awkward fingers brushing curved metal.

He almost shouted with hope as he straightened, but there was a lot he had to do before hope was justified. The water was almost above the pipe across the door. There was a gap behind the pipe. He pulled the crowbar from his knapsack and jammed the sharp end into the gap. He braced the crowbar vertically, its hook at the top of the door.

Again, he groped in the water. Groaning from the weight, he lifted the tank and used its straps to attach it to the crowbar, suspending it above the water. He took the plastic explosive from the knapsack and wedged it between the tank and the door. He yanked the roll of duct tape from his knapsack and secured the tank's rod so the nozzle was pointed at the middle of the tank. Next, he taped the lever on the rod's handle in the open position. Gas escaped. When he clicked the tank's igniter, the torch flamed, burning into the tank.

The water pushed at him as he fought to return to Amanda and Vinnie. He was reminded of nightmares in which he struggled to hurry somewhere but his legs were trapped. Seeing the reflection of the torch behind him, he pressed his shoes against the floor and urged his legs forward through the deepening water. Breathing furiously, he rounded the storage tank. The force of the water pressed Amanda and Vinnie against it.

"Close your eyes! Cover your ears!" he shouted.

Amanda didn't hesitate.

"Vinnie, can you hear me? Close your eyes! Cover your ears!"

Stupefied by his pain, the morphine, and the cold, Vinnie pressed his hands against his ears.

Balenger did the same. The water was at his chest. The torch, he thought. How long will it take to burn into the tank? One, two, three, four. It should have exploded by now. Seven, eight, nine. Did the tank fall into the water? Did the water rise high enough to put out the torch? Thirteen, fourteen.

The world became loud and bright. Even with his eyes closed and his hands over his ears, Balenger felt deafened and blinded. A force lifted him at the same time it seemed to suck the life from him. Weightless, he couldn't breathe. He dropped, pressure squeezing him. Up and down, right and left, these suddenly no longer had meaning. As chaos propelled him, he struck something, gasped, inhaled water, and continued speeding forward.

I'm in the tunnel, he realized. The door blew open. The water's flooding into . . . The chaos spun and tossed him. Banging against a wall, he inhaled more water and found that his face was above the surface. The green-tinted roof of the tunnel sped over him. Rats surrounded him. Two were on his chest.

He saw a swiftly approaching corner. His shoes rammed into it. The flood twisted him, propelling him down the continuation of the tunnel. Underwater again, he banged against a wall and strained not to breathe. At once, the feeling of weightlessness returned. He arced into a wide space, arms flying.

An impact jolted him. He rolled, stopping on his back, and struggled to clear his lungs as water sprayed behind him. Rats scrambled over him.

Boards. Somehow boards were above him. He lay on wet sand. A broken, rusted grate was next to him.

My God, he realized, the force of the water rammed the screen off a drain tunnel. It threw me onto the beach. I'm under the boardwalk.

62

Clang.
  Clang.
The wind carried the noise of the sheet metal flapping in the abandoned condominium. Balenger recalled the unease he'd felt when he heard it tolling seven hours earlier.
  Clang.
Rain came through cracks in the boardwalk, falling on his face. He groped for his gun, which remained in his holster. But the darkness was no longer green. His night-vision goggles had been torn away, and yet he could see a little. Lightning. The flames in the upper stories of the hotel. Balenger forced himself to sit up. Diane. Vinnie.

He searched among the debris. More rats scurried away. The five-legged cat lay motionless, its neck at an unnatural angle. A shape was sprawled near water spewing from the tunnel. Balenger dug his hands and knees into the sand, crawling toward it, only to stop in horror when he realized it was a mummified corpse. Again, something in his mind seemed to tilt, like ball bearings shifting weight.

To his left, he saw two other sprawled shapes. One of them was blonde. Fearful that this too was a corpse, he approached.

The shape moved. He increased speed, reaching it, turning it.

"Diane."

"No," the shape whispered.

Next to her, Vinnie lay unmoving. Balenger checked his mouth to make sure nothing blocked it. He turned him onto his stomach, pressing his back, trying to push water from his lungs.

Vinnie coughed, expelling fluid. Balenger kept pressing.

"Diane, we can't stay," Balenger said.

"But I'm not —"

"Ronnie will come. We need to get out of here." Balenger tugged Vinnie to his feet. "Help me, Diane."

As lightning flashed, she and Balenger held Vinnie between them. They did their best to hurry, but Vinnie's shoes kept dragging in the sand. Balenger stumbled and dropped to one knee. He gathered the strength to stand. Ten steps later, all three of them fell, exhausted.

Balenger looked around. "Ronnie'll soon be here. Need to hide. We need to . . .

That trough in the sand ahead. Diane, do you see it?"

No response.

Rain poured through holes in the board-walk.

"Help me drag Vinnie," Balenger said.

With the last of their energy, they pulled him into the trough.

"Lie down next to him," Balenger said.

"But —"

"I'll cover you. The beach'll seem flat. Maybe he won't see you."

"Our tracks."

"The rain's washing sand into them, hiding them."

"What about you?"

"I'll make him follow me in a different direction. Diane . . ."

"I'm not Diane."

"I love you."

"I wish I *were* Diane." She kissed his cheek.

He made her lie in the trough, then covered her and Vinnie with sand, just enough to hide them, a fake grave to prevent a real one.

He left their faces exposed.

"Cold," she said.

"I'll lead him away. Count to three hundred," Balenger said. "Then try to find help.

If it isn't safe for you to crawl out by then, I failed, and it'll *never* be safe."

"Diane was lucky to have you."

"Was? I don't understand. You've still got me."

He turned, somehow mustering the resolve to go back the way he had come — toward the drain tunnel. The debris. The rats. The mummified bodies. The rain was indeed shifting sand into the footprints. He summoned all his will and stepped onto the beach, walking toward the violent waves. Lightning cracked, but he no longer flinched.

63

A few yards from the surf, he turned and faced the boardwalk. Beyond it, flames burst from the Paragon's upper stories. The fire and the storm struggled with each other. In this deserted area, at this late hour, with the storm hiding the fire from the rest of the city, it would take time for firefighters and police to be alerted and arrive. Balenger couldn't depend on anyone for help.

To the right, lightning silhouetted the skeleton of the abandoned condominium. He heard the clang of the sheet metal.

He unholstered his gun and stuck it behind his belt at his spine. Then he spread his arms, making himself as visible as he could. His aggressive posture said everything. Come for me, Ronnie. See if you can take me.

Thunder rumbled as Ronnie appeared at the top of the boardwalk. Flames silhouetted him, making it seem that he stepped from hell. He stood at the collapsed rail, staring down toward the surf. His night-vision goggles were like hatches over his soul, making him look monstrous. Slowly, steadily, he came down the stairs, his shotgun in his hands.

The thunder reminded Balenger of a giant's steps. Murderous resolve made tall, thin, fifty-seven-year-old Ronnie assume a Titan's stature. The darkness of his Kevlar vest was emblematic of the terrible power he exuded. He strode with the weight of robbed innocence and a stolen childhood, of a lifetime of pain and anger, of terror and death. As he neared Balenger, his blank face communicated an emptiness that could never be filled.

"I'm sorry for what was done to you, Ronnie!" Balenger knew that he couldn't be heard in the storm. He wanted to keep Ronnie coming nearer, to make Ronnie curious about what he yelled. "I hate you, but I'm sorry for that little boy!"

Ronnie kept approaching, relentless, implacable: an executioner.

"Is this where Carlisle died?" Balenger shouted, rain pelting him. Ronnie was probably still too far away to hear. That didn't matter. He wanted Ronnie to see his lips moving, to wonder what he was saying, to keep approaching.

Come closer! Balenger thought. Most gunfights occurred within five yards. Even

451

then, adrenaline unsteadied the shooters' hands and often made them miss. Balenger's hands were shaking and numb from the cold. He couldn't possibly hope to shoot Ronnie from any distance. In contrast, Ronnie's shotgun could finish him at forty yards.

Closer!

"Is this where the old man blew his brains out? After he realized the extent of what you did, he became more terrified of you than he was of going outside! He escaped from the hotel! Did he find your shotgun? Did he take it with him? He hoped to protect himself on the beach! But as he stood here shaking, as he saw you coming in the rain, he realized he was damned! So he shot himself!"

Silhouetted by lightning, Ronnie narrowed the distance between them.

"The shotgun in your hand! Is that the one Carlisle used to blow his brains out?"

Thirty yards away, Ronnie stopped.

No! I need you closer!

"Is this where it happened? Is this where he did it? The father you always wanted! *Is this where you scared him into killing himself?"*

Thunder overwhelmed his words.

A flash of lightning paralyzed Ronnie for a

moment. Then he stepped nearer, wanting to hear what Balenger said.

"What a wonderful son you were!" Balenger shouted. "He gave you a chance for a new life, and you paid him back by filling *his* life with terror!"

Twenty yards away, Ronnie stopped again. Evidently he was now close enough to have heard. *"Sister Carrie,"* he shouted.

Balenger was startled by the incongruity of the statement. "What?"

"Dreiser's novel! When your friend talked about it, he said almost everything that matters! Our bodies and our surroundings doom us! He forgot to say that the *past* dooms us!"

"Not always! Not if you fight it! But that hellhole of a building sure can trick us into believing that!"

Lightning again paralyzed Ronnie. *What's wrong with him?* Balenger wondered. *Why isn't he coming closer?*

The goggles! Balenger realized. When the lightning flashes, the goggles need a moment to adjust! The lightning causes a flare that temporarily blinds him!

Ronnie lifted the shotgun to his shoulder.

As lightning cracked, again blinding Ronnie, Balenger pulled his gun from behind his back and charged. Ronnie came out of his paralysis and shifted his aim.

453

Balenger dove to the sand, shooting upward. Ronnie's shotgun blast hit behind him. Balenger fired toward Ronnie's face.

Then his pistol clicked on empty, its slide back. No more ammunition.

Did I hit him? Balenger rolled. A blast struck next to him, pellets hitting his calf.

He came to his feet, hobbling, trying to lead Ronnie away from the boardwalk.

A groan behind him made him turn. Lightning showed Ronnie sinking to his knees. His shoulder was bloody where one of Balenger's shots had hit him above the Kevlar vest. A raging figure stood behind him, swinging a two-by-four. Diane. Swinging. Shrieking. The shotgun went off, blasting into the sand, as Diane swung the board like a baseball bat. The flames in the hotel showed a chunk of bloody hair flying into the rain. In a Windbreaker, with only a nightgown covering her legs, both garments clinging to her, soaked, she swung the board again, whacking the rear of Ronnie's skull so hard that he dropped forward onto the beach. She stood over him, hitting, hitting, stopping only when the board snapped. Then she cursed and plunged the sharp end into his back.

Ronnie shuddered and lay still.

Amanda stood over him, sobbing. Balenger hobbled toward her.

"Is he dead?" she asked.

"Right now, he's entering hell."

They clung to each other, trying not to fall.

"He put a lot of others through it. Now it's *his* turn," she said.

"Because of something that wasn't his fault. A Fourth of July weekend a lifetime ago." Balenger was sickened.

Clang.

The wind whipped the flap of sheet metal.

Clang.

It tolled for Ronnie, for his victims, for the Paragon Hotel.

Clang.

Balenger watched the flames in the upper stories. "Diane," he said.

"I'm not Diane."

He stared at her. He touched her cheek.

"I know," he said, finally believing it. "God, how I wish."

"You were ready to die to save me."

"I lost Diane once. I couldn't bear to lose her twice. If I couldn't save you and Vinnie, I didn't want to live."

"You haven't lost me."

Sorrow made him feel choked. "We'd better go. We need to help Vinnie."

They stumbled through the dark rain toward the boardwalk. When they reached the

hollow in the beach, Vinnie was unconscious. They lifted him from the sand.

"Do I hear . . ." Amanda turned.

"Sirens."

Out of breath, they staggered with Vinnie,
following the boardwalk toward the sound.
Balenger's legs didn't seem a part of him,
but he kept struggling forward just as
Amanda did. He looked at her. How he
wished she was Diane, or at least that he
could *believe* she was Diane.

Delirious, he must have said that out
loud, because Amanda turned to him.
"Keep remembering, I'm not her, but you
haven't lost me."

They reached stairs to the boardwalk.
Avoiding broken planks, they ascended
wearily, sinking to their knees, then continuing upward. The light of the flames grew.
Balenger felt a warm wind from the fire.
Then the wind was hot, although Balenger
couldn't stop shivering. The sirens wailed to
a halt. Firemen jumped from a truck. Policemen scrambled from cruisers.

The top of the hotel's pyramid caved in.
Sparks flew. Consumed by fire, the sixth
level collapsed. There go the gold coins,
Balenger thought. He remembered the
double eagle in his pocket. The words on it:
In God We Trust.

Policemen ran to them, one of them shouting, *"What happened to you?"*

As Balenger slumped to the ground, he heard the *clang clang clang* of the tolling sheet metal. Another section of the building collapsed. But hell had many levels. So did the past. "What happened to us?" he murmured. He could barely force the words out. "The Paragon Hotel."

Author's Note:

An Obsession

With the Past

As every author knows, the most frequent question we're asked is, "Where do you get your ideas?" Creepers. Although I wasn't familiar with that term until recently, my fascination with the concept has gripped me for most of my life.

When I was nine, my family lived in a cramped apartment above a restaurant that catered to drinkers from the area's numerous bars. (This was in a city called Kitchener in southern Ontario in Canada.) I often heard drunks fighting in the alley beneath my bedroom window. There was plenty of fighting in the apartment, as well. Although my mother and my stepfather never came to blows, their arguments made me so afraid that many nights I stuffed pillows under my bedding to make it look as if

I slept there while I lay awake under the bed.

I often escaped that apartment and wandered the streets, where I learned the secrets of every alley and parking lot within ten blocks. I also learned the secrets of abandoned buildings. In retrospect, I'm amazed that I didn't run into fatal trouble in some of those buildings. But I was a street kid, a survivor, and the worst that happened to me was a cat bite on a wrist and a nail through a foot, both of which caused blood poisoning.

Those abandoned buildings — a house, a factory, and an apartment complex — fascinated me. The smashed windows, the moldy wallpaper, the peeling paint, the musty smell of the past, lured me back repeatedly. The most interesting building was the apartment complex because, although deserted, it wasn't empty. Tenants had abandoned tables, chairs, dishes, pots, lamps, and sofas. Most were in such poor shape that it was obvious why the objects hadn't been taken. Nonetheless, combined with magazines and newspapers left behind, the tables and chairs and dishes created the illusion that people still lived there — ghostly remnants of the life that once flourished in the building.

I felt this more than I understood it. Treading cautiously up creaky staircases, stepping around fallen plaster and holes in floors, peering into decaying rooms, I gazed in wonder at discoveries I made. Pigeons roosted on cupboards. Mice nested in sofas. Fungus grew on walls. Weeds sprouted on watery windowsills. Some of the yellowed newspapers and magazines dated back to when I was born.

But no discovery meant more to me than a record album I found on a cracked linoleum floor next to a three-legged table that lay on its side. Eventually, I learned that it was called an album because, prior to the 1950s, phonograph records were made from thick, easily breakable shellac, had only one song on each side, and were stored in paper sleeves within binders that resembled photograph albums. At the time of my discovery, discs of this sort (which played at 78 rpm) had been superseded by thin, long-playing, vinyl discs that were far more sturdy, had as many as eight songs on each side, and played at $33^1/_3$ rpm.

I'd never seen an album. When I opened its cover, I felt an awe that was only slightly reduced by the scrape of broken shellac. Two of the discs were shattered. But the majority (four, as I recall) remained intact.

Clutching this treasure, I hurried home. Our radio had a record player attached to it. I switched its dial to 78 rpm (a common feature in those days) and put on one of the discs.

I played the song repeatedly. Today, I can still hear the scratchy tune. I've never forgotten its title: "Those Wedding Bells Are Breaking Up That Old Gang of Mine." An Internet search tells me that the song was written in 1929 by Irving Kahal, Willie Raskin, and Sammy Fain. Melodic and rhythmic, it was an instant hit, recorded frequently over the years. But at the time, I knew nothing of that. Nor did I understand the emotions of the lyrics, which described the loneliness of a young man whose friends are all getting married. What captivated me was that scratchy sound. It came palpably from the past and served as a time tunnel through which my imagination could travel back to other years. I visualized the vocal group in unfamiliar clothes, surrounded by unfamiliar objects, singing out-of-fashion music in a setting that was always fuzzy and in black-and-white. Regrettably, I don't recall the group's name. So much for immortality.

Since then, I've obeyed a compulsion to investigate many other abandoned buildings, not to mention tunnels and storm drains, although I never again found anything so memorable as that phonograph album. I assumed that my traumatic childhood accounted for my fascination with crumbling deserted structures and that I was alone in my obsession with links to the past. But I now realize that there are many like me.

They call themselves urban explorers, urban adventurers, and urban speleologists. Their nickname is creepers. If you type "urban explorer" into Yahoo, you'll find an astonishing 170,000 Internet contacts. Type that name into Google, and you'll find an even more astonishing 225,000 contacts. It's a reasonable assumption that each of these links isn't represented by just one lonely explorer. After all, nobody's going to put together a site if he/she doesn't have a sense of community. Those hundreds of thousands of contacts are *groups,* and logic suggests that for every one that publicizes itself, there are many others that prefer to be hidden.

Those who wish to remain anonymous have a good reason. Bear in mind, urban exploration is illegal. It involves the invasion of private property. Plus, it's so unsafe it can be deadly. The authorities tend to insist on jail terms and/or serious fines to discourage it. As a consequence, many of these Web sites emphasize that explorers should get permission from property owners and that they should always follow safety precautions and never do anything against the law. Those warnings sound socially responsible, but my assumption is that for many urban explorers, part of the appeal is the risk and thrill of doing what's forbidden. It's significant that their slang term for entering a deserted building borrows from the covert-ops military expression for invading hostile territory: infiltration. As the Web site *www.infiltration.org* indicates, the objective is "places you're not supposed to go."

Creepers are mostly between the ages of eighteen and thirty, intelligent, well educated with an interest in history and architecture, often employed in professions related to computer technology. They share a worldwide interest, with groups in Japan, Singapore, Germany, Poland, Greece, Italy, France, Spain, Holland, England, Canada, the United States, and several other countries. Australian groups are fascinated with the maze of storm drains under Sydney and Melbourne. European groups favor abandoned military installations from the world wars. U.S. groups are drawn to classic department stores and hotels abandoned when social decay led to an exodus from cities like Buffalo and Detroit. In Russia, creepers are obsessed with Moscow's once-secret multi-level subway system intended for evacuating Cold War officials during a nuclear attack. Deserted hospitals, asylums, theaters, and stadiums: Every country offers plenty of opportunities for urban exploring (see Mark Moran's essay, "Greetings from Abandoned Asbury Park, NJ," at www.weirdnj.com).

One of the first urban explorers was a Frenchman who in 1793 became lost during an expedition into the Paris catacombs. It took eleven years for his body to be discovered. As a character in *Creepers* indicates, Walt Whitman was another early urban explorer. The author of *Leaves of Grass* worked as a reporter for the *Brooklyn Standard*, where he wrote about the Atlantic Avenue tunnel. Touted as the first subway tunnel anywhere when built in 1844, it was discontinued a mere seventeen years later. Before it was sealed, Whitman trekked through it. "Dark as the grave, cold, damp and silent," he wrote. "How beautiful look earth and heaven again, as we emerge from the gloom! It might not be unprofitable, now and then, to send us mortals, the dissatisfied ones at least, and that's a large proportion, into some tunnel of several days' journey. We'd perhaps grumble less, afterward, at God's handiwork."

But Whitman didn't get the point of urban exploration. He saw the tunnel in negative terms. For a true devotee, however, the cold, damp, silent darkness of a tunnel or an abandoned apartment complex or a deserted factory is exactly the goal. The spooky attraction of the eerie past: I suspect that's what a much later explorer felt in 1980 when he uncovered that same Atlantic Avenue tunnel 119 years after it was barricaded and forgotten.

A major modern instance of urban exploration occurred recently in the Paris catacombs. Those catacombs are part of a 170-mile tunnel system beneath Paris, the consequence of quarry work that over many centuries provided building materials for the city. In the 1700s, some of the tunnels were used to store thousands of corpses when Parisian cemeteries exhausted their space. In September of 2004, a French police team on a training exercise found a fully equipped movie theater among the bones. Seats had been carved into the rock. A small adjoining cave functioned as a bar and restaurant, with whiskey bottles on display along with professional electrical and telephone systems. Another major example occurred in Moscow in October of 2002 when Chechen rebels seized control of a theater. After the military surrounded the building, a Russian urban explorer guided soldiers inside through a forgotten tunnel.

Some of this is adventuring in a basic sense. But I think that there are also psychological implications. As I note in *Creepers*, our world is so fraught with elevated threat levels that it makes a lot of sense to retreat to the past. Old buildings can be a refuge, drawing us back to what we imagine were simple and less stressful times. In my youth, the deserted apartment complex provided an escape from the turmoil of my family. I was a time traveler, finding sanctuary in a past that appealed to my imagination and in which there were never any arguments.

In my youth. As an adult, I now have a different perspective, one with deeper, less comfortable implications. To me, old buildings have become like old photographs. They remind me how swiftly time passes. The past they evoke draws attention to my ultimate future. They are an opportunity for reflection.

I recently had the chance to visit the high

school I attended more than forty years ago. A part of it had burned to the ground. Most of the remainder has been boarded shut for a decade. When I entered, a hazard team was checking for asbestos, lead paint, and mold, prior to the school's renovation. It's amazing what years of disuse can do, especially when broken windows allow rain and snow to intrude. In disturbingly silent hallways, the hardwood floors were buckled. Plaster drooped from the ceilings. Paint strips hung from the walls. But in my memory, everything was clean and well maintained. I envisioned students and teachers filling the noisy corridors. The trouble is, many of those students and teachers have long since died. In the midst of decay, my imagination conjured youth and the promise of hope, gone just as the school would soon be gone.

I wonder if deserted buildings are vessels to which children bring a sense of wonder and adults bring their unacknowledged fears. When I obeyed the compulsion to visit that wreck of a school, was I unintentionally confronting my own mortality? But my visit had a safety that urban exploration doesn't. Infiltrating forbidden sites, investigating the decay of the past, creepers flirt with danger. Any moment, a floor might give way, a wall topple, or a stairway collapse. Creepers challenge the past to do its worst. With each successful expedition, they emerge victorious from another confrontation with age and decay. For a handful of hours, they live intensely. Obsessed with the past, perhaps they hope to postpone their inevitable future. Or perhaps they feel reassured that the past lingers palpably into the present and that something about *their* past might linger after they're gone.

When my fifteen-year-old son Matthew was dying from bone cancer, his most plaintive statement was, "But no one will remember me." *Memento mori.* Maybe that's what urban exploration is all about. Is an obsession with the past another way of hoping that something about us will linger, that years from now someone will explore where we lived and feel our lingering presence? That phonograph album I found. The distant hiss I listened to just as someone listened to that same platter decades earlier. "Those Wedding Bells Are Breaking Up That Old Gang of Mine." It's a song about time, which is basically what all stories come down to. In the lyric, a young man says he's got a lonesome feeling. But as I think back to that apartment complex and the deserted rooms I wandered through —

the abandoned sofas, chairs, lamps, and pots — I didn't feel alone.

— David Morrell
Santa Fe, New Mexico

Resources

Visit the following Internet sites for more information about urban exploring. They are representative of thousands of others. Some have links to other sites.

www.infiltration.org
www.jinxmagazine.com
www.urbanexplorers.net
www.forgotten-ny.com (To find a similar site devoted to your area, try an Internet search by typing the name of your region and putting "forgotten" or "abandoned" in front of it.)
http://users.pandora.be/a-p/index.html
http://catacombes.web.free.fr
www.caveclan.org
www.deathrock.net/ariadne/ruins.html (Look in "Amusement Parks" for photographs of Asbury Park, then and now.)
www.weirdnj.com (Mark Moran's Asbury Park essay is in "Abandoned.")
http://urbanexploration.org/2005/site mapgraphical.htm

About the Author

David Morrell is the award-winning author of *First Blood*, the novel in which Rambo was created. He was born in 1943 in Kitchener, Ontario, Canada. In 1960, at the age of seventeen, he became a fan of the classic television series *Route 66*, about two young men in a Corvette traveling the United States in search of America and themselves. The scripts by Stirling Silliphant so impressed Morrell that he decided to become a writer.

In 1966, the work of another writer (Hemingway scholar Philip Young) prompted Morrell to move to the United States, where he studied with Young at Pennsylvania State University and received his M.A. and Ph.D. in American literature. There, he also met the distinguished fiction writer William Tenn (real name Philip Klass), who taught Morrell the basics of fiction writing. The result was *First Blood*, a novel about a returned Vietnam veteran suffering from post-traumatic stress disorder who comes into conflict with a small-town police chief and fights his own version of the Vietnam War.

That "father" of all modern action novels was published in 1972 while Morrell was a professor in the English department at the University of Iowa. He taught there from 1970 to 1986, simultaneously writing other novels, many of them national bestsellers, such as *The Brotherhood of the Rose* (the basis for a top-rated NBC miniseries). Eventually wearying of two professions, he gave up his tenure in order to write full-time.

Shortly afterward, his fifteen-year-old son Matthew was diagnosed with a rare form of bone cancer and died in 1987, a loss that haunts not only Morrell's life but his work, as in his memoir about Matthew, *Fireflies*, and his novel *Desperate Measures*, whose main character has lost a son.

"The mild-mannered professor with the bloody-minded visions," as one reviewer called him, Morrell is the author of twenty-eight books, including such high-action thrillers as *The Fifth Profession*, *Assumed Identity*, and *Extreme Denial* (set in Santa Fe, New Mexico, where he now lives with his wife, Donna). His *Lessons from a Lifetime of Writing* analyzes what he has learned during his more than thirty years as a writer.

Morrell is the co-president of the International Thriller Writers organization. Noted for his research, he is a graduate of the National Outdoor Leadership School for wilderness survival as well as the G. Gordon Liddy Academy of Corporate Security. He is also an honorary lifetime member of the Special Operations Association and the Association of Former Intelligence Officers. He has been trained in firearms, hostage negotiation, assuming identities, executive protection, and offensive-defensive driving, among numerous other action skills that he describes in his novels. With eighteen million copies in print, his work has been translated into twenty-six languages. Visit him at www.davidmorrell.net.

We hope you have enjoyed this Large Print book. Other Thorndike, Wheeler or Chivers Press Large Print books are available at your library or directly from the publishers.

For more information about current and upcoming titles, please call or write, without obligation, to:

Publisher
Thorndike Press
295 Kennedy Memorial Drive
Waterville, ME 04901
Tel. (800) 223-1244

Or visit our Web site at:
www.gale.com/thorndike
www.gale.com/wheeler

OR

Chivers Large Print
published by BBC Audiobooks Ltd
St James House, The Square
Lower Bristol Road
Bath BA2 3BH
England
Tel. +44(0) 800 136919
email: bbcaudiobooks@bbc.co.uk
www.bbcaudiobooks.co.uk

All our Large Print titles are designed for easy reading, and all our books are made to last.